Praise for *Swear on This Life*

BOOKLIST, TOP 10 WOMEN'S FICTION OF 2016

GOODREADS BEST ROMANCE OF AUGUST 2016

"*Swear on This Life* is Renée Carlino at her finest. Raw, real and gripping; I read it in one sitting."

—Colleen Hoover, #1 *New York Times* bestselling author of *It Ends with Us*

"This bestselling author knows how to deliver a literary punch, and *Swear on This Life* is her strongest yet."

—*Redbook*

"Mysterious and compelling, *Swear on This Life* is the epic love story your summer needs."

—*Bustle*

"Carlino fans will love this one, and so will readers who have not yet made her acquaintance. The tale is engaging and paced to keep the pages turning long after the lights should be out."

—*Kirkus Reviews*

"[Readers] will find themselves simply smitten by both the novel in front of them and the story within the story. Romance readers and women's fiction fans should snap up this charming love story."

—*Booklist*

"Romance fans will find this heartfelt story of resilience and first love hard to put down."

—*Library Journal*

"Mesmerizing. A story of love and redemption, Renée Carlino's novel is a perfect reason for staying up too late to read."

—*Shelf Awareness*

"I love the juxtaposition of the story within a story, and I'm addicted to Emi and Jase's ill-fated love."

—*Heroes and Heartbreakers*

"A beautifully written second-chance romance that stays with you long after you're done."

—*Vilma's Book Blog*, 5 stars

"Carlino's writing will transport you."

—*Book Baristas*, 4.5 coffee cups

ALSO BY RENÉE CARLINO

Sweet Thing
Nowhere but Here
After the Rain
Before We Were Strangers
Swear on This Life

WISH YOU WERE HERE

A Novel

RENÉE CARLINO

ATRIA PAPERBACK
New York London Toronto Sydney New Delhi

ATRIA
PAPERBACK

An Imprint of Simon & Schuster, Inc.
1230 Avenue of the Americas
New York, NY 10020

First Atria Paperback edition August 2017

ATRIA PAPERBACK and colophon are trademarks of Simon & Schuster, Inc.

For information about special discounts for bulk purchases, please contact Simon & Schuster Special Sales at 1-866-506-1949 or business@simonandschuster.com.

The Simon & Schuster Speakers Bureau can bring authors to your live event. For more information or to book an event, contact the Simon & Schuster Speakers Bureau at 1-866-248-3049 or visit our website at www.simonspeakers.com.

Manufactured in the United States of America

10 9 8 7 6 5 4 3

Library of Congress Cataloging-in-Publication Data

Names: Carlino, Renée, author.
Title: Wish you were here : a novel / Renée Carlino.
Description: First Atria Paperback edition. | New York : Atria Paperback, 2017.
Identifiers: LCCN 2017015209 (print) | LCCN 2017021315 (ebook) | ISBN 9781501105838 (ebook) | ISBN 9781501105821 (paperback) | ISBN 9781501105838 (ebook)
Subjects: | BISAC: FICTION / Contemporary Women. | FICTION / Romance / General. | FICTION / Romance / Contemporary. | GSAFD: Love stories.
Classification: LCC PS3603.A75255 (ebook) | LCC PS3603.A75255 W57 2017 (print) | DDC 813/.6—dc23
LC record available at https://lccn.loc.gov/2017015209

ISBN 978-1-5011-0582-1
ISBN 978-1-5011-0583-8 (ebook)

For Rich, the best brother in the world.
I love you, even though you're Mom's favorite.

WISH YOU WERE HERE

1. Little Flags

Tuesdays were tortilla soup days at Blackbird's Café. They offered unlimited refills for a lousy four ninety-five. It was awesome if you were a tortilla soup lover. It was some kind of evil if you were a waitress there.

The restaurant's trick was that the bowls were wide and shallow, making it appear like a massive amount of soupy goodness, when really, each bowlful amounted to just a few thinly spread ounces. The problem with said plates disguised as bowls is that they were impossible to carry on a tray; the soup just sloshed from side to side, predictably spilling over the lip each time you traipsed from the kitchen to the customer's table, no matter how steady your hands were. Jack, the owner, and his fat "little" brother, who went by Jon-Jon (ridiculous, I know), insisted that we carry the trays up high, like waitresses on roller-skates at a goddamn carhop. *It's part of the charm*, they said. The word *charm* was used loosely to justify the outdated décor, in my opinion.

If you ordered the "bottomless" tortilla soup bowl, you

had to shamefully raise a miniature flag on a tiny flagpole screwed to the end of your table. It was an abominable mechanism, truly, but it achieved Jack and Jon-Jon's desired effect: no one ever, not even a three-hundred-pound man with a passion for Tex-Mex, would raise the flag more than twice; it was too humiliating.

Unfortunately, this type of ploy to get people into the restaurant without the business losing money didn't draw a high-tipping clientele, so Tuesdays were a bust for the waitresses at Blackbird's. We made no money and we always went home with a healthy amount of tortilla soup splattered on our white tuxedo shirts. (Yes, we wore tuxedo shirts and bow ties in a pie-and-fry diner; more of that charm I guess.) But this particular Tuesday was the worst.

"I FEEL LIKE I'm in hell. Have you seen the guy at table twenty-three?" Helen, my best friend, roommate, and fellow waitress, said to me in the side station.

I peeked around the wall and spotted a gray-haired man eating by himself. "Yeah, what about him?"

"He asked for an avocado al dente. Who the fuck uses the term 'al dente' to describe an avocado?"

"You know what he means though, right?" I was laughing but Helen was serious.

"Yes, but this isn't Spago. He'd be lucky to get a green avocado at this place."

"It's not that bad," I said as I filled a plastic cup with Coke. The fountain dispenser started huffing and puffing little bursts of air. "Fucking shit, the CO_2 is running out. Can you go tell Jon-Jon?"

"Sorry, I have to get twenty-one's order." As Helen left the side station, I watched her hips sway from side to side as she breezed into the dining room. Helen knew she had a good body and that men gawked at her. She walked slowly and rhythmically, which made me think she liked the attention.

I, on the other hand, walked fast everywhere, with my shoulders slumped and my head down. People would always say, "You're a pretty girl, Charlotte. Why do you walk like an old man?" My response was usually something like, "I don't know, it's just the way I walk." Lame, I know, but I didn't put much thought into how I was perceived. Probably because the only thing I really liked about my entire body was my long, reddish-brown hair. I had big brown eyes that my brother called "poop colored" and freckles that, thankfully, were fading as I got older. Still, if you asked me to draw a self-portrait, I'd unconsciously add the freckles. It's like that Freudian theory that says you're a perpetual child in your own mind.

"Did I hear my name?" Jon-Jon was suddenly standing inappropriately close to me as I unscrewed the large CO_2 cylinder.

"Can you fix this?" I was bent over with my ass in the air.

"You seem to be doing a pretty good job."

I popped up straight. "Why are you so pervy? You're gonna get sued one day." Had I not been fired from two jobs already that year, I never would have put up with Jon-Jon's crap, but I needed the money and I was not in a position to lose another job. I think it goes without saying that waitressing wasn't my career of choice, though that wasn't my biggest problem. I had a degree in nutrition and my real estate license, and I was a certified massage therapist. See a pattern? At one point I actually thought I wanted to become a horse jockey. I'd never even been on a horse, but repeat viewings of *Seabiscuit* were enough to persuade me.

"Relax, Charlotte, out of the way." Jon-Jon moved his tubby little body in front of me and took over replacing the cylinder.

I looked into the dining room to see raised flags on three of my tables. It was time for some ingenuity. I found a large pitcher under the dishwasher's station. "Can I use this?" I held it up to one of the busboys.

"Sure, Gutterfoot," he said. Did I mention that everyone at Blackbird's called me Gutterfoot? Directly underneath the big metal trays where we stacked dirty dishes was a one-foot-by-one-foot drain where we scraped all the nasty food that was left on the plates. Sometimes it got clogged, and very rarely, a waitress would step in it. Some shitty Tuesday when I was in a hurry, I was that waitress, and the damn thing was practically overflowing with what looked like vomit. It wasn't actual vomit, of course, but if ever you need something to really resemble vomit, a mixture of soup, meatloaf scraps, pie, soda, and beer is pretty much as close as you can get. The sludge went halfway up my right calf, but I just pulled my foot out and smiled, briefly thanking some higher-up somewhere. On any other day of the week, this incident would have enraged me, but it was a Tuesday. I thought for sure I'd get sent home and be relieved of my duties as soup peddler. I was wrong. Jack said we were too slammed, so I had to stay and distribute bottomless bowls of tortilla soup with a sopping-wet pant leg and shoes filled with rotting food sludge. Naturally, I got nicknamed Gutterfoot.

I took the pitcher and began ladling tortilla soup into it when Jon-Jon found me. "Charlotte, what are you doing now?" he asked.

"I have a bunch of refills. This'll make it faster and easier."

"You know you've been on thin ice since the closet caper, right? We don't serve soup via pitcher," Jon-Jon said.

"I'm being efficient! And, anyway, the closet stunt was Helen's doing." We always got blamed for each other's mistakes because we were inseparable. A couple of weeks before, when our shift had gotten slow, she'd told me to find Jon-Jon and ask him if he'd fixed the door to the linen closet. I'd known she was up to something.

When Jon-Jon had opened the closet, Helen jumped out and yelled, "Wah!" He'd fallen back on the floor and clutched his heart immediately; a man with his kind of dumpy little body was totally a candidate for sudden cardiac arrest. Luckily we hadn't been responsible for his untimely death . . . yet.

"You were part of it," he said.

"No, I really wasn't."

Helen came bouncing through the kitchen. "Dude, you have flags up on, like, every one of your tables. People have no dignity."

"I'm going, I'm going."

Jon-Jon was right. Tortilla soup should not be served via pitcher, but if anyone asked, I would say it was part of the charm at Blackbird's.

After our shift slowed down, I pulled a little closet caper of my own. I knew when Helen went on break that she'd sometimes make out with Luc in the linen closet. They'd been sucking each other's faces off for about six months. He was a French dude who had flunked out of some hoity-toity pastry school in France and now was stuck at Blackbird's, making pies for the masses. He was actually surprisingly proud of his job, despite the fact that he made minimum wage. His pie technique was incredible, and he had the freedom to make every kind of pie he wanted. Somehow, this aroused Helen. I tried not to judge, but I could barely watch Helen's face whenever Luc said anything. He pronounced her name *Huh-leen*, and every time he said it, she practically had an orgasm.

The first time they met, he'd kissed her hand and whispered in her ear, "You and I would make beautiful babies." Helen had turned into a pile of goo, and she was Luc's ever since. He'd helped both of us get hired at Blackbird's—I was between careers, and Helen hadn't landed a substantial acting gig in eight years—so I just rolled my eyes and kept my mouth shut whenever I saw Helen throwing him seductive looks.

But when I swung the linen closet open, it was just Helen sitting on a stool, puffy-eyed and holding a bottle of vodka she'd clearly swiped from Jon-Jon's famous Bloody Mary bar.

"What are you doing?"

"Luc broke up with me." She sniffled.

"What? Just now? Why?"

"He was rambling something in half French, half English, so I didn't catch it all. Something about a ship running its course, and overripe peaches. He was smiling the whole time, that bastard." She took a swig and hiccupped.

"How do you know he was breaking up with you?"

"Because he said, 'Huh-leen, it was a beautiful think, you and me, but eet is over.'"

She unintentionally made Luc's accent sound Mexican, and it made me laugh. "I'm sorry, but honestly, you're better off. I mean, those bright-pink tennis shoes and that permanent five-o'clock shadow . . . come on. I bet he wears Speedos."

"He does!" She burst into tears.

I bent and hugged her around her shoulders. "Don't worry, babe; there will be other, less stinky fish in the sea."

She straightened up. "He smells, doesn't he?"

"Like body odor mixed with pie dough. It's offensive."

"I need a rebound." Her eyes shot open and she raised her index finger to the closet ceiling. "That's it, we're going out tonight."

I shook my head. "I'm too tired, and you shouldn't be going out tonight, either. It won't make you feel any better. The first night of a breakup should be about Chinese food, ice cream, and bad TV."

"I'll let you dye my hair tomorrow," she offered.

"Wait. Really?"

Helen nodded like an excited puppy.

"Ugh. Deal." I had been contemplating going to cosmetology school, but I didn't have enough people to practice on. Helen changed her hair color after every breakup—it was currently a pale shade of purple—but she'd never let me near her hair before.

"I'm thinking chartreuse," she said, rising from her stool.

"Chartreuse will look great on you!" I gave her a bone-crushing hug of gratitude. "We'll get some Manic Panic tomorrow. So, where do you want to go tonight?"

"Ladies!" Jon-Jon barked. "Out of the closet. Do I have to remind you that this is a place of business?"

We peeked our heads around the door. "We weren't doing anything, Jon-Jon. We just wanted a break in peace," I said.

"Well, take your break outside. You two are getting phased for the night." He made a circular motion with his hand in front of his face, which was the symbol for, *Wrap up your tables because you're going home*.

"Thank you, Jesus!" Helen shouted. Once the rush was over, every waiter wanted to get phased. You didn't really make any money after the dinner rush, and the waiters who had to stay late ended up doing boring side work, like filling up saltshakers and ketchup bottles. It sucked.

"Did we decide where we're going tonight?" I asked Helen while we wiped down our empty tables.

"How about Villains?"

I gave her a wide grin. "Perfect."

2. Muse

Villains was an unpretentious tavern with live music about five blocks from our apartment in the Arts District of Downtown LA, where Helen and I had been living together for the last eight years. I'd heard of other people's friendships imploding after they became roommates with their BFFs, but Helen and I were always joined at the hip. We'd known each other since we were little kids growing up in the same suburban cul-de-sac, and we'd been together through twelve years of grade school and four years of college at UCLA. If we had any problem, it was that we were maybe *too* comfortable with the idea of becoming spinsters together.

Helen loved Villains because, deep down, I was pretty sure her Plan B was to become some rock god's muse. Whenever we'd go to a concert, she'd stand in front of the crowd near the stage and sway back and forth in an attempt to get the attention of the lead singer. It wasn't subtle. I'd usually sit at the bar and watch the spectacle from afar.

When it came to dating, I always waited to be approached.

I'd had boyfriends, but nothing had lasted longer than a year. I had a way of turning every date into a yearlong relationship instead of getting out early, when I knew it wouldn't last. I just couldn't get into the one-night-stand scene. But Helen had no rules about anything. I envied her for that.

After our shift ended, we went back to our apartment and peeled off a layer of tortilla soup, got ready, then headed to Villains around ten. I was wearing my party uniform—black blouse and jeans—and Helen was in a red, high-waisted, A-line skirt and sleeveless white blouse with platform heels. She always looked way hipper than me.

Once inside the bar, she shouted, "Damn it!" I followed her gaze to the stage where an all-girl band was setting up.

"Bummer," I said.

"Let's leave, Charlie. This is lame."

"No, I like it here. It's so close to our apartment. Don't make me go back out there."

The lead singer approached the mic and tapped on it. "Check, check." When she tore off a crazy guitar riff, Helen's face lit up. "Okay, fine. We can stay for a while, but we're getting shots!"

Remember how I said Helen had no rules? She liked attention, and it didn't matter who it came from. We sat at the bar and took shot after shot, forgetting all about tortilla soup, Luc, and the messiness of our lives. An hour into the set, Helen left me to approach the stage. She stood near the front and tried desperately to get the lead singer's attention, but the woman wasn't having it. Maybe she was straight? After more shots and watching Helen's pathetic attempts to catch the singer's eye, I found myself sitting in a booth, comforting a rejected—and very drunk—Helen.

"Why doesn't anyone want me?" she slurred. "Not even that gay chick with the guitar."

"Well, no one hit on me either."

"No one ever hits on you, Charlie! You're standoffish!"

"What? No I'm not," I whined.

"Your eyes scream, 'Stay away, I hate one-night stands.'"

"Everyone hates one-night stands. They're awkward as hell."

"You're just a prude."

"Ugh. Let's go home, I'm over tonight, and I don't want you throwing up in this bar." Between Helen, my brother, my mom, and Helen's mom, I got enough crap about the state of my love life.

"No, I wanna dance." Helen slid out of the booth and fell directly on her ass with a thump. I pulled her up by the armpits, wrapped my arm around her waist, and started dragging her toward the door. We were making a scene, but Helen was finally getting her wish: the lead singer was staring at her, along with everyone else in the bar.

"I got it, I got it," she said.

"I don't think so, babe. You can't even walk." I propped open the door to the bar with my foot and led her out onto the street.

"I think I got roofied," she slurred as her head lolled against my shoulder.

"I think it's the ten shots you took, not to mention the vodka from earlier."

We turned a corner and I looked up just in time to see a guy standing directly in front of us with his head down, staring at something written on his palm. "'Scuse us," I muttered, trying to navigate around him, but he was standing in the middle of the sidewalk, holding a bag full of what looked like Chinese takeout.

"Yum, is that Chinese food?" Helen asked.

The guy looked up at her strangely and then looked down at the bag in his hand. He was wearing shorts, flip-flops, and a black hoodie, which shadowed his eyes. Not the most fashion-conscious outfit. "Oh this? Yeah, it is. Are you hungry?"

I started pulling Helen forward. "Come on," I whispered. "You can't eat some random guy's Chinese food on the street."

She stumbled but caught herself before falling over.

The man walked to her other side. "Let me help you," he said.

"No, no, we're fine," I protested, but Helen had already slung her arm around his shoulder. She reached up and pulled his hood back, and he turned toward her, nonplussed, his striking brown eyes wide with curiosity. He was undeniably good-looking, and would be in anyone's book. "I'm Adam," he said. "Let me help you."

"Nice to meet you, Adam. I'm Trixie and that's Dottie. I think we got this." I said.

Adam grinned. Two deep dimples punctuated his cheeks. "Trixie and Dottie, for real?"

"Yep," I said curtly.

Helen rolled her eyes. "That's Charlotte and I'm Helen."

I elbowed her in the ribs. She leaned in and whispered, "He has Chinese food and he's cute." She said the last part a little too loud, which made Adam smile.

"Adam, do you live around here?" I asked.

"Yeah, I live on Molina."

"Why were you headed in the opposite direction then?"

He looked straight ahead so I couldn't see his face. "I must've gotten flipped around."

I looked at him curiously. *Maybe he's new to the neighborhood? That would explain why I haven't seen him around.*

"You wanna eat at our apartment?" Helen slurred.

"That's okay," Adam said. "I'll just walk you to your place."

"It's right up here." I pointed to the steps leading to the front door of our building. "This is good here; I'll get her up the rest of the way."

He stopped, looked at the side of our building, and crooked his head. "Ahhh, man, I love that mural. It's like wolves dancing in a bed of flowers."

I followed his gaze to the large, abstract mural that took up the whole side of our building in a riot of grays, pinks, oranges, and blues.

"We always thought those streaks were blood," Helen said, making sweeping motions with her hand.

"That's a pretty gruesome interpretation. Those are pink and red flowers, obviously," he countered. "Their beauty is meant to emphasize the equally wild beauty of the wolves."

I tipped my head and squinted. "Now that you mention it, they do look like flowers. But why are the wolves angry if they're dancing in a field of flowers?"

"Maybe they're allergic," Helen offered.

"Who says they're angry?" Adam replied. "The flowers are rising up from the ground to embrace them. To me, they look happy."

I stared at him as he stared at the mural, completely transfixed. Silence washed over us as we stood in the street, two best friends and a stranger sharing an oddly sincere moment together.

"Well, it was nice meeting you, Adam," I said, gently breaking our collective daze. "Thanks for your help."

"No problem. It was nice to meet you, ladies." He nodded at us, gave a little wave, and headed up the street. But as we turned and made our way up the stairs, we heard Adam call out, "Oh, I almost forgot!" He jogged back toward us, pulling a take-out container from his plastic bag. "Here, I told you I'd share." He held the little carton out to me and looked into my eyes with total sincerity. He pushed his thick, wavy brown hair back with his other hand, and I felt something pull within me.

"That's okay."

"No, we'll take it!" Helen swatted at the box, ripping it from Adam's grasp.

He chuckled at her and then turned his attention back to me. I couldn't pull my gaze from his, from that face full of kindness, those eyes that turned down slightly at the corners, giving him a slightly sad air. I should've felt uncomfortable, but I didn't.

You know when you're looking at someone and you can't help but smile at how oblivious they are to their own charm? That's what was happening to me, and it was making me feel . . . happy. Euphoric. Something indescribable. It was like we already knew each other, like we had met in a previous life. Memories that didn't exist began exploding in my mind like fireworks.

I smiled at him; he smiled back. There was some sort of

affinity between us, but I didn't know where it was coming from, exactly. I didn't know this guy half an hour ago, but now I *needed* to know him.

He glanced past me at the mural, and then he searched my eyes, squinting. "Have we met before?" he asked. *Is he feeling it, too?*

"No, I don't think so."

"But you seem so familiar to me."

"I know, right?" I said with conviction.

He reached out for a handshake, the whole time never taking his eyes off mine. "Maybe we both have familiar faces."

"Like, average faces?" I asked.

"Yours is anything but average." I felt that same pull again. I let him shake my hand for an unusually long time while he continued studying me. He turned it over, palm up, and ran his index finger across it. "Long life line," he said.

"Thanks. I think." If he wasn't so adorable and if I wasn't feeling the magnetism so fiercely, I'm sure my subconscious would have been screaming, *Is this guy a serial killer?*

Helen yawned audibly and I realized Adam and I were just standing there, staring at each other in a trance.

"Bye, Adam," I whispered.

His kind eyes crinkled. "Bye, Charlotte."

I swallowed and pulled my hand out of his. After he turned to head down the street, Helen said, "What on earth was that?"

"What do you mean?" I was still blinking out of my trancelike state.

"He could have impregnated you with that look."

I jogged up the stairs to our apartment. "Yeah, he was kinda . . ."

"Hot!" Helen blurted.

I was going to say *strange*, even though I liked that about him.

She went on. "Did you see the way he looked at the mural?"

"Yeah, I thought it was sweet."

Helen stood near the door, waiting for me to unlock it. "You should have asked him out. I would have been all over that guy if he looked at me like that."

"Too late, I guess."

Once inside, Helen hopped up on the countertop, which sat in front of the sliding glass door that led to a small balcony overlooking the front of our building. She tore open the Chinese takeout box and began eating directly from it with the chopsticks Adam had given her.

"I can't believe you're eating that," I said from the couch.

"It's delicious!" she mumbled through a mouthful of noodles.

I rested my head against the back of the couch, closed my eyes, and yawned. "I think I'm gonna go to bed."

"Oh my god!"

"What?" I turned around quickly.

"Look, look, there he is!" Helen was pointing toward the sliding glass door.

I popped up, slid the door open, and ran out onto the balcony. From our second-story apartment you could see all the way down to the corner, to where Adam was standing stock-still, gazing up at the street sign.

"What's he doing?" Helen asked, joining me on the balcony.

"I think he's lost."

"Should we help him?"

"Adam?" I called out. He turned around and began shuffling toward our building.

"Now you can get his number," Helen said under her breath.

"Look at him, he has no idea where he is," I said.

"Maybe this is some weird act."

"Adam? Are you okay?" I shouted

"Yeah. I haven't lived here that long and I forgot my phone." He was looking up at us from the street.

Helen leaned into me. "Help him. Let him use your phone."

"I'll come down and help you," I said.

As I was walking toward the door, Helen followed me out. "Tell him he can use your phone in exchange for a kiss."

"Not if you're going to be watching us from the window, weirdo."

I don't know what changed inside of me; maybe it was his sweet smile as he stared up at me like a lost puppy while clutching his Chinese food, or maybe I was tired of always being the one to sit back and watch.

His eyes were wide when I met him on the stairs in front of the building. I held my phone out. "You want to punch your address into the GPS?"

Taking it from my hands he said, "Yeah, thanks so much."

"Sure." He handed me the Chinese food to hold as he

read an address off his palm and plugged it into the maps app on my phone.

"So you're brand-new to the area?" I asked.

"Uh huh, yeah . . . sorta. Okay, left, left, right three blocks, left, then right. Left, left, right three, then left, right." He was studying the screen.

"You live right by Bar Kenner, in those brick lofts?"

He gave me a thumbs-up. "You got it."

I raised an eyebrow. Those were very expensive lofts. "That's pretty close," I said.

"You go there? Bar Kenner?" he asked.

"Yeah, Helen and I go there after work sometimes."

He smiled when he noticed I was staring at his mouth. "You want to go there and get a drink?"

Oh my god, he's asking me out. Be cool. "Sure. When?"

"Right now?" He shrugged, revealing his dimples again. "Life's short."

I took my phone back and looked at the time. It was eleven thirty. "It's kinda late."

Coward! I shouted inwardly.

"Go ahead! Go!" came a voice from above. No, it wasn't God; it was Helen, standing on the balcony—eavesdropping, of course.

"I'll sweeten the deal and let you have some of my cold kung pao chicken."

"That's very enticing," I said.

"I mean, I understand if you can't," he said, picking up on my hesitation. "It's late. Rain check?"

"Go with him!" Helen shouted.

"Sure. Do you want my number?"

He looked around and shoved his hands into his pockets

like he was searching for a pen but coming up short. That's when I made the decision.

"Screw it. Let's get a drink now. Wait here, I need to grab a sweater."

"I'll be here," he said.

I ran back to the apartment, a huge smile on my face.

3. Soul Affinity

I took the stairs two at a time and burst through the door. Helen was waiting for me. "He's precious, all doe-eyed and unassuming," she said. I ran around searching for a sweater while she continued talking. "He must have a decent job; he's wearing a Tag watch, and those lofts near Bar Kenner are super expensive."

"The watch doesn't exactly fit his style. Maybe it was a gift?"

"He was just running out for takeout." She braced my shoulders, stopping me from spinning in circles. "Don't be standoffish. This guy seems nice. Plus he's hot. Did I mention that?"

"Why do you and my brother insist on bringing up how standoffish I am?"

"Because you have a pretty bad track record. It's time to change that. Just go have a drink with him and be chill."

"It's late and he's a stranger. We just met on the street. Am I not allowed to be a little nervous?"

"Text every five minutes if that makes you feel better. I'll stay up. Besides, it's only two blocks away and you'll be in public. You've done way shadier stuff than this. Remember when you met that guy at the Museum of Death?"

"Ugh, don't remind me."

"Wasn't he wearing a dog collar?"

I was still rummaging through my closet for the perfect sweater, trying to ignore Helen. "Yes, yes he was."

"What was the thing about his name?"

I laughed. "He told me his name was Atticus Danger and then I saw his ID; it said Albert Davis. Part of the skull and bones tattoo on his forearm rubbed off when I spilled my margarita on him at dinner."

"And you're worried about this guy? Just take an Uber if he creeps you out that bad."

I gave her pistol fingers, even though I had already made up my mind. "That's a good plan. I'll go."

"I'm proud of you. You never do anything fun. Ooh, maybe you guys will bone!"

"Let's not get ahead of ourselves. I'm going to have a drink. Stop pimping me out." I hurried to the door. "If you don't get a text from me by two a.m., file a missing persons report."

I heard her cackling gleefully as the door shut behind me.

Adam watched me closely as I made my way down the stairs toward him for the second time that night. "You look lovely."

"I just put on a sweater."

"Well, you look lovely in that sweater."

"Thank you."

He took my hand in his. "Come on."

I pulled him the other way. "It's this way."

"Oh right, ha! Just testing you."

I honestly didn't know what I was thinking, leaving my house at almost midnight on a dark street, four blocks from Skid Row, with a stranger. I guess my intuition wasn't sounding any alarms when it came to Adam.

We found two seats at the bar and ordered the same glass of wine, so Adam suggested we get a bottle. "Why not?" I said, fully throwing caution to the wind.

"So, Charlotte, tell me about yourself. What do you do?"

"Well, I work at Blackbird's, that shitty restaurant on Fourth. But I'm saving up to go to cosmetology school."

"Blackbird's? The place with the Bloody Mary bar and those weird flags?"

"That's the one!" I said, with equal parts triumph and embarrassment.

"Good tortilla soup, though, right?"

"Unfortunately, yes." Time to change the subject. "What about you, Adam?"

"I used to be a lawyer, actually."

"A lawyer?" I didn't expect that.

"Yeah, corporate litigation. The really depraved kind." He smirked.

"What, did you find God or something?"

"Yeah, something like that." He reached out and touched my bottom lip with his thumb. I had been chewing the inside of my mouth, a lovely habit I acquired as a toddler. "You're gonna chew your mouth off."

"I always do this."

"It's cute."

"It's kind of gross."

"You're right, it's disgusting," he said, but I could tell he was kidding.

"Hey!" I protested, and we both laughed. "So you were working as a corrupt lawyer and then you found God and quit? How do you afford that fancy Chinese take-out?"

He stared at me intensely for a moment. "Do you want to come over?" *Whoa. That was abrupt.*

"Um, what? To your house?"

"Yeah! Do you want to have a sleepover?" He waggled his eyebrows. *Oh my god, this guy is forward.*

"Honestly, that kind of freaks me out, Adam." Truth be told, I totally wanted to have a sleepover at his house, but it was a little soon. Even by Helen's standards.

"Okay, we'll just have the wine then." He took a sip as if he were totally unfazed by my rejection. "To answer your question, I'm taking a break from work. And I paint."

"Houses?"

He laughed. "No, artwork."

"Oh, that kind of painter."

"Are you an art fan, Charlotte?"

"Who isn't?"

"A lot of people, unfortunately." He laughed. "Tell me more about your life, your family. How do you like to spend your time?"

He watched me like he was trying to commit everything I said to memory. There were things I noticed about him as he sat there, engrossed in my ramblings. First of all, he was insanely handsome. His skin and hair were just dark enough to make the brown of his eyes seem impossibly light, and he was tall and slim while looking strong and capable all at once.

It's incredibly sexy when a man is as comfortable in his

skin as Adam was. His motions were smooth, from the way he lifted his wineglass to his mouth to the way he gestured with his hands. There was an ease about him. And he was spontaneous and fun. It excited me.

"My mom and dad are still happily married, living in Thousand Oaks, where I grew up. I have a little brother, Chucky, who's in school studying to be a dentist, just like my dad. Total golden boy. He's kind of a dick. I'm close to my mom because she gets me, but my dad has always been hypercritical, at least of me. He calls me Paper Doll."

"What does that mean?"

"It means he thinks I'm fickle. Like I'll float away in a gust of wind."

"Wow. That's kinda harsh."

"Well, I guess I am a bit scattered."

"You don't seem like that to me."

"You don't know me that well."

He smiled like he thought that had no bearing on the situation.

"Boyfriend?" he asked.

"No. You?"

"I'm straight."

I punched him in the shoulder. "I mean, do you have a girlfriend?"

He smiled. *God, those dimples. Those lips.* I couldn't look away from him; it was as if we were inhabiting our own little vignette, separate from the rest of the bar. He squinted and then shook his head.

"What?" I asked.

"You're really beautiful, Charlotte. And . . . I want to kiss you."

"This is moving really fast, Adam," I stammered.

"Life's short," he said again, looking intently into my eyes, entranced.

I held up my palm. "Not mine."

"Braggart," he whispered as he leaned in, watching my mouth.

We met halfway and suddenly we were kissing. Slowly, delicately. No other body parts touching but our lips.

He pulled away and opened his eyes. "Do you want to come to my house and have a sleepover?"

"You asked me already."

"What was your answer again?"

"My answer was yes, absolutely, without a doubt. Let's go back to your place."

He pulled out his wallet and threw some money on the bar before holding up the bottle of wine to the bartender. "Can we take this?"

The bartender pushed the cork back into the half-empty bottle and then placed it in a paper bag and handed it to Adam. "See you soon, Adam," he said.

"Yeah, you too, man."

"Do you know him?" I asked.

"Sure. He's the bartender here." He held out his hand to help me off the stool. "Come on, kid, let's have a pajama party."

We walked hand in hand toward Adam's apartment building. "You don't seem lawyerly," I said.

"What's lawyerly? Like, douche-y?"

"No, like . . . disciplined. Tightly wound. High-strung. You were roaming the streets in the middle of the night, wearing flip-flops and offering Chinese food to strangers."

"You must not know very many lawyers. Anyway, now I'm roaming the streets in the middle of the night, wearing flip-flops, carrying Chinese food, and holding your hand. I win. And there's nothing more lawyerly than winning."

I laughed. "Should I prepare myself for a ridiculously clean and organized loft? Like, will I have to take my shoes off?"

"It's a total mess. I'm actually a little embarrassed," he said, but I don't think he was truly embarrassed. He just seemed too confident to be embarrassed about anything.

Adam stopped suddenly when he spotted a BMW parked crookedly in a space on the street in front of his building. It was decorated with several orange envelopes, which I recognized as parking tickets. "Shit, I didn't even notice those earlier." He began pulling the envelopes off one by one until he was holding a healthy stack.

"Is that your car?"

"No, I'm going to pay this poor fool's parking tickets. Yes, it's my car, silly."

"Are you going to pay those?"

"No. I'm going to throw them away."

"You're not serious."

"I am. I've learned lately that I only have so many fucks to give. I'll move my car tomorrow, but tonight, I don't give a fuck about these parking tickets, or the car."

"What do you give a fuck about?"

"Getting to know you." He squinted. "Maybe even painting you." I didn't believe for one second he was going to throw the tickets away, but I was getting the sense that Adam was undergoing some sort of change in his life. People who become lawyers aren't the type to forget their phone at home and amass a ton of parking tickets. I wondered what happened at his job that had turned him into the person in front of me at that moment.

When we got to the top of the stairs, he stared at his keys for a while. "Here we go," he said, but the first one didn't work. The second one opened the door. "You know the bartender at that bar we were just at, but you don't know which key opens your front door?" I teased. He just winked at me.

It was a traditional high-beamed, open loft space with big floor-to-ceiling windows overlooking the street. The other walls were exposed brick. There were canvases, tarps, and paint supplies everywhere—literally hundreds of paintings just leaning in stacks against the walls. Other than a few kitchen appliances, a dresser, and a small table with two chairs, there was only a bed. No other furniture. The bed was unmade. I noticed the first four paintings I saw were of women. One in a park, one in a taxi, one lying across a bed in a flowing orange dress, and one looking out onto the ocean.

The loft was, in fact, a mess. It wasn't filthy—it was actually quite clean—but there were items strewn about everywhere. I spotted a bra hanging over the chair near the table. I spun around and glared at Adam.

"You never answered me. Do you have a girlfriend?"

"No, that's my friend's. She models for me."

"It looks like you have a lot of friends who model for you," I shot back.

He looked at me curiously. "Does that bother you?"

"No," I said lightly, suddenly feeling insecure.

"Are you hungry? I'm starving. And we need to finish

this." He held up the bottle of wine. "Plus, this is the best Chinese food ever."

I had a feeling I was heading straight for bedpost-notch town. I'd never been there and frankly never wanted to go down that road. Until I met Adam.

"Okay," I said. So what if he slept with a bunch of girls and then painted pictures of them? He was an artist. Isn't that what artists were known for? Weren't they so romantic that they'd cut their own ears off and mail them to the women they loved?

Wait, that's not romantic; that's insane.

Helen's dumb bucket list had all kinds of things wrong with it, including being someone's muse. If I became Adam's muse, just for one night, would I get an ear in the mail the next day?

I banished my crazy thoughts and continued to walk around Adam's apartment. His paintings were gorgeous—truly stunning. They were current but also felt classic, in the way that figurative paintings sometimes are. Some of the portraits were photorealistic, and others were intentionally out of proportion, like a Picasso. I wondered if my image would ever get lost in a stack somewhere in his cluttered loft.

I followed him into the kitchen area. He dished the food out onto two plates and then stuck them in the microwave. When I leaned against the counter near the microwave, he took my hands and spun me around to lean against the counter on the other side. "You shouldn't stand near the microwave when it's on."

"Why?"

"It'll cook your brains."

"You don't actually believe that."

He opened his eyes wide. "Yeah, I do."

I chuckled. "So, what's the plan?"

"We're chilling. We're hanging out," he said with his back toward me.

"This feels way too comfortable for two people who don't know each other at all."

He looked back at me. "We don't know each other?"

I laughed, but it didn't seem like he was kidding. He smiled, finally. "It does seem like that, doesn't it? Let's embrace it. We're getting to know each other. What else would you be doing right now?"

"Um, sleeping? It's pretty late."

"I'll sleep when I'm dead." He took two steps before I was pinned against the counter, his body pressed to mine. "If you don't want to be here, I understand. I can walk you home."

My head tilted back and I looked him in the eyes. Our faces were inches apart, and then centimeters, and then millimeters, and then we were kissing.

I was dizzy when he pulled away. "I'll stay for a while," I said.

"Good, let's get naked!"

"I don't think so."

The microwave dinged. "Okay, let's eat then."

I was in love with his spontaneity. I envied it. We sat at the small table, drank wine, and ate the warmed-up Chinese food.

"So tell me everything about you, Adam."

"Well, I'm twenty-nine. I grew up in Northern California. My dad was one of those guys who got in early on a

little company called Google, so we had lots of money growing up."

"Oh that little company? Yeah, I've heard of it. Go on."
Jeez, this guy must be loaded. No wonder he paints all day.

"I went to law school here at Loyola, and that's about
it. Up until now, my adult life has always been about work,
work, work."

"You always painted on the side, though?"

"No, I just started a year ago. I just have an affinity for it."

I looked around. "You're kidding me. You painted all of
these in a year?"

"I'm fast."

"I guess."

"Not at everything though." He winked.

Adam didn't have any framed pictures of family or
friends anywhere. In fact, it looked like he didn't really live
there, like maybe it was just his studio. "Do you live here?"

He laughed. "Yes. Why would you ask that?"

"Well, there's not really any personal items around."

"What, like tchotchkes?"

"Yeah, or vacation pictures."

"I had a really boring life when I was a lawyer. I thought
I was doing the right thing all that time, billing hours and
living for work, but then . . ." He hesitated. "One day, I just
sort of woke up and realized I didn't want to waste another
minute of my life. I had been working so hard to make
money, but I had no time to spend it. I lived and worked
in a high-rise downtown, but when I 'woke up,' I realized I
was suffocating. I bought this place, quit my job, and started
painting. And I've never been happier."

I was dying to know what had triggered his breakthrough

moment. I had a feeling I wasn't getting the whole story, but I didn't want to pry.

"Do you have siblings?" I asked.

"No, I'm an only child. My parents were of the mind-set that people should do one really well."

"Did they?"

"I'll let you be the judge." Before I could ask another question, he said, "Do you like donuts?"

"Yes."

"What's your favorite?"

"Uhhh . . . maple bars, I guess?"

"Shut up, me too! I know this place that's open twenty-four hours. They make maple bars as big as my arm. Wanna go?"

"Now?"

"Yes, now. Why do you think I brought it up?"

"Okay. Can I use the bathroom?"

"Of course." He pointed to the only other door beside the front door.

Once there, I checked my hair and reapplied lip gloss. I stared at myself in the mirror and mouthed, *What are you doing?*

"Come on, Gidget! Let's get those donuts!" he called from the kitchen area.

"One sec!"

When I opened the door, he was standing on the other side with his shoulders slumped. He looked dejected. He raised his gaze from the floor to my eyes.

"Hi," he said, his voice low.

"What's wrong? You were excited about donuts thirty seconds ago."

"I'm still excited about the donuts. I just got sad thinking that this night will eventually have to end."

My heart thumped. "Well, let's make it last as long as possible."

He smiled. "I'm in. Oh, and you're beautiful. Did I tell you that already?"

I didn't say anything. He could tell me as many times as he wanted to.

"Donut time," I said.

We held hands down the stairs. At the bottom, I realized it had gotten way colder out. "Oh shit, I forgot my sweater."

"I'll get it." He quickly ran back up and returned with my sweater and a backpack.

"What's in there?"

"Just some stuff. You want to help me?"

"Help you what?"

"Paint something. We have to be fast, though."

My heart raced. "What?"

He pulled me along, "Come on, kitten."

"You promised me donuts." I was suddenly worried about getting arrested.

"Your payment for being my assistant will be a giant maple bar. I'll even feed it to you."

4. Blind Eye

We ran down the street, hand in hand, but at the end of the block, he pulled me back from the curb and slapped his hand over his chest like he was having a heart attack. "Oh jeez, I thought there was a car coming. Sorry."

It was completely quiet out—not a car on the road or even the sound of one in the distance. At least he was being careful? We crossed the street and then he stopped in front of a concrete wall about two blocks down from his loft. "I only have enough paint for a small one." He removed two small cans of paint and about twelve brushes. Then he started painting frantically.

"Holy shit. What am I supposed to do?"

"Keep watch." It felt like the craziest thing I had ever done, but it wasn't like he was defacing the building; he was creating art.

He was hyperfocused. His hood was up and he was humming a mindless tune. "I think this will make sense someday," he mumbled.

After what seemed like hours, I turned around.

"Voilà," he said.

It was a profile of a man, wearing a black suit and top hat and looking down at his feet hovering off the ground. The only other color Adam used was baby blue to paint a stunning set of wings sprouting from the man's back. "Wow. That's breathtaking, Adam. What is this?"

"It's a man with wings, genius."

"I know that, genius, but what did you mean when you said it'll make sense someday?"

"Did I say that?"

Behind him, I saw headlights in the distance. "We better go. Are you going to sign it?"

"Nope."

I looked at it one last time. Adam's brushwork bore a striking resemblance to the mural on the side of my building. "Adam, did you paint those wolves on my building?"

"What wolves?"

Guess not. "Let's go." I took a picture of it with my phone and texted it to Helen.

> Me: Adam just painted this!

> Helen: Glad you're alive. It's not even 1 am yet so I haven't reported you.

> Me: I'm going to get donuts now.

> Helen: With spontaneous artist dude?

Me: Yeah, my dad would be over
the moon.

Helen: Yeah, he would disown
you.

Me: I like him, H.

Helen: Figures. Does this mean
I'll see you in the morning?

Me: ☺

Remember when I said I was a bit scattered? It wasn't just when it came to jobs. I had a slew of strange ex-boyfriends, too. There was George, who liked to wear my underwear . . . everyday. Not just to prance around in—he wore them under his Levi's at work. As a construction worker. That didn't go over well with his co-workers once they found out. He works at Jamba Juice now. I don't think anyone cares about what kind of underwear he wears at Jamba Juice.

Then there was Curtis. He had an irrational fear of El Caminos. Yes, the car. He just hated them so much that he became really fearful of seeing one. He'd say, "I don't understand, is it a car or a truck?" The confusion would bring him to tears. When we were walking on the street together, I had to lead him like a blind person because he didn't want to open his eyes and spot an El Camino. If he did, it would completely ruin his day. He would cry out, "There's another one. Why, God?" And then he would have to blink seven times and say four Hail Marys facing in a southerly direction.

I don't know what happened to Curtis. He's probably in his house playing video games and collecting disability.

After Curtis came Randall, who will never be forgotten. He was an expert sign spinner. You know those people who stand on the corner spinning signs? Randall had made a career of it. He was proud and protective of his title as best spinner in LA. I met him when he was spinning signs for Jesus Christ Bail Bonds on Fifth Street. He was skillfully flipping a giant arrow that said, "Let God Free You!" and his enthusiasm struck me. I smiled at him from the turn lane. He set the sign down, waved me over, and asked for my phone number. We started dating immediately. He called himself an Arrow Advertising executive when people would ask what he did for a living. He could spin, kick, and toss that sign like it weighed nothing. But when he'd put his bright-red Beats by Dre headphones on, he could break, krump, jerk, turf, float, pop, lock, crip-walk, and b-boy around that six-foot arrow like nobody's business. He was the best around and I really liked him, but he dumped me for Alicia, who worked at Liberty Tax in the same strip mall. She would stand on the opposite corner, wearing a Statue of Liberty outfit, and dance to the National Anthem. They were destined for each other.

After Randall was Paul. Ugh, Paul. That, I will admit, was completely my fault. I had zero foresight with him. Helen and I were working at this massage place called Dharma. She was the receptionist and I was trying to build a clientele there. You know what they don't tell you in massage school? They don't tell you that bad things are happening in some of the nicest massage establishments. They don't tell you that no matter where you work, you will occasionally get that random guy who thinks you'll give him a happy ending for an extra twenty. Helen jokingly called Dharma the best little whorehouse *not* in Texas.

Paul came in one day and seemed like an absolute gentleman. Good-looking, too. I gave him a massage and then he asked if he could take me out. We started dating pretty seriously . . . or so I thought. Every once in a while he'd come into Dharma on his lunch break and we'd have a quiet little romp while listening to the trickling sounds of some Zen meditation soundtrack shit they'd pump through the place on a loop.

One day, when I was late and Helen was home sick, the back-up receptionist told me that Amy, another therapist who we called Airbag Amy because of her enormous fake breasts (and because we hated her), was using my room for a client. "Why?" I had said.

"The client said the bed was better."

Something made me walk through that door, some force I couldn't fight. It was truly divine intervention that led me to Airbag Amy riding Paul, reverse cowgirl style, on my massage table, her giant tits bouncing like vulcanized rubber. I quit the little whorehouse that day and never saw Paul again. Bullet dodged.

I hadn't won any awards for picking men, so a part of me was just waiting for the other shoe to drop with Adam.

We arrived at Donut King, located in a short building among tall ones. It looked like an afterthought of a building. There was no door, just a window and a line halfway down the block.

"I didn't even know this place existed."

"It comes to life at night," Adam said.

"You bring all your dates here?"

He shook his head.

"There are a lot of paintings of women in your loft," I remarked.

"They're just women I see on the street and stuff."

"So you don't date them?"

"I don't think I would make a very good boyfriend, small fry."

Uh-oh. Do I want to know why? Wait, did he already forget my name? Is that why he keeps calling me all these weird nicknames?

"Why do you say that, Adam?"

"I'm a little forgetful, in case you haven't noticed. Not good with anniversaries, birthdays, in-laws, parking tickets. You know the deal."

"Were you always forgetful?"

He didn't answer me. I stood there awkwardly.

"I was dating a runner when I worked at the firm. Her name was Keri, and every weekend we'd get up early and go for a run. We ran by this place at seven in the morning once and there was a line wrapped around the building. As we passed by, Keri looked at the line, rolled her eyes at me, and said something about them being gluttonous pigs. I remember just really wanting a donut." He looked down at me and smiled. "I'm glad I'm here with you."

"What happened to Keri?"

He stared past me down the street, looking wounded. "She left me about a year ago, right after I quit the firm."

"I'm sorry," I said.

"Don't be. Her loss." He smirked. "Honestly, I could have been better to her."

We were getting close to the order window when he slipped a hand behind my neck, leaned in, and kissed me. The lady behind him bumped hard into his backpack, which forced Adam to stumble into me. He reached one hand out to the wall behind my head and the other snaked around my waist so I wouldn't get crushed against the brick wall. It was a somewhat athletic move. I felt completely safe and cocooned by him.

His eyes were wide open. He looked furious.

The lady leaned around him and said, "Sorry about that."

His body relaxed. He let go of me, turned toward the woman, and smiled. "No worries."

I was in awe of his self-control.

I could not figure Adam out. All I knew was that I liked him. One minute he'd be totally focused, and the next he'd be onto another subject. I couldn't tell if he was truly free-spirited or working toward it. He seemed like a typical guy his age, but I suspected he was grappling with something from his past.

We ordered two maple bars and headed back to Adam's loft. At the top of the stairs was a woman standing near his door, holding a cat. "Oh shit," Adam said.

My stomach sank. I thought for sure it was his girlfriend, or a disgruntled ex. "Hi, Adam. Foxy was out on the ledge meowing for the last half an hour."

He ran up the stairs toward the woman. "Come here." He took the fluffy black cat from the woman's arms. "Awh, I'm sorry, Foxy," he told the cat.

I stood a few steps below Adam. The woman was wearing a thin robe. She leaned around him and waved. "I'm Stacy, his neighbor."

"Oh, hi, I'm Charlotte. His friend."

"It's late. I'm sorry we woke you, Stacy," Adam said.

"You can't forget to close the bathroom window, Adam. Foxy can jump out here." She pulled a Post-it from her robe pocket. "I wrote you a note to put in the bathroom."

"Thanks." He took the note from her and gestured for me to come up. "Come on, let's go inside."

I hadn't noticed before because of all the clutter, but once I was back in his apartment, I realized there were little Post-its on various items throughout his apartment, reminding him to do random things like eat, buy food, and shower. When my grandmother got dementia and we'd go see her in the convalescent home, she would always call me by my mother's name because she remembered my mom from thirty years ago, but couldn't remember what she ate for breakfast. We had to put Post-its on pictures around her room to remind her of everyone's names. She still forgot.

Adam set Foxy down. "I better close the window before I forget." I picked up the cat. She purred. Adam called back, "That's Foxy Cleopatra! Get to know each other."

He had a cat. I always went for guys with dogs. I always thought dog people were more normal, but they're not. In fact, they're less normal. One time, George (the panty man) asked me to take his Labrador, Lucy, to the groomer while he was at work. When I picked her up, she was wearing a pink bandana with cherries on it. The groomer told me that Lucy had a fungal infection in her ears and recommended sixty-dollar eardrops and a cup of plain Yoplait with each meal. "You gotta be kidding me! Yogurt, for a dog?" I had said.

"It's a yeast infection. Like what women get, but in her ears."

"I'm sure it will run its course," I had said.

Her smile faded. "Is that what you do when you have a yeast infection? Let it run its course?"

"She's a dog."

I unleashed the puppy police with that statement. "How could you be so heartless? That poor animal is relying on you to take care of her."

I was about to tell the woman it wasn't even my dog, but I thought she'd probably try to have me arrested for dognapping. "I don't have sixty bucks."

"We take Visa and MasterCard."

When I told George about the incident, he said I was insensitive. And he never paid me back the sixty bucks. Dog people.

I had a cat named Ginger when I was a kid. He was orange. I named him when I was three, before I knew Ginger was a girl's name, according to most of the world. Anyway, when I was around eight, a raccoon attacked fierce Ginger. He came walking up our driveway with part of his intestines hanging out, dragging on the concrete. My dad said he'd be fine. No one believed my dad. Ginger somehow managed to climb into the rafters of our garage. I was 99 percent sure he was going there to die, but he didn't. He spent seven days licking his wounds until he healed himself. Cats are awesome! We had a lot of respect for Ginger after that, even though he was kind of an asshole.

"Oh my god!" Adam slammed the refrigerator door closed and my attention was suddenly directed to him standing in the kitchen, shocked.

I set down Foxy Cleopatra. "What?" I began walking toward the refrigerator.

He stood in front of it, blocking it. "No! You can't look in there."

I started feeling sick to my stomach. "What, what is it?" *Is it a human head?!*

He slowly moved out of the way. "You're gonna find out eventually." He looked down at the ground as I reached for the handle. I was trembling. This was suddenly getting very strange.

I opened it and looked in. There was nothing unusual. Adam leaned in, near my ear, and whispered, "Champagne. We haven't had Champagne tonight."

"You scared me!" I shouted. I grabbed the bottle and pulled it out.

"What'd you think you'd find in there?"

"You don't want to know."

In the kitchen, we ate the giant maple bars and drank Champagne from the bottle.

We were hopped up on sugar and Adam seemed fidgety. "Bathroom break. I'll be right back," he said.

"Okay." He handed me his phone. "Here, it's hooked up to the speaker up there. You want to put some music on?"

"Sure."

The picture on the screen saver was of Foxy. Maybe cat people are a little weird, too. Who just hands over their phone like that? He was hiding nothing from me, but he was still a mystery.

I picked Paul Simon, and "Obvious Child" came on. Adam yelled, "Good choice!" from the bathroom. He came out wearing only a white T-shirt and boxers. My mouth fell open in shock.

"What?" he said.

"What happened to your clothes?"

"I took them off." He squinted, confused. "Why are you dressed like that? It's the middle of the night."

I paused for a minute, unsure of what he meant. "This is the same outfit I've been wearing all night. How should I be dressed?"

Something flickered in his eyes. "Sorry, I bet that seemed weird. That was my lame attempt at a joke. Shall we get comfy?"

5. Stranger Things

"What the hell," I said. I kicked off my shoes, peeled off my jeans, and pulled my shirt over my head. I was standing in a black lace bra and underwear set.

"Wow."

"Wow?"

"Yeah, wow. By the way, have I told you how beautiful you are?"

I turned up the volume. "No!" I yelled over the loud music. "Tell me again, Adam!"

"You're insanely beautiful!" he shouted. He pulled me toward him and I was yanking his T-shirt off. He had *muscles*. If you must have a one-night stand with a strange artist-man who paints murals in your neighborhood and seems kind of weird, muscles help. I moved my fingertips across the ridges on his stomach and up his arms to his defined biceps. He laughed.

"Ticklish?" I said.

He guided my hand to his mouth and pretended to bite my fingertips.

A second later we were dancing like lunatics in front of the big window and then we took turns sliding across the wood floor in our socks. We ate more Chinese food and drank more Champagne and spun each other around until we collapsed into a pile on his bed. Then we were kissing and it wasn't slow anymore. It was frantic and passionate. We were tugging at each other and rolling from one side of his bed to the other. He was on top of me and I was yanking his boxers off with my toes, pulling them down his butt.

He jolted upright and grabbed my foot. "How are you doing that?" He inspected my feet. "Oh my god!" Holding my foot up, he said, "How are you doing that with these sausage toes?"

"Hey! I like my toes."

"They're adorable, but they look like they belong on a fat toddler."

We were both laughing, but I felt vulnerable, so I sat up. "Let me see your feet."

"I have beautiful feet," he said and it was true. The bastard could have been a foot model.

"Damn you."

"Come here, let me see those little Jimmy Deans."

"Leave my toes alone!" I tried to scurry off the bed but he caught me. He was sitting on the edge, pulling my arm back. He spun me around and his face was level with my belly. He kissed it, slowly, while running one hand up the inside of my thigh. There was no more talking after that.

He pulled me to straddle him and then he gently unclasped my bra and began kissing my breasts. I arched my back and let my head fall. A moment later, we were completely naked, rolling back onto the bed. I tried to pull him on top of me, but he turned us over again so that I was on top of him. I leaned forward and clicked off the bedside lamp. The light from the street reflected off the ceiling, creating a cool glow in the large loft space.

Remember what I said about one-night stands being awkward? It wasn't awkward with Adam. Usually teeth clash or heads bump or hands go the wrong way. It's like when you're walking down the street and you veer to the right to get out of the way of the person coming toward you, and then they veer to their left, mistakenly, and then a series of awkward jerky movements ensue, making you both feel like jackasses.

It was nothing like that.

At first we were just kissing; I was feeling a tad self-conscious about being naked on top of him. And then he was inside of me, coaxing me to move. "Sit back," he whispered.

I sat up and let my hair fall down my back. He gripped my hips hard as I began to move above him. He met my movements with ease.

Blissfully, he watched as I moved. My self-consciousness slipped away. I closed my eyes. When I slowed the rhythm, he flipped us over. He hovered over me, full of strength. We were connected, so close, and he was kissing my neck and nibbling at my ear and then his mouth was on mine. He picked up the pace and I could feel my body tingling. I was coming apart, letting go with a stranger. I couldn't believe how easy he made it all feel. Once there was no stopping it, my back arched off the bed, my neck went rigid, and one quiet "Oh" slipped from my mouth, almost painfully, before I felt myself pulsing all around him.

"Oh god," he murmured, and then he thrust one last time and collapsed on top of me.

When I opened my eyes finally, he was holding himself above me, staring down.

"What?" I said.

He squinted slightly, as though he were trying to recall something. "How long have we been in love?"

My throat tightened. I *felt* like I was in love with him, but I didn't even know him. It was just lust, ecstasy, some weird trick our brains played on us right after sex, but the look on his face was so sweet, sincere, genuine. I reached up and ran my hand through his hair.

"It's been years now. Five, right?"

"Yeah, I think so, but I'm bad with anniversaries, remember?" He smiled.

We were role-playing and I was into it. Most of the men I dated would have shied away from this type of thing . . . afraid it would lead to something permanent. I wanted to pretend for just one night that we were in love . . . that I was his muse.

We lay in bed next to each other, naked, holding hands, staring up at the ceiling.

"Do you believe in reincarnation?" he asked.

"I'm not sure," I said. "I guess I believe that our energy is everywhere, even after we leave the physical world. Like our souls leave some residual imprint on the people we knew, or something."

"Explain."

I turned toward him, propping my head up on my hand. "Your art, our memories, the memories people have of us . . . it makes us immortal. When you love someone, whether it be your family, friends, partners, whatever, it's like planting a little seedling of yourself inside of their hearts."

"I like that," he said. "Tell me about us. How'd we meet?"

I searched his eyes. "I can't believe you don't remember."

He smiled as if to say, *you know I do.* "I just want to hear you tell it again. I love the way you tell it."

"We met at a museum . . . the Getty." I had to think on my pudgy toes, but I was getting a chance to describe exactly what I wanted. My fantasy.

"The Getty . . . right. Go on," he said.

"We were both completely mesmerized by that Edvard Munch painting. What is it?"

"*The Scream?*"

"No, *Starry Night*," I said.

"That's Van Gogh, kitten."

I reached across him for my phone on the bedside table. "I swear to god, Munch also painted a *Starry Night* and it's at the Getty. We met in front of that exact painting." I Googled it and handed him the phone. He stared at the screen.

"Yes, I remember now. What were you wearing?"

"A red dress. I had my hair up, Audrey Hepburn style."

"That's right. And you were staring at the painting for a long time." He closed his eyes. "I wanted to kiss the back of your neck."

"You didn't, though; you just said something absent-mindedly like, 'It's not as starry as the Van Gogh version.'"

He laughed. "Sounds like something I would say."

"I agreed with you and then you asked me out on a date. I politely declined."

"How could you?"

"I was playing hard to get."

"Of course you were."

"But then you followed me through the whole museum, making silly comments about the artwork. We played I Spy in the Italian Romanticism section. You kept hinting at boobs and penises. I told you to grow up, so you disappeared for a bit and then you found me a little while later, staring at the illuminated manuscripts. You tried to act cultured and sophisticated. You pointed out some crap about the fine brushwork detail and we both started laughing. That's when you asked me out again and I said yes."

"And for our first date I took you to—"

"Pink's Hot Dogs!" I shouted.

"Gross."

"I know, I was deeply disturbed, but you just kept saying it was an institution."

"You know I don't eat pork, silly," he said.

"They're all-beef hot dogs," I quickly replied.

"After Pink's, I brought you here and we made love."

"No."

"No?"

"You were the perfect gentleman. You drove me home, walked me to the door, and kissed me on the cheek. Then you asked me out on a second date."

"It's because I really liked you."

"I pulled you inside my apartment and had sex with you on my kitchen floor."

He turned and looked at me with wide, shocked eyes. "You did not."

"I know, I'm teasing. We ended up going out the next night. And we've been together ever since."

"Didn't I take you to the Griffith Observatory a couple of months later?" he asked.

"Are you being silly? That's where you told me you loved me for the first time."

I expected at some point for him to start laughing like it was all ridiculous, but he didn't.

"I didn't forget that. I was just testing you," he said.

"Remember you were looking into a giant telescope and you pulled away and said, 'Darn, there's not enough,' and then I said 'What?' and you said, 'There aren't enough stars up there to match the reasons why I love you.'"

"God, I'm romantic when I want to be."

"Yes, you are."

He leaned over and kissed me. "I'm sure I've told you a million times, but I'll tell you again. Your body is perfect." He smoothed his hand down my side to my hip as we lay face-to-face.

I traced my finger along his chest muscles across the small tuft of hair. "You're not so bad yourself."

"Do you know why I paint?"

"Because you're damn good at it."

He laughed once. "No, that's not it."

I pulled the sheet off the bed and wrapped it around my body. I went to the window and bent near a stack of canvases propped against the glass. "You painted this one because you liked the color of this woman's hair." The woman in the painting was standing in front of Adam's building.

"Maybe," he called out from the bed.

"You must enjoy it?"

"I do."

"Have you ever tried to get a show or sell any of these?"

"Not really. It doesn't really matter to me."

"They're beautiful, Adam. The world should see them." Glancing at the clock, I noticed it was almost three. "Shit, I need to text Helen."

I stood up, facing the window, and turned to find Adam standing right behind me. His eyes were wide. "What are you doing?" I asked.

He blinked. "Painting," he said, but he wasn't. He was just watching me.

"There you go, being romantic again."

"Guess so."

"I need to call Helen." I tried to walk past him, but he pulled me against his body and kissed me.

When he stepped away, he said, "Who's Helen?"

"My roommate."

He smirked. "You mean I'm not your roommate?" He was still playing. *Maybe we'll do this all night. I wouldn't mind.*

"No. Remember we decided to live separately?"

"I can't imagine why," he said earnestly.

A quiet alarm went off on Adam's phone. He stared at it. "What's that for?" I asked.

"Nothing. No big deal. I'll be right back." He went off to the bathroom and I texted Helen.

> **Me: Staying here tonight.**
>
> **Helen: You okay? Code word?**

Helen and I had code words for everything. It was usually an old pet's name or a line from one of our favorite movies. Growing up, Helen's family had Maltipoos. It's a mix between a Maltese and miniature poodle . . . damned dog people and their overbreeding. Anyway, they had a little black Maltipoo named Major. He would have been adorable if he weren't an incessant humper. It was just vile; truly, the dog was persistent and fanatical about humping. Witnessing Major molest everything in his path was traumatizing. He was constantly in motion, his little butt pumping in and out. There was clearly something wrong with him. He humped everything from stuffed animals to vacuum cleaners to any leg he came in contact with. Helen and I hated that dog. We called him Major Humperdinck. After high school it became our code for *I totally want this guy to hump me*. I know, we were disgusting girls.

> **Me: Major.**
>
> **Helen: Major What?**
>
> **Me: Don't . . .**
>
> **Helen: I'm calling the police.**
>
> **Me: Major Humperdinck**
>
> **Helen: I knew it. Well, have fun . . . slut.**

But I wasn't a slut. I was Adam's long-term girlfriend that he had met at the Getty. When I put down the phone, I noticed he was standing near the window, gloriously naked. I lay back on the bed and watched him look out onto the street.

"Oh my god, honeybuns, you should see this. There's

a couple down there. I think . . . I think they're falling in love," he said.

"What if they look up and see you flashing them? Isn't that voyeurism or something? You could get arrested."

"It's exhibitionism, not voyeurism. They can't see me anyway. They're too busy being all crazy in love with each other to notice anything else."

"What are they doing?" I didn't get up. For some reason, something kept me there, on the bed, watching him in all his innocent wonder.

"Ah, this is so sweet. Oh, they're dancing now, under the streetlight. Holy shit, he's getting down on one knee."

"He's proposing to her?" I asked.

"Wait, I'm a great lip reader. I can tell you what he's saying. Okay, he's saying, *I know we only just met, but I think you're amazing.*"

"Wow, what a coincidence," I said.

"Wait, there's more. He's saying, *I want to spend the rest of my days with you.* Oh my god, kitten, he did it."

"What, what?" I shouted, caught up in the moment.

"He asked her. He said, 'Marry me?'"

I finally jumped out of bed, dragging the sheet behind my naked body.

I stood in back of Adam, wrapping my arms around his middle as he faced the street. Just as I was peeking over his shoulder to see what he was watching, he turned and wrapped himself around me. "You missed it," he said. "They're gone."

"I missed it, dammit. Where'd they go?"

"Probably to have sex somewhere."

"Or maybe get a donut and celebrate?"

"Yes, they probably went for a donut." He laughed and then kissed my nose. "Let's dance."

We swayed back and forth until we were kissing again. He lifted me with ease to straddle him, then he pushed me against the glass of the front window. "Someone will see us," I said.

"So what? It's the middle of the night. Don't we do this? Isn't this what we do?"

"What, Adam?" I said huskily, trying to catch my breath as he ran his tongue across my neck and up to my ear.

"Stay up all night, talking, making love?"

I squirmed. "Yes, we do."

He pushed harder against me. "Let's be in the moment." I shivered from his voice near my ear. He pulled the sheet around us as he gripped my bottom, pressing me into the glass. Gliding into me with ease, he buried his face in my neck and whimpered. "God, you feel so good." He looked up; we were face-to-face. There was curiosity in his eyes.

Something hit me. Adam had done this before, clearly. I looked around the room quickly. Any one or every one of these women in the paintings had probably been pressed against this window, just like this, while Adam moved slowly, in and out, professing his undying love to a person he didn't know.

He finished and then breathed into my neck while he held me.

I kept still, squeezing my eyes shut, forcing the tears back. This is the part about one-night stands that I hate. In the end, everyone is just pretending.

The rumble of Adam's chest shook my body as he began laughing. I felt as if I were going to throw up. He set me down. "We probably looked like a ghostly blob in that white sheet, fucking against the window." His humor suddenly seemed less charming and more callous.

"Mmmhmm," I said, a sullen note in my voice.

He stood up and took a step back, recognizing the change in my demeanor. "What's wrong?"

"My name is Charlotte." My stomach was twisting in knots.

"I know," he said. "What's wrong, Charlotte?"

Still leaning against the glass, I wrapped the sheet around my body. Adam stood naked, facing me. "Nothing," I mumbled.

"Something's wrong." With his thumb and index finger he pinched my chin, tilting my head up to look him in the face. He was smiling with his eyes, with utter sincerity and warmth.

He leaned in with confidence and kissed me, slowly, sweetly. "You're stunning and that was beautiful and I loved every second of it. I'm sorry you didn't like it. Did I hurt you?"

Was it true? Was it a line?

"No, but are you going to paint it?"

"Paint what?"

"Us, what we just did?"

He shook his head. "No."

"No?"

"No. I don't need to. I'll never forget it and it's sacred."

He paints to remember?

I wanted to believe him. I wanted to believe the stranger I had met on the street hours before wasn't just playing me. I wanted to believe he was falling for me. I kissed him, dropping the sheet and wrapping my whole body around him. My chest shook from the emotion. He held me tightly to him, rubbing my back as he carried me to his bed and lay me down. I was so bone-achingly tired that nothing felt real. It was all dreamlike.

He kissed my nose. "You should get some sleep," he said. "I'll make you breakfast when we get up."

"Things will be different in the morning," I said.

"Why?" He slid under the sheet next to me. I put my head on his chest and he held me like we had been sleeping that way for years.

The glow of dawn began to invade the loft, unwelcome and painfully bright. We were fighting sleep but completely calm, wrapped in each other.

"Have I asked you to marry me?" he said sleepily. We were back on.

"Every day," I replied.

"Well . . ."

"I always say not yet."

Adam was dozing off and slurring when he said, "Why?"

I'm certain he was asleep when I finally replied, "Because I don't want you to stop asking."

6. Just a Dream

Hours later, I was startled awake by the sun blasting through the large loft window. I was naked and alone in Adam's bed. I glanced down at my buzzing phone and noticed three missed calls, all from my mom. I quickly texted Helen.

Me: I'm fine. Thanks for caring.

Helen: You guys bone?

Me: I'll call you later.

Helen: That's a yes, Major Humperdinck.

Me: Stop texting me.

**Helen: Your mom called here twice.
Said your phone was off.
I told her you were at church.
HAHAHAHAHAHAH!**

Me: I'll call her in a sec.

"Adam?" I called out, but he didn't answer. I figured he was in the bathroom.

I dialed my mom's number. She picked up on the first ring. "Church? Please. You'll have to tell Helen to come up with something better than that."

"I went to get donuts." I was trying to rush the phone call before Adam came back into the room. "What'd you call for?"

"Nice manners. I just called to say hello. Am I allowed?" she snickered.

"Of course. Sorry, Mom. I'm fine, really."

"Are you still coming to dinner tonight?"

Right then Adam walked into the room and looked at me peculiarly. "Hello," he said in a timid voice.

"Ummm . . ." I was tongue-tied.

"Did I hear a man's voice?" my mother said.

"No. Um, so yeah, I'll be there for dinner. What time?"

"Around six?"

"That works," I said. Adam was still staring. He walked over and picked up my clothes and set them on the bed before heading toward the kitchen. *That was weird.*

"Love you, Mom, I gotta go."

Just then I heard a loud crash punctuated by a breathy groan from Adam in the kitchen. I ran toward the commotion, sporting just the sheet. He was buckled over, grumbling, "Fuck, fuck!"

I ran around the bar and put my hand on his back. "Oh my god, are you okay?"

He was wincing in pain, holding his hand to his head. "Adam, did you cut yourself?" I looked in the sink at the broken glass and then at his hand. There was no blood. "Adam, I said are you okay?"

He was groaning, clenching his jaw. "I'm okay," he said finally. "I just . . . too much alcohol last night, not enough sleep."

"We didn't drink that much."

"You know, you're not really my girlfriend." And then he glanced toward my clothes on the bed. "I don't need your help, okay?"

I stared at him for a moment, then stood up and pulled the sheet tighter around me. "Trust me, I wasn't confused by last night."

I rushed over to the bed, fighting back tears, grabbed my clothes, and went into the bathroom. *What the fuck is happening?*

When I walked out of the bathroom, he rose from the kitchen floor and rushed to the door to head me off. "Tell me something."

"What?"

"Why did you lie?"

"What do you mean?"

"That story . . . of us being together . . ."

I was starting to feel sick to my stomach. "You lied, too."

"Why'd you do it?"

"Because you wanted me to? Because I wished it were true?"

He shook his head, pinning me with his stare.

"I'm sorry." I meant it. I was sober and it all seemed so stupid now.

His expression softened. He reached out to touch my face but pulled back. "I think you should go," he said.

"I'm already one step ahead of you."

I opened the door and left without looking back.

ONCE I GOT home, I proceeded to mope around my apartment while Helen watched me like a hawk. I had told her everything, watching her face transform from totally excited to completely horrified.

"Did you get his phone number?"

"I know where he lives, Helen. I don't need his phone number. Also, I never want to see him again."

She was sorting laundry on the couch, looking on while I opened the refrigerator, stared into it uncomprehendingly, and closed it. Over and over again. But there was no point; I had no appetite.

"I think you should go over there and be like, what's up? Tell him you're a grown-up and you know what a one-night stand is. He didn't have to be a dick."

I replayed the night and morning in my head. "The weird thing was that he seemed more disappointed than rude."

"Some guys just aren't straight up about it. They like to make girls feel stupid so they'll leave without being told."

"Oh, he *told* me."

I opened the refrigerator again.

"You're letting all the cold out, Charlie."

"Do you want to have dinner at my parents' tonight?"

"Chuck the Fuck gonna be there?" She was referring to my golden-boy brother.

"Who cares?" I said flatly.

"I just hate how your parents dote on him right in front of your face."

I plopped down on the couch next to her folded laundry. "Mom doesn't."

"No, I guess not. Pops is just hard on us." My parents treated Helen and me like we were sisters. Helen sometimes called my mom "Mom" and my dad "Pops," though I don't think he was very fond of the nickname. Growing up, she had spent many weekends at our house, so it was just natural, but I think my dad felt that Helen and I had an unhealthy relationship. Maybe we did, but I didn't care; she was my only friend.

7. That Computer Thingy

I was still in a mood when we got to my parents' house. My mom was asking me a million questions while she cooked beef stroganoff, which I hated, by the way. My brother Chucky loved it, so she made it every time she thought he was joining us for dinner.

"Is Chuck even gonna be here?" I asked her while I hovered around the stove and Helen sat on the countertop, checking her phone.

My mom ignored me. "Helen, get off the counter and help Charlotte set the table."

"Should we set a spot for the prince?" Helen asked.

My mom smiled. She actually loved Helen. "Set two extra spots. One for Charles and one for the new girl he's dating."

"Ew, gross, who would date him?" I asked, rolling my eyes.

Chucky never showed up, even though he technically

lived at home. He had zero respect for my parents and they gave him everything, including all of their attention.

The first thing my dad said after kissing me on the cheek and taking his seat at the dinner table was, "When are you girls gonna get serious?"

"What do you mean, Pops?" Helen said.

"I mean, are you going to work at Blackbird's until they run out of that tortilla soup?"

"Honey," my mom said.

"No, I'm serious, Laura. These girls are gonna squander their twenties playing games at a diner while they date and date and date some more." He shook his head. "How come we never meet any of these guys?"

My mom answered for me. "We have. We met that one boy, with the neck tattoo."

I looked at Helen. "Curtis."

Helen laughed hysterically. "You met Curtis, the guy who used to cry when he saw an El Camino?"

"It's not funny, Helen," I said, "he had a serious phobia. He could barely leave his house."

I thought about the night before with Adam. He would have seemed suitable to my parents. Too bad he dogged me.

Helen knew I was thinking about him. She was staring at me from across the table.

"It's too bad you never got to meet Adam, Laura," Helen said.

"I've never even heard of an Adam," my mom replied.

I tried not to make eye contact with my mom.

"Helen," I warned through clenched teeth. My mother caught my eyes. "What?" I said to her.

"Tell me about Adam."

My mom was sincere but my dad, on the other hand, was shaking his head, slurping up his dinner and trying to ignore us.

"He was a lawyer," I said.

"A lawyer?" my mom said. Both of my parents perked up.

"I went on one date with him, Mom." I didn't mention that it was the night before. That would have been too uncomfortable, even for Helen.

"Why? What did you do?" my dad said.

"Nothing. I don't think he liked me that much."

"How could he not?" My mother was shocked. "You're beautiful and smart."

"Thanks, Mom," I said into my bowl of stroganoff.

"Of course, leave it to Charlotte to finally find a nice lawyer and then send him running for the hills."

"How's the dental business, Dad?" I tried to change the subject.

He looked up at me. "Great, as usual. Charles is very lucky that he'll inherit the practice, but he's also worked his ass off for it."

Helen chimed in, "Adam was an artist, too. A painter."

Why was she stuck on this topic? I felt bad enough.

"That's romantic," my mother mused.

"Yeah, so romantic," my dad said sarcastically.

"Let's stop talking about this," I begged.

"Well, I know you don't want to talk about it anymore, but I signed you up for that computer match thingy."

Why is it that so many people over the age of sixty refer to everything on the Internet as some sort of "computer thing"?

Helen was trying to contain her laughter. "Laura, do you mean Match.com?"

My father was groaning audibly now.

"Yes, that's it. Charles helped me put up her profile."

"Oh my god, Mother. Are you kidding me?"

Helen jumped out of her seat and started running toward the computer in my dad's home office, which was right off the dining room.

"Get out of there, Helen," my dad yelled, but she ignored him.

I chased after her, but she stuck her arm out, blocking me from the monitor. "No, I have to see it!" she shouted.

"Stop it, girls," my mother chided.

"Move, bitch." We were very mature for our age.

"This is the best day of my life. Your mommy made a Match profile for you!"

"Actually, Chuck made it," my mother yelled from across the hall.

Oh shit.

Helen typed my name in quickly. My prom picture from nine years ago popped up on the screen. My brother had cropped Steve Dilbeck out of the photo the best he could, but you could still see Steve's arms wrapped around my purple chiffon–clad waist. "You're joking. You're fucking joking."

"Language, Charlotte!" my dad yelled.

"Mom," I cried, "he used my prom photo! What is wrong with him?" I still had braces at eighteen. I had to wear them for seven years because my orthodontist said I had the worst teeth he had ever seen. You know how sharks have rows of teeth? Yeah, that was me. I blame my mother and the extended breastfeeding for that one, too. My brother, Chuck the Fuck, used to tease me, saying it was leftovers of the dead Siamese twin I had absorbed in utero. My brother's an ass, so it's pretty awesome that he set up this handy dating profile for me. In case you hadn't noticed, our names are Charlotte and Charles. Just more parental torture. Would it be dramatic to call that child abuse?

Underneath my prom photo, I read the profile details while Helen laughed so hard she couldn't breath.

My name is Charlotte and I am an average twenty-seven year-old. If you looked up the word mediocre *in the dictionary you would see a picture of me—more recent than this nine-year-old photo, of course, because at least back then I hadn't inked my face like an imbecile.*

Did I forget to mention that I have a tiny star tattooed under my left eye? Yes, I'd been drunk at the time. It was a momentary lapse of judgment. It would actually be cute if it was a little bigger, but it's so small that most people think it's a piece of food or a freckle. I cover it up with makeup.

I like junk food and watching reality TV. My best friend and I like to drink Champagne because it makes us feel sophisticated, then we like to have a farting contest afterward. I've had twelve boyfriends in the last five years so I'm looking for a lifer. It's not a coincidence that I used the same term as the one for prisoners ineligible for parole.

"Chuck the Fuck," Helen squeaked through giggles.

I turned and glared at her. "He still doesn't know that you watched him jerk off like a pedophile when he was fourteen."

"He's only three years younger than us."

"Four. And I *will* tell him. I'll unleash Chuck the Fuck on you if you don't quit."

My breasts are small and my butt is big and I have a moderately hairy upper lip. I also don't floss, clean my retainer, or use mouthwash with any regularity.

"God, my brother is so obsessed with oral hygiene!"

"That's what stood out to you? He said you have a mustache." Helen grinned.

"Girls, get out of there and come clear the table," my dad yelled.

"What do you think the password is?"

"Try 'Fatbutt,'" I said.

"Yep, that worked. Okay, I'll change your profile while you clear the table."

My parents had retired to the living room while I cleaned up and Helen tried doing damage control for the sake of my love life.

"I have a good picture of you from Facebook," she said. "Oh my god, Charlie, you have three messages from men who want to date you."

"Read them to me," I called out.

"Okay, this is from Rod in Hollywood. It says, 'Charlotte, I'm dying to see your ink. I also like your candor. Can we chat?'"

"What does he look like?"

"Oh no, his entire face is tattooed."

"Move on. Read the next one."

"This is Ben in Encino. He says, 'Charlotte, hit me up, yo.'"

"Next!" my mother and I said in unison.

"Okay, this is Charles from TO. It's your brother." Helen starts chuckling. "It says, 'Hey Fatbutt, guess you figured out the password. Please don't trick any poor fools into dating you by lying about your disgusting habits and sick-ass halitosis. Love, Chucky.'"

"Bastard," I said under my breath.

"Charlotte Ann Martin!" my father scolded from the other room.

I didn't think he could hear me.

"Okay, I'm fixing it," Helen said.

The picture she changed it to was of me in a skimpy bikini, standing in a house in Cabo, holding an ice pack to one eye and frowning. Our families were on vacation there the year before. I had gotten stung by a bee on my forehead and my entire left eye had swollen like a puffer fish.

"That picture?"

"You look vulnerable and cute and your body looks hot."

The new profile details read:

I'm Charlotte, 27, and mildly allergic to bees, but I do love being outside, going to the beach, live music, baseball, and dining out! I love life and adventure, especially when I have someone to share it with.

"I like it, but baseball?"

"You love going to baseball games," Helen said.

"Right, but I wouldn't call myself a fan. I don't even know any of the players on the Dodgers."

"Listen to me. Guys like girls who are willing to watch sports with them. I wouldn't be caught dead at a baseball game, but you love that shit."

"Honestly, it's the butts in the baseball pants I love."

"Nevertheless, Charlie, you only have so many angles. Would you rather I include your proclivity for men with debilitating phobias and cross-dressing fetishes?"

"Fine, leave the baseball thing."

When we left my parents' house that night, my mom told me to be patient and my dad said, "You better figure it out. Your college fund is gone and I can't help you out of a pickle."

I hugged him even though I felt wounded. "I will, Dad. I'm gonna be a hairdresser."

"What, like how you were gonna be a real estate agent?"

That stung.

Helen tugged on my arm. "Come on, Charlie. Bye Pops, bye Mom, we gotta go."

Sometimes she saved me from their scrutiny, and I did the same for her with her parents. We relied on each other a lot. Maybe too much.

8. Jedi Mind Trick

A week later, I was checking Match.com. I laughed out loud at a message I had gotten.

> *Charlotte, hello, my name's Seth Taylor and I'm also mildly allergic to bees, love baseball, and have asshole family members who think they're hilarious. (I caught on pretty quickly to your original profile details.) I live south of LA. I'm not great at emailing or texting, so if you want to talk, here's my number. I'd love to chat with you.*

I was sitting on the couch in our apartment, waiting for his profile picture to load.

"Oh my god."

From the bathroom, Helen yelled, "What? Is he ugly? Or is it an old guy?"

I was speechless. Seth Taylor was *hot*. Like, surpassing a ten on the range of hotness into *he would never give me the time of day* territory. Of course he posted a picture of himself lying on a beach, shirtless, with an adorable sleeping black Lab splayed across his twelve-pack abs. I wanted to be lying across his twelve-pack abs. I'd polish his twelve-pack abs with my tongue if I could.

"No, he's cute!" I called out. "But he's a dog guy."

Helen came out of the bathroom and looked over my shoulder. "He's gorgeous."

"He would never like me," I said.

"Give it a chance."

It was a Monday at ten in the morning. "Do you think it would be weird to call him now?" I couldn't take my eyes off his photo. He had short, golden-brown hair, blue eyes, and a perfectly scruffy jawline. He had a playful expression in the photo, like those people who can smile with just the corners of their eyes.

"You should call him. He's gonna get snatched up. And look, he's younger than you, you cougar."

"He's two years younger than me," I protested.

"Call him!" Helen messed up my hair, then skipped off to her room.

I dialed his number. "Hello," he said. His voice was deeper and smoother than I expected. It radiated through me.

"Hi."

"Hi."

I should have written down at least five go-to lines before I dialed his number.

"I'm Charlotte. I'm the girl you messaged on Match."

"Hi, Charlotte, I'm Seth."

Awkward silence. "Hi, Seth."

"Well, I think we've gotten the introductions out of the way. Your profile was pretty brief, although I did appreciate the prom picture that was up before this new one, which, by the way, is hot, even though you're holding an ice pack to your face."

He called me hot. Is that good or bad? Stop overthinking this, Charlotte, and talk to the poor guy. "Oh, thank you. That first profile was my brother's creative genius."

"I figured. I'm actually the youngest with three sisters— so I fully understand how sibling love works."

"Three sisters? My goodness. That must have been interesting."

"There was a lot of drama and fighting over the bathroom. I'm also very skilled at painting nails and picking out accessories."

"I just realized I didn't look at your profile details. All I saw was your picture and the message you sent me."

"You should have done your research. We might have nothing in common. I can read it to you if you want?"

"Sure." *This is weird.*

"'I'm Seth Taylor, I enjoy hunting large endangered species and finding ways to get out of paying my taxes. I'm better looking than most people and I hate everyone under the age of eighteen and over the age of fifty-five. I own a lot of button-down stripies and my favorite cologne is called Sex Panther, which is made with little bits of real panther so you know it's good. Hit me up.'"

There was no way I could contain my laughter. Before I even responded, I went to his profile on my laptop and saw zero description, so I knew he was making the whole thing up.

"What do you think?"

I was still laughing. "Sex Panther sounds delicious."

"Women like it, sixty percent of the time, every time."

"All right, I found your real profile but there's no description, clever guy."

"Well, I can tell you about myself. I lied about the little bits of panther; everything else is true. What else do you wanna know?"

The conversation was picking up with ease. I felt comfortable talking to him. He seemed down-to-earth and fun.

"Where do you live, what do you do? What do you like to do for fun? Is that your dog in the profile?"

"Yes, that is my dog, Obi-Wan, and he's awesome. I live in Encinitas. Do you know where that is?"

"Yeah, on the coast, right? In San Diego?"

"Yep. I'm embarrassed to admit this but I'm living with my parents until I finish school."

Ugh, he's still in college at twenty-five?

"What else?"

"I like baseball and I like to surf. But let me tell you more in person. Can we meet tomorrow night?"

The invitation was completely abrupt. "Um, well . . ."

"I mean, I have to take off right now. But I wanted to plan something . . . with you."

"Yeah, sure, where do you want to meet?"

"How about you text me an address and I'll meet you there at seven tomorrow?"

"Okay. Sounds good."

"Looking forward to seeing you in person."

"Likewise." We hung up.

I screamed with excitement and then Helen and I danced around the apartment. Adam would soon be a distant memory once I went out with cute and clever Seth.

THE NEXT DAY, Helen picked out a slutty outfit for me to wear, but I chose to go with jeans, a sweater, and flats. We were to meet at Villains. I figured I better keep it close and safe so I could call in reinforcements if I needed to.

When I got there, I took a seat at the bar and ordered a glass of white wine. I checked my phone and looked around every five minutes. Five minutes turned into thirty minutes—and no Seth.

I texted Helen.

> Me: I'm getting stood up. He's still not here.

> Helen: He lives far away. Text him or give him another twenty.

> Me: This is beyond rude. He should be texting me.

After an hour, three glasses of wine, and no food, I began Googling convents in the area. Not surprisingly, there weren't many. Helen hopped onto the stool next to me and put her arm around my shoulders. "Awh, Charlie, I'm sorry."

She peeked at my phone. "You going to marry God now?"

"I'm thinking about it."

"Stop drowning your sorrows in that wine. Let's go home. We have to do brunch tomorrow at the restaurant and you know how Jon-Jon gets when we show up hungover."

"I only have so many fucks to give, Helen, and Jon-Jon

is not one of them." I used Adam's line because it was true. I needed to prioritize.

She pulled the glass out of my hand and downed the rest of it. "Let's make a deal. We'll get wine tomorrow after work and scroll through Match.com together and look for nice boys . . . for both of us."

"No," I barked. "As a matter of fact . . ." I hit the Match .com app on my phone and immediately deleted it. "I'm over it. I'm taking a break from dating. Giving myself six months, minimum."

Helen laughed. She didn't believe me, but I had suddenly and finally acquired some resolve after being a flake for so long. Getting dropped on your ass by two men back to back will do that to you.

9. [...]

Six months later . . .

Six months into my celibacy, I was still slinging fries at Blackbird's. Helen had managed to date a busboy, a cook, and the UPS delivery man. He serviced Blackbird's while sweet Helen serviced him in the supply closet. She rebounded about ten times after Luc while he watched on with indifference. She told me I needed a rebound, too, but from what? A one-night stand and getting stood up almost immediately after by a hot guy with abs?

One Tuesday my mom came down for dinner at Blackbird's. After our shift she was going to follow us back to my apartment so I could touch up her roots. I was muddling through the beginning of cosmetology school but losing interest with every day that passed, much to the surprise of no one.

I looked over to where my mom was sitting and noticed she was lowering and raising the stupid little tortilla soup flag like it was a toy. Approaching her table I said, "Are you bored?"

"Not at all, sweetie." My mom had the most pleasant speaking voice and the kindest eyes. She made everyone smile. Helen always said my mom and I were alike in that way. I hoped it was true.

I sat down next to her in the booth, feeling suddenly curious about her at my age. I realized I had never asked her, "What did you want to do when you were younger, Mom?"

"What do you mean? Like, travel?"

"No, as your career?"

She sighed. "I wanted to do so many different things. But times were different back then. I was married and pregnant by twenty-one, and your dad was in dental school. I worked at Penny's for about six months and then I was your mom . . . and then Chuck's mom."

"What were the *so many things* you wanted to be?"

Jon-Jon walked by, paused, and looked over at me. "Sitting on the job, are we?" he said.

"I'm taking my fifteen-minute, mandated-by-law break right now with my mom. Helen is covering my tables." Jon-Jon never offered breaks even though he knew we were supposed to get them.

"You need to run that by me first," he said.

"I couldn't find you. Papi said you were in the bathroom for half an hour."

He scowled before walking away.

"What's his problem?" my mom said.

"Well, that's him," I pointed to his frumpy, fat butt and permanent wedgie as he walked away. And then I pointed to his older brother, Jack. "And that's his brother, who is the owner of this restaurant. Jon-Jon has worked for him for fifteen years." Jack was an extremely handsome forty-something. He owned three different Blackbird's locations and Jon-Jon was just the manager of one.

"Oh, I see. Sibling rivalry," my mom said.

"Yeah, I know how it is."

"Why do you talk like that, Charlotte?"

"Because Chucky is the golden boy and I work at this place." I waved my hand around vaguely. "Look around. Look at what I'm wearing." I pointed to my bow tie.

"I love you, Charlotte. I know your dad is hard on you, but I wouldn't care if you served tortilla soup for the rest of your life. I just wish you and Helen weren't perpetually single."

None of the relationships I'd had were worth discussing with my mom; they'd only met Curtis by accident.

"Everyone says Chucky is so good-looking and smart and was such an athlete. Dad didn't go to a single one of my soccer games in high school because I wasn't good enough. Chucky got all the girls in high school. The boys just thought I was awkward."

She huffed. "Have you looked in a mirror lately? You have grown into a gorgeous young woman. Would you have some confidence, please? Sit up straight."

I was taking slouching and bad posture to a whole new level. "I just feel like I'm at a dead end."

"Well, it's time to make a goddamn U-turn, kid. By the

way, I might have gone on your computer dating thing." She shot me a sheepish look. "Don't be mad. Helen told me you stopped using it after that Seth guy stood you up."

"Yeah, I changed my freaking phone number the next day, too. Clean slate."

"Hmm, that explains it."

Jon-Jon was back. "Is that fifteen?"

I looked at my imaginary watch. "Nope, only twelve."

He shook his head and walked away. I looked over and noticed Helen flirting with a patron.

"See, Helen has confidence," my mother said.

"She's a freakin' actress. Anyway, what were you gonna say about the dating site?"

"There was a message from that boy. The one who stood you up. He said his dad had—"

"Wait. How do you know about that?"

"Helen told me."

I caught Helen's attention and mouthed *I'm gonna kill you.*

She shrugged.

"Anyway," my mother went on, "Seth's dad had been in a car accident. He's okay but he had to have surgery."

All of a sudden my mom knows all about Seth's family life? Seth, whom I don't even know?

"So what, Mom. I'm over dating."

"He's very cute. He apologized profusely and said he tried calling you. That must have been around the time you changed your number. I wondered why you did that."

"I have to get back to work."

"Hold on. About a week ago, he messaged again and

said he was hoping you still checked the site. You should go on and read the messages."

"Maybe," I said. I kissed her cheek and walked away.

BACK AT OUR apartment, as I put color in my mom's hair at the kitchen table, Helen went onto my Match profile from her laptop on the couch.

"Awh," she said.

"What! Read it to me."

She cleared her throat and began. Her back was to me so I couldn't see her face but she sounded emotional from the very beginning. "*Dear Charlotte, I cannot tell you how sorry I am that I missed our date. My dad was in a car accident about twenty minutes before I was set to leave. I was so worried about him. It was pretty bad, and he had to have surgery.*" Helen started sniffling.

"What, Helen? Jeez."

"He put up a picture of him in the hospital with his dad."

"Keep reading."

My mother sniffled. I spun her chair around. "Are you kidding? Are you crying, too?"

"He just seemed really worried about his dad."

I shook my head. "Keep going, Helen."

"*Will you please consider giving it another try?* And then he sent another message just last week. *Hey, Charlotte, just wondering if you're still on here? I'm giving this one last shot. I'd love to meet you. I'd love to take you out. That is, if you've found it in your heart to forgive me.*"

I walked over to the couch while my mom was processing. "God, he is good-looking, isn't he? Maybe I'll message him."

"Charlotte, my scalp is starting to burn."

"Shit."

I rinsed out my mom's hair and it was definitely more orange than red. I styled it and then showed it to her in the mirror. I knew I had messed up, but she just said, "I love it!" She hugged me with fervor. Maybe she was too easy on me. Maybe my dad was right. After all, I fucked up her hair and she hugged me anyway.

After she left, Helen waved the phone in front of my face while I did the dishes. "Stop that and call him."

"Fine." I dried my hands and went over to the couch. "Get out of here," I told her. She scurried off to her room, but I knew she'd still be eavesdropping.

I looked up Seth's number and called him. He answered on the first ring.

"You called!" he said triumphantly. "Can you meet me in Lake Elsinore tomorrow, Charlotte?"

Jeez, just like that. This guy is a character. "Um, hello, hi, how are you? How is your dad?"

"Hello, hi, I'm good. My dad is good. I want to meet you. I'm glad you forgave me. In six months, no one on any website or in life has intrigued me as much as you, and I can't get your picture out of my head. Do I sound stalkerish?"

"Yes."

"Well, come to a baseball game tomorrow and we'll meet and enjoy the great American pastime together."

"A baseball game in Lake Elsinore? What, like, Little League?" *Oh my god, he has a kid.*

"The San Diego Padres have a minor-league team called The Storm that plays there."

I was confused. "Is it like *Bull Durham*?"

"Yeah exactly!" He sounded excited that I knew what he was talking about. "You wanna go see a game?"

"Um . . ."

All of a sudden Helen popped out from behind the couch where she was hiding. She pointed to the phone at my ear and mouthed, *Yes!*

"Can my friend Helen come?"

"Why not? Okay, so I'll leave two tickets at will-call for you. It starts at six. See you there?"

"Okay."

He hung up right after that. I hit end on the phone and looked up at Helen. "What did he say?" she asked, brushing out her wet hair.

"I thought I heard you in the shower. How long were you hiding behind the couch?"

"Never mind that. What did he say?"

"Not much. We're meeting him at a baseball game. He said he'd leave two tickets for us."

"I can't believe you told him I was going. I'm not going," Helen said, rolling her eyes.

"You have to. I don't even know him. This is the weirdest thing in the whole world. I'm gonna drive an hour and a half to go watch some minor-league baseball game with him? What if he stands me up again?"

"You went home with Adam and boned all night in his loft and you think that's any safer than meeting a dude in a public place where there are thousands of spectators?"

"Why do you always bring up Adam?" I moved off the couch and headed to my room.

"Wait, where are you going?" She stalked after me. "I

bring it up because you were different afterward and every time I mention his name, you act like it wasn't just some one-night stand."

I turned around in my doorway and stared her down. "I felt extremely rejected by him, okay? I don't like talking about it."

She put her hand on her hip. "It's been way too long to still be thinking about him."

"I liked him and he threw me out . . . made me feel like an idiot."

She was looking at me cautiously, treading lightly. I knew she could hear the self-reproach in what I was saying and in how I acted right after that night with Adam. "I could tell he liked you, too, Charlie . . . as much as you liked him. It just wasn't meant to be. Something was up with him. Who knows what."

I nodded. Tears filled my eyes.

"Don't feel bad anymore, okay? I'll go with you to the game tomorrow even though I hate baseball. I'm sorry I've been giving you so much shit lately. That guy looks really cute in his profile. He seems to like animals and he wants to go to a ball game with you, and he didn't even mind that you wanted to bring your friend. It's a good start."

"I know, but who knows anything anymore. I attract the weirdest fucking people. I'll try to be in a better mood tomorrow."

"Okay, you still wanna go out tonight?" she asked.

"No, I have the breakfast shift."

Helen went off to bed and I went into my room and searched for Seth's profile on Facebook and Instagram, but there was nothing.

THE NEXT DAY at work, I tried to ignore the first-date nerves. The dickhead who requested the al dente avocado from Helen was back, and giving me an earful about how his poached eggs were too stringy. I ran my ass off for him, trying to make sure they got his eggs right the second time, and then he tipped me a dollar twenty-five on an eighteen-dollar check.

When I told Jon-Jon, he said, "He's a regular, Charlotte. Make the man happy. So what about the tip?"

"I work for tips, Jon. I know that doesn't matter to you, but he's extremely disrespectful to the waitstaff here, especially the women. You never have our backs."

"Do you know how many people would kill to have your job and the great shifts I give you?"

It's terrible, but I wished our closet caper would have at least hospitalized him for a bit of time. I wasn't sure I could deal with another six months in that place, with those stupid gimmicks and Jon-Jon's bad treatment.

"I don't think we should have the tortilla flags anymore, and these outfits are lame."

"Charlotte." He braced my shoulders. I shuddered at his touch. "File a complaint with Jack if you're that unhappy."

"Maybe I will."

"You're phased. Get your tables closed out."

"I made twelve bucks this morning and I had to drag my ass out of bed at five thirty."

"Not my problem," he said, walking away from me.

Why couldn't I just quit this stupid job? Oh I know, because I have to pay rent.

10. Storm Chasing

Helen and I left our apartment around four and headed toward Lake Elsinore, which is in the middle of fucking nowhere. We hit tons of traffic but managed to make it to the small, minor-league stadium by six. We were both in jeans and T-shirts, trying to play the part of a couple of girls going to see the game, although we did spend a little extra time on makeup and hair. Chucky would have been proud of how thoroughly I flossed.

As we made our way toward our seats, I kept searching for a dude who looked like Seth's profile picture, but it was hard to pick out faces among the hordes of moms, dads, and little kids.

We found our seats but there was no Seth. There was no one else even sitting in the row with us. I felt my stomach sinking. What if it was a joke some tween, bored out of his mind, decided to play on my poor rejected ass, just to see if I'd be dumb enough to drive over a hundred miles to a baseball game. I could think of nothing but the worst.

My only relief was that someone had purchased our tickets for us.

"Guess he's not here yet," Helen said. "Kind of lame to be late to a date after you stood the girl up the first time around."

"Maybe he hit bad traffic? He was coming from the other direction." I couldn't believe I was making excuses for him.

"You're too easy on people, Char. If he's late today, you can pretty much guarantee he's the perpetually late type. And a horrendous flake."

I shrugged and focused my attention on the walkway above us, hoping to see a six-foot-two, handsome guy coming our way.

"You want me to go grab us some beers?" Helen asked.

"Okay," I said. The game was under way. The Lake Elsinore Storm were out on the field, and some team from Modesto was at bat. Helen returned a few minutes later with two large draft beers and two hot dogs.

"Yuck, you know I hate hot dogs."

"Fine, don't eat it; I'll give it to Seth if he ever shows." Helen leaned into my face. "I can't believe he's not here yet. What a dick."

"I'm gonna drink this whole beer in one gulp," I said, staring off into space. Getting stood up twice by the same person was pathetic.

"Hold on. Don't overreact yet." She looked at her watch. "If he's not here by six thirty, we can get up and leave." The Storm was up to bat and there was a player warming up in the batter's circle. He had a perfect ass and Helen was watching him. "Or we can stay and watch the game." She wiggled her eyebrows. "Ohhh, baseball pants. Sigh."

"It's only the bottom of the first inning. I'll give him until six forty-five." I looked at the flexing muscles in the player's arms as he did a few practice swings. "Or maybe we should just hang out for a bit and enjoy the show, like you said."

"The game, you mean?"

"Yeah, the game." I grabbed my beer from the cup holder and began sipping when the announcer's voice came over the speaker.

"Leading off for the Lake Elsinore Storm, number twelve, center fielder Seth Taylor!"

"WHAT?" Helen and I both shouted. Just before Seth left the batting circle, he turned around and glanced up at me. It was the first time I saw his face in real life. He grinned and then threw his hand up in a brief wave before turning back and heading toward the plate.

If I had to guess what I looked like, I would say I probably resembled one of those Chihuahuas with the abnormally large alien eyes that you see on greeting cards.

Helen elbowed me. "Did you wave, stupid?"

My jaw was on the floor. "Oh my god. He's literally and figuratively out of my league."

"Oh shut up! He was totally smiling."

"Let me watch, be quiet. Oh man, look at his butt. This is so not fair. This is God's comedy. I have a muffin top and look at him, he's perfect."

"Charlotte, you do not have a muffin top. Stop that."

Seth was down in the count when he hit a blooper deep into right field. "It's gonna drop, it's gonna drop!" I yelled as I got to my feet. It did drop. Seth rounded second base and headed for third. "Go, Seth! Go!" All the fans in the stadium were screaming for him. The right fielder fired it to third base but Seth dove and was safe by what looked like an inch.

"That was amazing," Helen said. "He looks so coordinated. I bet he's good in bed . . . all long and athletic." She shivered. "God! Gives me the chills."

I watched him get to his feet and brush his hands down the front of his uniform. He high-fived the third-base coach and then looked up at me with wonder, squinting. I wanted to know what he was thinking. I couldn't wait to talk to him. He scored a minute later and jogged back to the dugout without glancing my way.

For the rest of the game he didn't look up at me, but he did go four for four. He dove twice, fielding hits. He had an amazing game. He was easily the best player on either team.

"I can't believe he's not in the majors. He's so good," I said, right when the game ended.

A lot of fans started getting up to leave.

"What are you gonna do? He kind of tricked you. Are you okay with that?" Helen asked.

"I don't know—hopefully he'll come out. I feel stupid just sitting here. Though my profile did say I liked baseball."

A second later he came out to the fence right near the on-deck circle. We were about five rows up. He clasped the chain link and leaned into it. "Hey, my little lucky charm. Get down here so we can officially meet," he called to me.

I stood and walked down the steps, praying I wouldn't fall, wondering what he thought of my body. "Hello," I said when I reached the fence.

He was searching my eyes. "I'm Seth." He wiggled his fingers through the chain link.

I reached up and shook one of his fingers like a moron. "I'm Charlotte."

"You're way prettier in real life."

"I do look better when I'm not in anaphylactic shock."

He laughed. "That's right, the bee sting. I thought it was cute." His mouth settled into a crooked smile.

"You're a professional baseball player?"

"You found me out. This is the minors, though. It's not that exciting."

"I think it's exciting. You told me you were in college."

"I am." He nodded, and then glanced back over his shoulder. "Backup plan. I could pull a muscle and this would all be over. Anyway, the pay's not that great. Doesn't that totally impress you?"

"You had an awesome game."

"Best game of my life, seriously. I hereby declare you my talisman. You have to come to every game from now on and sit in the same seat and wear that shirt and don't ever wash it."

I laughed.

"I'm not joking. Baseball players are serious about their superstitions."

"Maybe I will. I love talking to men through fences."

"Ah, you're a little live wire, aren't you? I like funny girls. Hey, can you give me ten? I'm gonna go shower." He pointed his thumb behind him.

"Sure, should we just wait here?"

He looked up into the stands. "That your friend?"

"Yeah, that's Helen."

"She's cute."

"You want to date her instead?"

"No, silly, I was thinking I'd bring my friend Roddy, the catcher. Introduce them, you know, so she doesn't feel like a third wheel?"

"That massive, bearded bear of a man?"

"Yeah, that's him. He's a gentle giant. Except up to bat." He rolled his eyes, understanding the double entendre. "I mean, in baseball."

"I knew what you meant. So where are we going? We can just meet you guys there."

"Okay, yeah. Pints and Quarts is our go-to. Let me get the address."

"I can pull it up on my phone," I said.

"Okay, cool. See you in a bit then."

"Good game, Seth!"

"Thanks, kid."

I headed back up the steps toward Helen, who was wearing one of those shit-eating grins.

"Well?" she said.

I pulled her by the arm to follow me. "Come on."

We headed toward the parking lot. "Are you gonna tell me what he said? I'm dying here."

"Helen!" I froze, braced her shoulders, and turned her to face me. "He doesn't know how hot he is."

"Oh, I love those types."

"Right?"

"Are you gonna see him again?"

"We're going to meet him and his friend right now."

"His friend?" She raised her eyebrows.

"Yes, the catcher, Roddy."

"That big guy?"

Helen had a type. I didn't, except that most of the guys I dated were bad for me in some way. Helen had a very specific physical type, at least when it came to the guys she dated for more than a week. They were usually on the darker side, small, thin, and foreign. She liked exotic men. Roddy was an all-American, redheaded, freckly, three-hundred-pound, six-foot-two catcher from Nebraska.

"We're all just going as friends. It'll be fun."

"You wanna be friends with Seth?" she said behind me as we walked to the car.

"No, I want to be held captive by Seth. I want Seth to do very bad things to me," I said.

When we arrived at the restaurant, the waitress seated us. We each ordered a glass of red wine and waited for the guys to get there. The door opened a few minutes later and in they walked. Several people at the bar clapped and cheered. It must have been a popular hangout for the players. Seth was wearing jeans and a plain T-shirt.

"Good lord, his forearms," I said as he walked toward me. He had this goofy smile that made him completely approachable even though he was a god. It belied his boyish innocence; he was unself-conscious. His hair was longer on top and messy and going in a bunch of different directions.

He high-fived a couple of people on his way over. Roddy got held up at the bar behind Seth. Helen leaned into my ear and whispered, "He's kind of geeky."

"There's nothing geeky about that body."

"You have a point. Where's the other guy?"

"At the bar."

Helen looked over to where Roddy was grabbing two beers. "Oh, he's not so bad."

Roddy had a beard and a very serious hard-part hairdo.

"He's like a giant hipster," I said.

Finally, Seth made it to our table. When I stood up, he immediately leaned in and hugged me. "Hey, kid."

"I should be calling you that. I'm older," I said.

He let go and stuck his hand out to Helen. They introduced themselves and shook hands. Roddy came over with two beers and handed one to Seth. "Ladies."

We all sat down and toasted. "To a great game," Helen said. "Cheers!"

After conversation picked up among the four of us and the drinks were flowing, Helen and Roddy were warming up to each other, and Seth and I were hitting it off, too. We agreed to come back that Saturday for a day game and then we would go out afterward.

At the end of the night, the guys walked us out to my little Honda Civic.

"You okay to drive?" Seth asked.

"Yeah, I only had a couple of drinks." I looked back over my shoulder at Helen and Roddy, who were laughing at something near the restaurant entrance. Helen had matched tequila shots with her three-hundred-pound counterpart. After betting she could outdrink him, he finally made her stop after four shots. He was basically unfazed by the alcohol, but Helen was in goofy mode.

"She's pretty hammered, huh?"

"Yeah, she's okay, though." We watched as Roddy bent and threw her over his shoulder like he was carrying a tiny sack of flour.

"They like each other," Seth said as we watched them.

"Yeah, she's great."

Turning toward me, he said, "I had a good time."

"Same here."

He leaned in and kissed me on the cheek. "So, Saturday?"

"Yeah, I'll see you Saturday."

Roddy came strutting over while Helen hung upside down behind him and punched his butt. "Let me go, you big oaf!"

"You like it, Tinkerbell." He chuckled from his chest, and it sounded like thunder.

When he set her down, she leaned up on her toes and kissed him on the mouth. Then they started making out right in front of us. *Oh god, Helen's in love.*

I whistled "Sittin' on the Dock of the Bay," while Seth stared at the ground with his hands in his pockets.

"Come on, Helen, wrap it up," I said.

Finally, they pulled away. "Okay, boys," she slurred. She walked to the passenger side and pointed at Roddy accusingly. "You're like a ginger Thor! That's who you remind me of." She was hysterical.

Roddy and Seth laughed. "See you later, ladies."

I got into the car and started it, then saw Seth running back toward my window. I rolled it down. "Hey." He took a deep breath. "Can I call you tomorrow, just to chat?"

"Sure," I said.

"Cool." He smiled.

My hands were gripping the steering wheel as I watched him jog away. "Go," Helen said.

I didn't move. "Go!" She repeated and then looked

over at me as I watched Seth. "Ooh, you've got it bad," she teased.

"Me? You were the one twisting tongues with Roddy."

"I like that big bear. He's brawny."

"Brawny! Ha! You amaze me."

Helen could love. Yes, she had a type but she found something intriguing in everyone she met, no matter what they did, how they acted, or what they looked like. She took all of these people that entered her life and she let each one touch her heart in some way. It made her beautiful because she was able to see the beauty in others. She took chances, she loved hard, and sometimes she fought hard and cried hard in the end. I had never been willing to let anyone see the real me until Adam, in that one night, under false pretenses. The one night I was just me. Maybe because I knew how that would end. But Helen was living her life and having fun, and I was just watching mine pass by from a safe distance.

Helen passed out twenty minutes after we left, so I blared the radio all the way home. As I drove, I tried to think of one negative thing about Seth but I couldn't. Still, I didn't feel that insane connection to him. I didn't feel the same as when I was with Adam that night, so many months ago.

IN THE MORNING, Helen dragged her feet into the kitchen. "You look pretty," I said. She had drool crusted on her face and mascara smeared down her cheek. Her blond hair was matted in the back and she was wearing flowery granny panties I recognized from when we were younger. "Why do you still have that underwear?"

"I don't know," she said through a yawn.

A minute later Roddy came out of her room, wearing nothing but a pair of boxer briefs.

"Oh . . . um . . . what the hell?" I said.

He walked up to Helen standing at the counter, wrapped his arms around her from behind, and rested his chin on her shoulder like they were a comfortable married couple. "Morning," he said to me.

"Morning," I replied, dumbfounded. "When did . . . I'm so confused."

Helen smiled. "We were on the phone late last night and I was like, what the heck, come over."

"Do you live near here?" I asked him, still in shock.

"About two hours away."

"That's not near here. You drove two hours in the middle of the night?"

"Totally worth it," he said, instantly. Helen giggled.

"I don't understand anything anymore," I said as I walked toward the door to leave for work. "Have fun, you guys." They didn't respond because they were already sucking face in the kitchen.

ON MY BREAK at work, I checked my phone and saw a new text from Seth. It was a screen shot of the Lake Elsinore Storm's game schedule.

I laughed and then dialed his number.

He answered by saying, "So you're coming to every game, right?"

"Why don't we start with Saturday?"

"I have a game tonight, though. What will I do without my talisman?"

"Keep your eye on the ball."

"Good advice. Are you working?"

"Yes, I work at a restaurant. More like a diner, actually."

"Sweet. I'll have to come in sometime."

"So Roddy was at our apartment this morning," I said.

"I know. He really likes Helen."

"I guess Match.com works in mysterious ways." I didn't want to draw attention to the fact that we were supposed to be on a date, and nothing had really happened for us, but he smoothed it out before I could even say anything.

"I like to take things slow," he said in a sincere voice.

"That's unusual for a guy."

"Not when he's tired of being single," he said.

"I don't understand."

"I mean, I don't know how to put this without sounding kind of arrogant but—"

I got where he was going with the conversation. "Getting laid is easy for you, is that what you were going to say?"

"Well, there's this group of women who come to the games."

"You have groupies?"

"Sort of."

"They must know you're on Match.com," I said.

"I did some mild Instagram stalking of you to make sure you weren't one of them. There's a necessary screening process before I date anyone."

I laughed. "And I passed the screening?"

"I did question that photo of you at the fair wearing a cow costume."

"Oh yeah, that. I worked as a cow at the LA County Fair last year," I said. I failed to mention that I was also a giant Hello Kitty that stood outside the Sanrio store at the mall. I almost died of a heatstroke because of the costume's improper ventilation. I've had a lot of jobs. Sanrio paid my medical bills, so that was good.

"Do you still have the cow costume?"

"No, I had to give it back."

"Bummer," he said.

"I know." Jon-Jon was glaring at me from behind the pie case. "Well, I have to get back to work. Not everyone can be a major-league baseball player."

He chuckled. "It's just the minors."

"See, I would have known that if I were a groupie."

"They're called Storm Chasers."

"Shut up."

"I swear to god." There was a second of silence. "I'll let you go. Can I call you after my game?"

"Sure."

Helen came in just before her shift started. She walked up to me in the side station and said very nonchalantly, "He asked me to move in with him."

"Excuse me. What?"

"Yeah, he asked me to move in with him." Her eyes darted to the ceiling and then to the floor before coming to rest on her fidgeting hands.

"What kind of person asks a woman to move in with him after one night? What did you tell him, Helen?"

"I told him yes."

"Are you out of your mind? You have seriously lost it. You met Roddy less than twenty-four hours ago, you psycho!"

She finally made eye contact. "I know, but I really like him."

"This is wild. Even for you, Helen."

"If it doesn't work out, I'll just move out."

"Well, don't expect to have a room in my apartment waiting for you if your little experiment blows up in your face." I started to walk away. I was so pissed.

"You're such a great friend, Charlotte," she snickered. "Just because you wouldn't do it, it's impossible for you to be happy for me?"

I turned around. "I think you're making a mistake. That's all. And I can't afford your half of the rent while you play house with Roddy, whom you met *less* than twenty-four hours ago!" I glared at her.

"You said that already."

I stomped my foot. "You don't even like baseball."

"I do now," she said defiantly.

"Well, I guess we'll see each other at the games then." I headed back into the kitchen and into the walk-in refrigerator to look for mayonnaise.

"Wait, Charlie. I'm not moving out today." Helen followed me in. I was standing precariously on a keg trying to reach the mayo on the top shelf. Helen was a bit taller than me and had longer arms. "Let me do that," she said.

"No! I have to learn to do things without you now." When I started to lose my balance, she braced my legs. "I got this, Helen!"

I jumped down with the mayo in hand and headed for the door.

Why did things have to change?

"Can we talk," she said as she blocked the exit.

"It's freezing in here. We're in a refrigerator."

"Is that why you're being so cold to me?"

Just then Luc, the pie guy, walked in to get something. "Charelette and Huh-leen, hello."

"It's Helen and Charlotte, Luc. You've been in this country long enough to know how to pronounce our names."

Helen was still very resentful. The walk-in was not a good place for her to be face-to-face with Luc. They had had sex in there, like, fifty times.

She was glaring at him as he searched for the butter.

"Let's get out of here, Helen."

"Fine." Once in the kitchen, she said, "You should go to the game tonight."

"Why?"

"Don't you want to see Seth?"

"I can wait," I said.

"That's the thing with you. You're always waiting. Waiting until something lands in your lap."

"I'm not going to stalk him. I don't want to seem desperate. You do whatever you want, but you have to understand that what's going on with you is not normal for most people."

"It's because you're insecure," Helen said.

"Quit fucking insulting me! It's because I don't even know if I like Seth yet."

"You slept with Adam after knowing him for five minutes."

"This isn't about sex. And Adam was different."

"Why?"

"I don't know."

"Then why don't you go look for him?"

"I'm done talking about this, Helen. Go to the game, I'll cover you. Move in with Roddy, I don't care. Do whatever you want, but you need to give me a month's rent to find someone to take your room."

"Do you really think I'm crazy, Charlie?"

Helen still had an adorable sprinkling of freckles on her nose leftover from childhood. I looked at her and thought about how soft and pure and sweet she was. How her innocence and faith made her beautiful. She still believed in fairy tales. And because of that, she would get hers.

"Honestly, yes, it's crazy. But I guess it's also a little brave. I just don't like to see you get hurt."

She looked down and then up again thoughtfully. "It's worth it to me, though."

"I know. I get it. Go, go to the game and see your man."

She skipped out of the kitchen and I was stuck slinging fries with Jon-Jon. "Thanks, Charlie," she called out.

I WALKED BY Adam's loft on the way back home. His car was gone and there was a FOR RENT sign in the front window. I guess that was that.

11. Oh Brother

Seth called after the game. "I went four for four again."

"Shit, maybe it's Helen," I said.

"I don't know. She was pretty cute cheering Roddy on. Did you hear?"

"Yes, of course. She told me right away, but I still can't believe it. Does Roddy do that?" I felt I needed to do some recon for my friend.

"No," Seth said adamantly. "He's, like, noncommittal. He's never even introduced a girl to his parents. They came to the game tonight and met Helen."

"Wow." As fast as it was moving, I guess it was real. "Well, it will either be beautiful and amazing or it will go down in flames."

"I think it will be beautiful and amazing," Seth said.

"Die-hard optimist?"

He laughed. "You make that sound bad. Oh hey, Obi-Wan wants to meet you," he said.

I rolled my eyes, thankful Seth couldn't see me. "Oh

yeah. Well, have him call me and we'll make a date." I had an instant flashback to the panty man and his dog obsession.

When we got off the phone, I got into bed and thought about the current state of my life. It wasn't that I hadn't been willing to give any guys a chance. Hell, I stuck it out with Curtis way longer than any normal person would have. Even as he'd bless himself over and over and do his strange rituals after seeing an El Camino, I would sit by and watch him and wait until he was done. I put up with the panty man stealing my most expensive underwear and I had put up with Paul's unwillingness to commit. I was a saint and I was also very seriously in denial. I knew none of those relationships would pan out, just like I knew none of my other careers would stick. That's why I was willing to waste my time with them. They were safe. And I feared permanence. No normal person would go home with a guy they found on a Los Angeles street in the middle of the night carrying Chinese food.

But I think I felt with Adam what Helen was feeling for Roddy. Too bad Adam hadn't felt the same way. Too bad Adam was gone. That combination of spectacular sex, the way he looked, the way he talked, the way he thought . . . I was hung up on him and still felt really defeated by him. My self-confidence, or at least the little I'd had, went in the tank after that night. Now Seth was here and I wouldn't even give him a chance to show me who he was.

SETH CALLED AGAIN a couple of days later but I didn't call him back. I came home from work on Friday and all of Helen's things were packed. Roddy was carrying boxes down the stairs. "Hey, Charlie."

"It's Charlotte." I couldn't make eye contact with him. I walked by Helen in the living room. "Doesn't he have a game?"

"Not tonight. They have a bye."

"Did you know what a bye was before this morning?"

She stood from her spot on the floor where she was packing up the last of her books. "Don't be an asshole, Charlotte."

Roddy came back in and stood at my side. "Can I talk to you outside?" he asked.

"Me?" I pointed to my chest.

"Yeah." He was apprehensive.

"Oh god, what now?" I mumbled, and then followed him. We walked out the front door onto the landing. A gust of wind kicked up the bottom of my dress, and I tried to smooth it down. "What do you want? It's windy and I want to go back inside."

"I know it feels like I'm taking your best friend away—"

"Did Helen fill your head with that crap?"

"No, it's obvious you feel that way; otherwise you wouldn't be acting like a five-year-old." He had a point. Roddy had a rumble to his voice that you could feel on your skin. It was mildly unnerving. "I just want you to know, I've never met anyone like her. I'm not gonna hurt her." He smiled sincerely. I looked into his light-brown eyes and saw someone speaking from the heart.

"How do you know?" I said.

"I just know."

When will I just know? I wondered. "Well, if you change your mind and decide to hurt Helen, I'll make it very hard for you to catch a ball ever again."

He smiled. "Something tells me I should take that threat seriously, even though I can eat your body weight in food in one day. I'm not going to change my mind."

When I went back inside, Helen was carrying her last box toward the door. "Chuck the Fuck called."

"Okay."

She set down the box. "Can I have a hug?"

I had been fighting tears since I walked in but once it was time to hug I couldn't hold back. I started crying. She pulled me into her body. "Fuck, you're still my best friend," she said near my ear. "One of us had to make the first move, otherwise we would have ended up like those weird, old, spinster couples who live together in a hoarderish apartment."

"We're not that old." I sniffled.

"It was time."

I nodded in agreement but couldn't say the words.

In less than a week, Helen had found someone as crazy beautiful and brave as she was. Within four days, she had quit her job and become someone's live-in girlfriend. I was going to be stuck ladling tortilla soup alone for eternity. It all seemed too fast, even for Helen, but what if it actually worked out?

After they left, I called Chucky.

He answered with, "Hey, Fatbutt."

"What's up Shitstick?"

"I heard Helen moved out."

"So what. Helen and I can live apart."

"That's not why I called. Jesus, why are you so hostile toward me, Fatbutt?"

"I don't know, Chucky, maybe because you call me Fatbutt."

"I just wanted to see if you wanted a roommate?" He actually sounded sincere.

"You?!" I said, like it was the worst idea I had ever heard.

"You'll get free cleanings from me and I'll pay half the rent and bills."

"Free cleanings? As in my teeth?"

"Yes, what do you think I'm talking about, stupid?"

"You're not going anywhere near my mouth, ever!"

"Charlotte, listen, Mom is driving me crazy with her hovering. I need to get out of here. I'll be making a ton of money once I pass my exams and go to work with Dad."

My brother had two months left of school and then his state boards before he could become a legit dentist. It was actually quite remarkable that he had handled living with our parents all that time.

"I know Mom still cuts the crust off your sandwiches. Don't expect that kind of shit around here."

"I told her to stop doing that. It's embarrassing. Please, just consider it."

I knew I could live with Chucky. That's one thing about siblings. You go through the gauntlet with them when you're kids. You've imagined strangling them so many times that by the time you're adults you're pretty much desensitized to their crap. I once made my brother walk home in the rain from high school because he told the guy I was dating that I wore dirty underwear. Chucky got pneumonia. My mom acted like he was dying. While he was home sick from school, he went into my room and deleted a twelve-page term paper I had to turn in the following day. I was so mad that I literally threw up in his face, though not on purpose.

I waited after that to exact my revenge. The day before

his big state championship wrestling match, I mashed up a bunch of laxatives and put them in his protein shake. That is how evil we had gotten. I actually wanted my brother to shit his singlet in front of the whole school. But he was onto me. He didn't drink it, thank god. After dumping out the shake, he spent the afternoon squirting hot sauce into all of my shoes while I was at math tutoring. I smelled like sriracha for the rest of senior year. We had grown up a lot since then.

"Fine Chucky, you can live here, but I have rules."

"You do not have rules. You're the biggest slob I know."

"I've changed. And anyway, this is my apartment so you're gonna follow my rules," I said.

"Fine. What rules, Charlotte?"

"I don't know yet, I'll have to think of them, but they're going to be strict."

"When can I move in?"

"Helen's gone. You can move in now." It felt like I was saying she had died. I felt sick.

"Well, I'll pack up my stuff and probably be down there on Monday."

"Okay." I actually couldn't bear the idea of being home alone all weekend but I couldn't say anything to Chucky about it. I couldn't admit that to him, or ask him to come down earlier, because I knew he would never let me live it down. "See you Monday."

I went into Helen's empty room, looked around, and cried some more.

A few minutes later I heard a voice. "Hello, anyone here? The door is open . . ."

I walked out to the front room and froze when I saw the figure standing in the doorway. I looked down at his hand gripping a bag of what looked like Chinese food, and for a moment I wished that it were Adam standing there.

"Seth, what are you doing here?" I wiped under my eyes, knowing I looked haggard from crying.

His large frame filled the entryway. "I hope I'm not being too forward by coming here," he said.

I wasn't sure what to say.

He held up the bag. "I brought dinner."

I walked toward the door slowly. "Is it Chinese?"

"It's Thai."

Thank god.

"Charlotte?" Seth was still staring at me, waiting for my approval.

I blinked. "I'm sorry. Yeah, please, come in. Sit down." I motioned for him to sit at the small table in the kitchen while I set out plates and flatware. "Would you like a beer or something?"

"I'm sorry. I should have called," he said, shifting uncomfortably in his seat.

"No, it's okay. I was just kind of out of it because Helen just left. We've been living together since we moved out of our parents' houses. I grew up with her three doors down, so this is going to be a huge adjustment for me." I handed him the beer.

"That's why I came," he said. "Roddy told me you were pretty bummed."

"But you don't even know me," I said as I stood next to him. As soon as it was out of my mouth, I regretted it.

He began to get up. "This was a bad idea."

Why did I have to sabotage everything? "Wait. Stay. Let's eat. I just feel like this is a little awkward."

When I sat down across from him, he took a slow sip of his beer, swallowed, and said, "I'm sorry. I've really never done anything like this. We had a bye today, I was bored, and I was thinking about you."

"It's fine." *He was thinking about me.*

"I should have asked you out on a real date tonight. I was waiting for Saturday but then Roddy and Helen were moving at warp speed."

"I know, you don't have to explain, and we don't have to move at warp speed just because they are."

He let out a long breath. "Okay. So we're good?"

"We're good," I said.

"Do you want to get out of here? You can throw this food in your fridge and eat it tomorrow," he suggested.

"Where do you want to go?" We hadn't opened the cartons of food yet, so I stood and started putting them back in the plastic bag.

"I don't know, but I feel like a restaurant would be better so this isn't so . . . awkward." He shot me a tight smile.

"I think you're right."

"Are you sure you want to go out?"

"Yes. I'm sorry I've made this uncomfortable. I know a great place. It has a really cozy vibe. Wurstküche. It's an exotic sausage grill, you'll love it."

He laughed. "That sounds terrifying to me."

"Come on." I nodded toward the door as he stood. "There's nice people, lots of craft beers. They've got hot dogs. Don't all baseball players like hot dogs?" Although I actually hated hot dogs, this place had the most amazing fries and dipping sauces, so that's what I'd get. "They have a sausage made out of rattlesnake."

"You're killing me. Not all baseball players like hot dogs and I'm not eating rattlesnake, but I'm willing to see what else they have."

"Perfect! Let's go."

I didn't even look in the mirror, let alone bother changing out of the black jeans and blouse I had been wearing all day. Seth looked casual in jeans, a short-sleeve button-down shirt, and white Converse.

We walked shoulder to shoulder, making small talk until we got to the stoplight across from where Adam's mural of the winged man was painted. I stared at the image, mesmerized by the fact that I had stood by while he had so effortlessly created such a powerful work of art.

Then, a block farther, I saw something else. And I was speechless.

I froze.

The wall opposite from Villains was newly painted with a giant mural. Seth was looking at me strangely as I stared at the artwork.

"What are you looking at, Charlotte?"

When I raised my head to meet his gaze, he looked concerned.

"Nothing, it's nothing. I'm okay. Let's keep going?"

My legs were shaking.

"What's wrong, Charlotte?"

"I need to sit down." I started to sway.

In one swift motion, Seth hitched his arm under me and brought me to his chest. "You're as white as a ghost," he said.

What I had seen was like nothing I knew possible. I couldn't make sense of it. In Seth's arms, I continued staring at the mural.

It was me, from the back, staring at Edvard Munch's *Starry Night* in the Getty Museum.

My long hair pinned up, exposing my neck through an open-backed silk red dress.

It was so realistic, so accurate. It looked like a photo, right down to a freckle I have on my shoulder.

I knew Adam had painted it, but why?

Seth's eyes narrowed, staring at me with genuine concern.

"I'm fine," I reassured him.

"You're acting strangely. I don't know what to make of what's going on. You can barely walk. Are you that upset about Helen? Is it a physical thing? Do you feel sick?"

"I just saw something that confused me on that wall, that's all," I said, my voice low and shaky.

"Are you going to tell me what's going on, Charlotte?" He wasn't angry; he was just trying to be empathetic.

It was hard for me to look him in the eye as I began the story so I focused on a manhole in the middle of the street. "About seven months ago, I met a guy." I hesitated.

"Continue," he said, a twinge of worry in his voice.

"I met him on the street. I went home with him and we had a very strange but special experience. Or so I thought."

"Let's find a bench and sit down. I really have no fucking clue what you're talking about."

We were now sitting against the wall where the mural was painted.

"I'm trying to tell you without making myself sound like a slut."

"I don't think you're a slut, Charlotte. Just tell me the story."

"I met a guy on the street. It was a whirlwind night. I went back to his loft. He was a painter. There were paintings everywhere. We had . . . sex, a whole bunch of sex."

Seth swallowed. "Okay, so what?"

"At some point in the night, he asked me if we were in love, like we were role-playing or something, and I told him this story that we were together and that we had met in front of *Starry Night* at the Getty. It's hard to explain, but it made sense in the moment."

"I thought they had *Irises* at the Getty?"

"No, Munch's *Starry Night*, not Van Gogh's."

"Oh. And . . . ?"

I pointed with my thumb behind me. "That was the story I told him. And today, just now, I discovered he painted a giant mural of it. I pass this wall all the time; it wasn't here before."

Seth turned around and looked at the mural. "It's beautiful." Then he looked back at me. "So, what happened?"

"I kind of fell for him that night, but he acted weird in the morning and accused me of being a liar. It was all very strange. Like I said, I thought we were just role-playing or something."

Seth swallowed. There was a long, uncomfortable silence hanging in the air between us. We both turned around and sat there staring at the mural for a long time.

After what felt like hours, Seth turned to me. "I'm gonna walk you home now, Charlotte. I think you should be alone to think about this. I'm not judging you at all, but you seem really affected right now, and it's been a long day for you."

The idea of being alone terrified me, and I wondered

if I was scaring Seth away. In fact, I *knew* I was. But I also wanted to do nothing but stare at the mural all night long.

We stood up. The little crosswalk symbol went on, motioning for us to walk. Seth grabbed my hand, and I looked down at my hand in his. I looked up to his face. He smiled. "I'm a good guy," he said. "I'm taking you home because your mental state concerns me. You seem really troubled. Maybe you need to call him, Charlotte. Get some resolution. Find out why he painted this mural seven months after he kicked you out of his apartment."

"You're right," I said, but I had no idea how I would find his number.

"I like complicated girls," Seth said, out of the blue, as we walked back to my apartment. "I like challenges and I like interesting people. That's why I was attracted to your profile. And then the other night I could just tell. That's why I'm here now. But you need to work this thing out, whatever it is you're going through. I don't want to pry. We don't know each other that well and I already feel like I've invaded your space tonight."

"Not at all, Seth. I don't know what I would've done if I'd been alone when I saw that mural. But I do need to get home."

Once we were at my door, Seth leaned down and kissed me on the cheek. "Do you want to come to my game tomorrow? We can talk this out afterward."

"Okay," I told him, but I wasn't sure if I still wanted to go.

When I opened the door to my apartment, Chucky was sitting at the counter, eating cereal. "Yay! Fatbutt's here!" he shouted through a mouthful.

"You still have a key?"

"You left it unlocked, dipshit."

Growing up, my brother looked like that kid on the cover of *MAD* magazine but with black hair. I still saw him that way, even though as a grown man he now looked like Jake Gyllenhaal. Yes, girls liked him, but he was arrogant and he had impossibly high standards.

"Are you eating my cereal?"

"I don't eat that sugary crap," he said.

None of his belongings were lying around. I walked back into Helen's room and saw that Chucky had moved all of his stuff in and unpacked in the two hours I was gone. His room was perfectly tidy. With wide eyes, I appraised him as I walked back toward the kitchen.

He looked up at me. "What?"

"It's clean."

"We're not kids anymore, Charlotte."

I opened the refrigerator in search of a snack and discovered hummus, yogurt, and a bowl of quinoa, along with a very expensive bottle of Champagne.

"What's all this?"

"I just made the quinoa; it's in there cooling. I'm thinking of making a quinoa and feta salad with olives tomorrow. And the Champagne is for you, my sweet, loving sister."

"Really, Chucky?"

"Will you call me Charles from now on? I don't really go by Chuck."

I leaned over and glared into his eyes. "Who are you and why are you wearing my brother like a suit?"

"Cut the shit, Charlotte." That was a commonly used phrase in my house growing up. I was a bit of a drama queen as a kid.

"Okay, brother. I will open my figurative, though not my real arms, to this new version of you. I hope it lasts. And thanks for the 'shampag-knee.'"

"You're so classy, Fatbutt. I'm glad we're gonna be roomies."

"Do you know how many years of squats I've done to firm up this ass?"

"Stop trying to get me to look at your butt; it's weird and gross," he said as he slurped up his cereal.

I smacked him in the head. "'Kay, dork, I'm going to bed."

"Nighty night."

"Night."

I didn't even wonder why Chuck had moved in that day instead of Monday, like he said he would. Only later would I find out that Helen had called my mom out of concern, and she had told Chuck to move into my apartment that day. Guess my mom knew as well as I did that I couldn't be alone.

I lay in bed all night and didn't sleep a wink. I couldn't get the image of the mural out of my head.

I knew I had to look for him, but where would I even begin?

12. Boy(s)

At some point just before dawn, I finally fell asleep. When I woke up in the morning, Chucky was already gone. He left me a note saying he would be training for the Iron Man triathlon the whole morning but had left the quinoa, feta, and olive salad for me in the fridge for lunch. I guess he really had changed. I was the only one who was still the same.

I decided that I would go to Seth's game after all, but before heading to Lake Elsinore, I drove by Adam's apartment and saw the same FOR RENT sign. I could also see through the window that the apartment was already vacant. I parked the car and knocked on his neighbor's door, the one who had given Adam that Post-it note about Foxy, but no one answered. I got back in my car and tried Googling "Los Angeles muralist" on my phone. There were actually quite a few hits about his murals, but no one knew his identity. I guess I never really would, either. Maybe he wanted it that way.

AT THE GAME that night, I retrieved my ticket at will-call and found Helen in the same seats we sat in before. She looked up at me as I shimmied sideways down the aisle. "I guess this is the girlfriend aisle," she said.

"Seth isn't my boyfriend, Helen."

"I know." She huffed. "Never mind." She was wearing a Storm T-shirt with Roddy's number on the back. It was one of those jerseys made for women. They're basically designed to make your boobs look big.

"Cute shirt," I said, but Helen ignored me. "I'm glad we're here together," I finally said after several moments of silence.

She turned to me. "I'm glad, too." She smiled. "I love you, Charlie."

"I love you, too." My eyes started to water.

The speaker crackled to life, announcing that Seth was up to bat. There were runners on first and third and one out. He hit a blooper to right center field that was caught pretty easily.

"Bummer," I said.

"No, it's good," Helen said. "It was a sacrifice fly. The runner on third tagged up and scored."

"Oh. Wow, Helen, I'm impressed. I was wondering why he high-fived the first-base coach before running back to the dugout."

"See, I'm learning. I really like it!" she said.

"I'm glad." I squeezed her hand.

Seth had another great game, and afterward we went to the same bar we had gone to before. Helen pointed out to me two Storm Chasers sitting at the bar. One was way too old to be a baseball groupie. She had to have been well over forty, with a soccer mom bob. Her cut-off jean shorts were rolled up her artificially tanned legs and she had a ton of Storm buttons pinned to her shirt. She was sitting with a smaller, dark-haired girl who could have been her daughter but was apparently old enough to be at the bar. They were glaring at us. Roddy and Seth tried to ignore them.

"They smell it," Roddy said.

"Smell what?" I said.

"Seth's move up." He arched his eyebrows like I should know.

Seth looked away shyly. "What does he mean?" I asked Seth.

"There's talk that I might get bumped up to the majors soon."

Helen clapped excitedly. "Oh, that's so great, Seth!" She was rapidly becoming a Storm cheerleader.

He smiled, embarrassed. "I don't know if it'll really happen."

"Don't be so humble," I said, though I actually really liked that about him. "You've done amazingly well. I wondered why you weren't in the majors the first time I saw you play."

"He was," Roddy answered. "He was with the Royals. You didn't hear the story?"

"All right, let's get this over with," Seth said, shooting Roddy a mock glare. "I played one season with them. In a crucial game, I made an error on a routine fly ball, which allowed the other team to score three runs in the top of the ninth. Then I struck out with bases loaded and two outs in the bottom of the ninth. We lost the game and our chance to go to the playoffs that year. So that's my fucking legacy." He seemed more amused than pissed.

"But you might have a chance to redeem yourself," I said.

"Maybe," he said, looking away absently.

I didn't know what to say, but Helen broke the moment of awkward silence. "What do the Storm Chasers have to do with him getting bumped up?"

"They follow our team and try to get in with the players who might make it onto the Padres," Roddy answered. "I'd bet that woman is trying to find a husband for her daughter."

We all laughed. "That's pathetic," Helen said. "And she doesn't have to glare at us."

"We should invite them over for a drink," I said.

"No!" Seth shouted.

"Come on," I pleaded. "I just want to know what their deal is."

"No, I really don't want you to," he said.

I turned to him and in a quiet voice said, "Did you already date that girl? Is that why?"

He nodded.

Roddy jumped up from the table. "Another round, ladies?"

"Sure," Helen and I both said quickly.

Helen, sensing that Seth and I needed a moment, followed Roddy to the bar.

"I know you've dated other people, Seth, and after last night, you know I have, too. I didn't assume you were a monk. Let's not make this into a big deal."

He smiled. "I appreciate you saying that, Charlotte. But I didn't want to invite her over here because she has an annoying voice. It's grating—seriously."

"How long did you guys date?"

"I took her out once. We didn't even kiss."

The girl seemed to sense that we were talking about her because, a second later, she was approaching us.

"Seth," she said, drawing his name out in a long whine.

"Hey, Marley," Seth said. I took a sip of beer and tried not to make eye contact with her. "This is my girlfriend, Charlotte."

I coughed and felt beer shoot up my nose. Trying to catch my breath, I reached my hand out toward her. "Nice to meet you," I said between throat clearings.

"Oh!" She shook my hand quickly but with a weak grip. She looked at Seth. "Move on fast, don't ya?"

He stood from the table. "It was nice seeing you, Marley. Charlotte and I have to take off." He grabbed my hand and pulled me toward the front of the bar. We passed Helen and Roddy on the way out. "Bye, guys," Seth said.

"Where are you going?" Helen asked.

"Home," I said.

"Bummer—I wanted to party!"

"Me and you can party, sweetie," Roddy said to her before leaning down and kissing her right below her eye. She giggled.

"All right. See you later then. Charlotte, are you coming to the game tomorrow before they go on the road?"

"Go on the road?" I asked.

Seth squeezed my hand. "Yeah, we'll be out of town for a couple of days."

I was the only one acting awkward about the whole situation and everyone else could tell. I wasn't going to be Seth's girlfriend for real or pretend to get a couple of Storm

Chasers off his back. I didn't like the feeling that I was being subtly manipulated into having a relationship with this dude because it would seem cute to go on a bunch of double dates with Helen and Roddy, and talk about how we'd be at home waiting while they were on the road. I hadn't even gotten to know Seth yet, but suddenly my world was revolving around his, around his schedule, and what he wanted.

"Oh well, you boys enjoy your time on the road. I won't be able to come tomorrow. I'm sorry." I was trying to be gracious and not lead Seth on, but I thought the three of them were being ridiculously pushy.

"Why?" Helen said.

"Because I have plans, Helen." My smile was gone and so was Seth's. He was squinting at me, trying to read my expression while he still gripped my hand.

"What do you have to do on a Sunday, Charlie?" Helen raised her eyebrows.

"It's okay," Seth said, shaking his head. "There's no pressure. It's a long trip to make two days in a row."

"Thank you." I was sincere. I looked him in the eye. "I really appreciate that. My brother just moved in and we're getting settled."

"What? Chuck the Fuck moved in?" Helen shouted.

We were standing near the entry of the bar. We kept having to dance out of the way of passersby to talk to Helen and Roddy, who were now perched on barstools.

"Well, I told you I can't make the rent on my own. Plus, he's changed. Kind of. I mean, he's still Chucky, but he's grown up a lot."

"Oh yeah, I could tell from that profile he wrote about you on Match.com," she said.

Seth and Roddy were quiet during my back-and-forth with Helen. "That was funny," I said.

"I didn't think so." Helen rolled her eyes and looked away.

"I thought it was funny," Seth added. "That's why I contacted her. Sense of humor goes a long way."

"Well, you guys have fun tonight." I detected a twinge of jealousy in Helen's tone. She was probably hurt that I had found a roommate so quickly, never mind that it was my own brother.

Seth pulled me out the door. "Bye," he called out.

He started heading toward his car, which was on the opposite side of the parking lot from mine. He was holding my hand and leading me along, like it was the most natural thing in the world. "My car is over here, Seth," I said, gesturing toward my Civic.

"Oh, you don't want to go back to my place tonight? I can bring you in the morning to get your car."

"No, thank you. I need to get home tonight. I'm fine to drive."

He turned and we walked in the other direction. Out of the corner of my eye, I could see his chest heaving. When we got to my car, I unlocked the door and leaned against it to face him. "I'm sorry, Seth."

"It's okay, Charlotte." He sounded annoyed.

"I'm not going to sleep with you after a couple of impromptu dates and ball games where you have to concentrate on playing and I'm sitting there watching you."

He squinted and I wondered if he was thinking about my one-night stand with Adam. "Do you even want me to call you anymore?" he asked.

My stomach dropped. "Well, yeah, of course I do."

"I'm not convinced."

I shook my head. Now I was annoyed. "I'm not sure I'm your type, Seth. I mean, I'm not going to get into wearing Storm garb with my daisy dukes, like Marley."

"That's not my type—otherwise I'd be dating *her*. I just wonder if you're hung up on that guy."

I shot him a look. *You know I am.*

I didn't say anything in response. Seth was almost a foot taller than me in flats. I had to look up at him and he had to drop his head for us to make eye contact. The parking lot light shone behind him, shadowing his face, making it hard for me to see his expression. I waited for him to say something else.

"I think you're beautiful. I know you have a sense of humor, yet I haven't seen much of it in person, and I don't know why. I can tell you're smart and savvy and you know a lot of things about the world, but you have such a low opinion of yourself. It baffles me."

What the hell? "Thanks for those observations, Seth."

"Wait," he answered immediately. "I'm just saying I find it odd. You don't seem to understand how people see you. How men see you. I think that guy might've made you feel bad about yourself."

A lot of guys have made me feel bad about myself.

"I don't want to make you feel bad about yourself." He stepped back into the light where I could finally see his face. His smile was tight but sincere, and I realized it was because he could see my face. And he knew I wasn't having it tonight. "Okay. Drive safe, Charlotte."

As he turned to walk away, I reached for his hand.

I stepped toward him. He was hesitant, waiting for me to make a move. "When will you be back?"

"Thursday," he said, his tone softening.

"When is your next day off?"

"Thursday."

"How are you going to school with such a schedule?"

"I do online stuff during the season and then go to classes in the off-season."

"Where?"

"UC Davis."

"Really? What are you studying?"

"Veterinary medicine."

"Huh," I looked into his gray-green eyes. "That's sweet."

He laughed once. "Thanks."

I leaned up on my toes and touched my lips to his, but he was holding back; I could tell. He was only matching my own motions, too afraid to push for more. We kissed for just a moment and then I pulled away. I could feel him leaning into me as I pulled back. He didn't want it to end but he was trying to have some self-control.

"How about Thursday then?"

He nodded. "I'd like that."

"I can meet Obi-Wan."

"He'd like that."

"Okay, then it's a date."

"Okay, see you Thursday." He leaned down and kissed my cheek.

"Good luck on the road."

I opened my door. Seth waited until I got in and started the car. He took a step back and waved as I drove away.

13. Things Change

I didn't hear from Helen all week. I felt like my heart was breaking, but thankfully Chucky was there for comic relief. We sat on the couch every night and watched TV. He even drank Champagne with me.

"This is actually really fucking delicious. Let's cook tonight and we'll drink the rest of this bottle. Want to?"

"Don't you have a girlfriend, Chucky? Why do you want to sit here and hang out with me?"

"I could say the same to you, Charlotte." He used my full name and I instantly felt bad for calling him Chucky.

He was standing at the bar, cutting tomatoes. I moved past him to look in the refrigerator. "Salad and salmon?"

"Yep," he said. He was trying to eat healthy for the triathlon. In the few days that he had been there, I was starting to feel healthier myself. It's not fair to say that Helen and I were bad for each other, but it was true that we had fallen into a lot of bad habits. And we hadn't been moving forward. She was right, it was time to put some space between us, otherwise we'd be perpetual twenty-one-year-olds, in dead-end relationships, goofing off in our pigsty apartment while the whole world was growing up around us.

"I'm dating someone, you know. He's out of town," I said after several moments of companionable silence.

"Helen told me." He went to wash his hands at the sink. "But she said you weren't serious about him. Not surprising. Have you ever been serious about anyone?"

When the hell did Helen talk to Chucky? "Not really. My track record sucks. I'm not good at picking them."

"Helen thinks this dude is a good guy."

"When did you have such a deep, meaningful conversation with Helen?"

"She came by when you were at work today." There was a small box on the counter. "I forgot to give this to you."

I opened the box and inside it was one of those best-friends trinkets. One half of a broken heart. Helen and I didn't have them when we were kids because we thought we were too cool. There was a small note inside.

Charlie. I don't expect you to wear this kid shit but it conveys a sentiment I want to get across to you. We're forever, you and me. Okay? Let's fucking go shopping soon and not act like strangers just because we don't live together. I get you and you get me more than anyone, BFF. Love you. Helen.

I started getting misty-eyed but Chucky slapped me on the back. "She's sweet. And hot. I wished I would've tapped that when I had the chance."

"Chuck, you never had a chance with her."

"Are you kidding? Helen was infatuated with me. She snuck into my room one night and tried to kiss me when I was thirteen."

I was shocked. "What a slut! I can't believe that. She never told me."

Chucky and I laughed. Helen was always boy-crazy in general. I don't think she had actually been into him, but I'm glad he didn't let her kiss him. Imagine living with that your whole life. Gross.

After dinner on the couch, I paused *Game of Thrones* right as Jon Snow was filling the screen. "Perfect view." I turned to Chucky. "Can I tell you something?" I couldn't believe I was confiding in Golden Boy.

"Go for it."

"A few months ago, I met this guy on the street a couple of blocks from here. I went to his loft and slept with him."

"Shocker."

"Shut up, Chuck. I liked him. He was spontaneous, kind of wild. He changed his whole life around in a year and spent every day doing exactly what he wanted to do: painting."

"Oh, another shocker," Chucky said. "Like Curtis and his video games? You sure know how to pick 'em."

"I know, I know. Just listen. Here's the thing. I fell for him . . . hard. We were acting like this couple who had been together for years. We acted like we were in love and it felt like we were. Then, the next day, he practically kicked me out."

"Was he a drug addict?"

"No. I told you, I went to his loft. It was nice. He was a corporate lawyer but quit his job to become a painter."

"Like a house painter?"

"No, like an artist."

"This is the weirdest one yet, Charlotte. Who pretends to be in love after one night?"

I shook my head. "That part is hard to explain, but it made sense in the moment. The point is, I really fell for him but I didn't think he was into me—especially after the next morning. But then I saw this new mural a few blocks away, painted on the side of a building. And it's of me. I can't get him out of my head now."

"And that's what's making it so hard for you to date the baseball player? Seriously?"

"I think so," I said.

"I don't. I think any normal, suitable guy is off limits to you because you think you're not worth it, so you have to obsess over crazies like this painter."

I shook my head. "I don't think so."

He grabbed my hand, which was weird.

"What are you doing, Chucky?" I scowled.

"Charlotte, listen to me. I was a shitty brother. I think I ruined your self-esteem or something. But you're gorgeous, okay? And you deserve better than some bipolar hipster artist guy."

I yanked my hand away. "Ew, Chucky."

"Oh, grow up, Charlotte. I just wanted you to know I don't think you're fat or dumb. Not really, anyway. My standards for women are high because I had an awesome mom and an awesome sister who showed me how smart and beautiful a woman could be. Inside and out."

"I'm actually going to start crying if you don't stop."

He laughed once and looked away. "I just wanted you to know, okay?"

I grabbed his hand back and squeezed it. "I think you're pretty awesome, too. I'm really proud of you for making it through dental school." At that point I really did start to cry, and Chuck's eyes welled up, too.

"Thanks, sis. Now can we go back to being assholes to each other? Just for fun?"

"Totally."

ON MONDAY, I did everything I could to find out more information about Adam. I learned that there was a man in the Los Angeles planning department fighting to protect the murals in the Arts District, and to restore some of the old murals that had been covered up in and around LA. I couldn't imagine someone coming along and covering up our frolicking wolves or the winged man . . . or the new mural of my alternate-universe romance with Adam.

I wrote a letter to the city and asked to sign the petition to protect our local murals. I wanted to keep the fantasy alive through Adam's art for as long as possible.

At work on Tuesday, I spilled an entire glass of water on a baby's head. The mother yelled at me for five minutes. I just kept saying, "At least it wasn't coffee." Jon-Jon wasn't amused.

I made it safely to Wednesday without Helen, and without walking past Adam's loft or texting Seth or bugging Helen about being lonely, but I *was* lonely. I watched TV that night and scrolled through Match.com posts on my laptop. Chucky walked by, dressed up in slacks and a button-down shirt.

"Where are you off to?" I asked.

"I have a date."

"Go, Chucky! Who is she?"

"This girl I've been seeing from dental school. Jenn."

"Okay. Well, if you want to bring her back here, text me and I'll get lost for a while."

"Really? You'd do that for me?"

"Please. I'd do that for *me*. I don't want to hear any of your weird sexcapades."

He chuckled. "Probably best. See ya."

He was out the door and I was alone again.

At nine, Chucky texted me to get lost, so I went out and got a donut. I told him to text me the all-clear once he was ready.

I sat on a bus bench eating a giant maple bar, wondering how to approach this thing with Seth. There were sparks, for sure, but something was holding me back from feeling fireworks. I wished I felt worthy of him. I wished that I thought I was as attractive as he was or had as much to offer. I was just a waitress, living with my brother in some crackpot apartment in a less-than-glamorous part of LA.

Halfway through my donut, I got a text from Chucky.

Chucky: It's all clear but Jenn's
gonna stay the night, okay?

Me: Sure, fine, whatever. Be home
in ten. Please be fully clothed.

Instead of going home, I walked past Adam's loft. His neighbor, whom I had met for two seconds, was coming out of the building. *What am I doing? I promised myself I wouldn't do this.*

"Excuse me? Hi."

"Oh, hey," she said. "Charlotte, right?"

"Wow, good memory. What was your name again?"

"Stacy." We shook hands. "I only remember because Adam remembered, and that was totally unlike him. He was looking for you for a while but said he couldn't find you."

What in the hell is happening?

"Why didn't he just come to my house? He's been to my apartment before, and I live just a few minutes away."

She gave me a long look. "You don't know, do you?"

"Know what?"

She stared at me for a few seconds, but I could see her mind at work, as if she were having a debate with herself. "I don't really think it's my place. Would you mind if I took your number so I can get in touch with him and see if it's okay to pass along his info?"

"Well, jeez. It doesn't sound like I was a person he wanted in his life."

"No, you don't understand. It's not my place to talk to you about this. He liked you a lot. He remembered you. That was amazing for Adam, at that time."

"Why was it amazing for Adam at that time? Is he mentally ill or something?" That would certainly explain a lot.

She pulled out her phone. "No, no, not at all. I'm sorry, I have to go meet my husband. Just let me get your number and I'll get in touch with you, okay? I promise."

"Um, okay. I just . . . he kind of rejected me."

"No," she said, shaking her head adamantly. "He was confused. I'll explain everything later."

I gave her my number and then stumbled home dumbfounded, but not before sneaking another glance at my mural.

14. Sabotage

Chucky and Jenn stayed in his bedroom and kept quiet all night. It wasn't any different from rooming with Helen. Even Helen would occasionally be brazenly loud with some guy she had brought home.

In the morning, I left early for work first thing. Around eleven, Seth texted me.

Seth: We still on for tonight?

> **Me:** I'm sorry. I think I'm going to pass tonight. Rain check?

Seth: Of course. Do you really mean it though . . . about the rain check?

> **Me:** Yes.

Seth: I have some news. I'm going to be a Padre. They're

**bringing me up. Starting me
in center field. It wasn't just
a rumor.**

> **Me: That's amazing, Seth! You'll
> be a major leaguer.**

And I'll never hear from him again.

I was genuinely happy for Seth. He deserved it. Soon there would be even more women flocking to him. He would be on television practically every night. People would recognize him.

My stomach started swirling around and around in circles. I needed to give him an out.

> **Me: You're probably not going
> to have much time once
> you've been moved up.**

Seth: My first game is tomorrow.

> **Me: Yeah, I mean, you're
> probably going to be
> insanely busy.**

He was on to me.

**Seth: Can I date you? Is that
all right, Charlotte? Or are you
not ready for that right now,
because I sense that you're
trying to get out of something.**

Me: I'm not sure.

**Seth: Come to the Padres game
Friday and let me know. I'll leave
you a ticket at will-call.**

I didn't go to the game that Friday night. And I waited and waited for Stacy to call me with news of Adam.

I stayed home, but I did watch the game on TV. I actually paid a hundred dollars for some baseball package through Direct TV because our local channel wasn't airing it, but I had to see him play. On TV, he was strikingly handsome. When he'd get up to bat I felt like I heard more women cheering than men, though maybe that was my mind playing tricks on me.

Chucky came home sometime around the fifth inning.

"Yo," he said as he walked by me toward his room.

"Yo."

When he came back out, he was wearing a red polyester tracksuit and had a bag in his hand. "I got you a present," he said. When I stood to take the bag from his hands I noticed that the name "Chuck" was embroidered on his jacket.

I cautiously removed the contents of the bag to reveal an identical tracksuit to the one he was wearing, except it had "Charlie" embroidered on it. "Oh my god, Chucky." I buckled over and started laughing.

"Screw Helen," he said. "We're roomies now."

"We're the Royal Tenenbaums!" I said, trying to catch my breath. "Thank you, Chuck. I totally thought you'd have Fatbutt embroidered on something the first chance you got."

"It crossed my mind."

Still laughing, I said, "We're gonna be a spectacle."

"It's fucking rad. Wanna go for a run?"

"I'm watching the game."

He turned around to look at the TV. "Your guy playing?"

"Not really my guy, but yeah, Seth's playing. I'm gonna go put this on now," I said.

"Cool." He sat down on the couch to watch. "It's Seth Taylor, right?"

"Yep," I called back from the bathroom.

"He's up."

I ran out wearing my new tracksuit. "Scoot, scoot."

Seth was down in the count when he smacked a high fastball clear to the scoreboard. Chucky and I jumped up and cheered. The stadium went wild and the announcer said, "What a way to make an entrance for Seth Taylor!"

Seth jogged the bases with a humble smile. I couldn't take my eyes off him. The camera panned to a group of giddy women sitting above the Padres dugout, shaking their stupid boobs at Seth as he ran toward them from home base.

"Jeez," Chucky said.

"Right? Buncha skanks."

"That's not really what I was thinking."

"What were you thinking?"

"I was thinking that dude can get anyone he wants."

"Awesome, thanks for the reminder."

"I'm just saying."

"Whatever. Let's go for a run."

We didn't talk at all during our run, but when we reached the stairs of our apartment, I said, "Do you think Seth and I should date? I mean, he'll probably stop calling me after this."

"Cut the shit, Charlotte," Chucky said as he passed me through the front door and headed toward his room.

After I showered, I dozed off in my room while reading a magazine. I was awoken at midnight by the sound of my phone buzzing on my nightstand. It was a text.

Seth: Hey pretty lady.

> **Me:** Hey

Seth: Are you sleeping?

> **Me:** Currently? Yes. I'm very good at texting while I'm asleep.

Seth: Smartass. I tried calling you earlier . . .

> **Me:** I went for a run then I fell asleep.

Seth: So you weren't at the game after all?

> **Me:** No. Sorry.

Seth: I thought for sure you were there.

> **Me:** Why? Because of the home run?

Seth: So you watched? ☺

> **Me:** I saw the highlights.

Seth: Oh.

I don't know why I lied.

                                        Me: Congrats.

**Seth: Thanks. I'll let you get
back to bed.**

                                        Me: Ok. Night.

Seth: Night.

Rejection would be hard, even for Seth Taylor, but I was selfishly too concerned about being rejected myself to think about his feelings. And I was annoyed that I hadn't heard from Stacy.

THE NEXT DAY I had to work a double. By the dinner shift I was ready to kill Jon-Jon. A customer found a roach crawling up the hostess stand, and when I told Jon-Jon, he killed it but wouldn't comp her meal. Of course I got no tip. There are roaches in every restaurant. You just hope they don't end up in the food. But still, people don't want to see them when they're eating.

When I got home late that night, I finally checked my phone. There was a text from Seth.

Seth: Missed you tonight. Went 0 for 4.

I didn't respond. I checked my voicemails. Surprisingly, I had two messages. No one ever called me, but my fingers were crossed that it was Stacy. The first one was from Helen. "Dude, what have you been up to? I miss you. Call me."

The next message was from my mom. "What in the hell do I have to do to get my children to call me?" She was missing Chucky.

I yelled from my bedroom, "Chuck, did you call Mom back?"

He came and stood in the doorway of my room. Through a yawn, he said, "Yeah, she's having empty-nester pains."

"That's pathetic. I figured it was more about you than me."

"Your boy had a shitty game."

"I heard," I said.

"Are you working tomorrow?"

"No, I don't work on Sundays. It's a holy day."

Chucky choked on his Kombucha. "You are the poster child of goodness and virtue."

I was brushing out my hair and inspecting the balayage I had done on it the day before.

"I thought you were gonna start being nicer to your landlord?" I said.

"Your hair looks good, Charlotte. Seriously. You kind of look like Lily Aldridge now."

"Who's that?"

"Some famous chick."

When Chucky left the room, I immediately Googled Lily Aldridge. She was a model and married to a rock star. I walked over to Chucky's room, where I found him dozing off in bed. I walked right up to him and smacked him in the head.

"What are you doing?" he shouted.

"You can't call me Fatbutt and then say I look like freakin' Lily Aldridge."

"Okay," he whined. "I take it back. You look like you ate Lily Aldridge."

"Fuck you, Chucky."

As I walked back to my room he called out, "Love you, Fatbutt!"

I plopped on my bed and called Helen back. "What up?"

"Hey. How are you?" I said.

"Good. Roddy just came back into town so we're making up for lost time. By the way, I think I want to go back to a natural color now that the chartreuse has faded. Can you come here and color it for me before Seth's game? Roddy has four tickets in the section where all the family members and wives sit. Wanna go?"

I hesitated.

"Don't say no," she pleaded.

"I'll come down tomorrow morning around nine and do your hair."

"And you'll go to the game?"

She wasn't gonna stop. "Yeah, I'll go."

I've got nothing else to do.

THE NEXT MORNING, when I arrived at Roddy and Helen's condo in San Diego, I was surprised to see a complete vision of domestic bliss. I knew they were in love, but I fully expected Helen to be living in Roddy's bachelor pad in transition. Instead, it was actually a really nice place, and I could see all of Helen's warm touches.

I followed her around the house as she pointed things

out to me. "And I got those throw pillows at Home Goods. Aren't they cute?"

"Yep."

"Come, I'll show you our room."

"I don't think I need to see your room, Helen." Helen was wearing a robe in preparation for having her hair dyed and Roddy hadn't come down the stairs yet.

"Come on, it's nice."

"Isn't Roddy up there?"

"He's fine. Babe!" she yelled. "I'm bringing Charlie up. Are you decent?"

"Come on up," he yelled.

Their bedroom was sprawling, with large glass doors leading to a balcony and a vast view of an unadulterated landscape. The bathroom was the size of my room in our LA apartment. I caught a view of Roddy in his boxer briefs, leaning over the sink, shaving. I quickly looked down at my feet.

"It's okay, they're basically shorts," Helen said.

"No, they're not." His back and butt were thick and muscular.

Roddy looked up at me through the mirror and smiled. "Hey, Charlotte."

"Hi, Roddy." I waved and then headed for the bedroom door, flushed all the way to my ears.

I dyed Helen's hair in the downstairs bathroom and blew it out into soft waves. When I was almost finished, Roddy came and stood in the doorway, gazing at Helen with such reverence that it actually made me emotional.

"I like it," he said. "This is the real you."

Helen nodded and then her eyes started watering. Her hair was back to how I remembered it growing up—a light, natural blond, her eyebrows just a shade darker, framing her green eyes.

"You look great," I said. "I haven't seen you like this in a long time."

She stood and went closer to the mirror. "Jesus, Charlie, you're a miracle worker. I never thought I'd see this hair again." I couldn't believe I hadn't fucked it up.

I was feeling good about myself, and feeling good about where Helen was with Roddy. But still, how in the world could two people know they'd be compatible after spending a few hours with each other?

When Roddy left the bathroom, I said, "How do you know, Helen? About Roddy?"

She shrugged. "I think I just finally figured myself out. I'm a fucking goofball and I was tired of being fake around guys." She shut the door to the bathroom and sat on the closed toilet seat. "When I first saw Roddy . . . well, you know, he wasn't really my type."

I moved to the other side of the bathroom, leaned against the sink, and crossed my arms over my chest. "So you decided to move in with him?"

"No. I was just fucking around, being myself. I thought nothing would come of it. But it was awesome, being myself with him. He just totally let his guard down, too. We goofed off that first night and we had crazy sex and then goofed off some more. I just kept wanting to relive it."

"Yeah, but that happens for a lot of people, Helen. They don't go moving in with each other."

"No, I've never been able to be myself around a guy and still love myself afterward."

"Hmm. I get it, I guess."

"Seth is genuinely a good guy, Charlotte. Why don't you give him a chance?"

"I know nothing about him."

"Try to get to know him."

I shrugged. "Maybe I will."

But the person I really wanted to get to know was nowhere to be found.

WHEN WE GOT to the game, we were ushered to our seats and soon discovered that Seth wasn't playing at all; they had another utility player in his position. "Why isn't he playing?"

"I don't know. It's a bummer, though. I wanted to cheer him on," Roddy grumbled.

We watched almost the whole game in silence. I think we all were wondering if Seth's major-league stint was going to be short-lived.

At the bottom of the ninth, the Padres were down by two with bases loaded and two outs. Then they brought Seth in to pinch-hit for the pitcher.

"Oh my god, the pressure," I said.

Roddy came back quickly with, "He can handle it. Come on, Seth!" he shouted.

"Come on, Seth!" I screamed. There was no way he heard me, but from my view it looked like he straightened his shoulders infinitesimally the moment I yelled. The first pitch was a strike. He stepped out of the batter's box, taking a breath, taking his time. He did a practice swing and then tapped the bat on his shoes and dug into the batter's box again for the next pitch. It was a high ball, outside. It looked like he was almost going to swing.

"Be patient, number twelve!" Roddy yelled. "That high-ball outside is his weakness," he said quietly to us.

The next pitch hung in the air, right at his shoulders. As if in slow motion, I watched Seth bend his knees, step forward, and swing right into the pitch with beautiful grace and ease. The stadium went crazy as we watched the ball sail all the way out of the park, past the center field wall. It was the farthest section, a generous four hundred feet to the wall, and Seth smacked the ball over it like it was nothing. A grand slam. He coasted around the bases, and when he tapped his toe on home plate, he kissed his hand and waved toward me. We made eye contact for a second. I smiled with such joy that I felt like an idiot.

"Wow," Roddy said. "They say it's harder to hit a home run at night here because of the marine layer."

"What are you talking about?" Helen said.

"To hit it out at the farthest part of the field, because the air is thicker. He really got ahold of that one."

Helen laughed. "It has to be because she's here." She patted me on the head.

"What, are you serious?"

"Maybe," Roddy said.

"That's ridiculous."

Helen leaned in and whispered in my ear. "Sometimes they just need to believe in it. It's a head trick."

She wasn't actually superstitious; she wasn't actually buying this crap. She was doing what a good baseball girlfriend would do: letting them believe. Letting them have faith. Wasn't that what I did for crazy Adam that one night?

15. Worship

When the game was over, we walked across the street to the lobby bar at the Omni hotel.

"He'll be over when he's done," Helen said when she spotted me looking around.

"Oh, I don't care," I said.

"Yeah you do."

Roddy was off talking to one of the coaches while Helen and I sat in round bucket chairs, watching swarms of fans gather around.

After my second drink, I yawned and thought I would give him another ten minutes and then head home. I didn't have any messages on my phone, so I figured he was busy with all the hype from hitting the walk-off grand slam. A moment later, I noticed Helen beside me look up and smile. Before I had time to turn around, I felt a big, warm hand on my shoulder.

"Charlotte?"

With the touch of his hand, something suddenly clicked for me, and I decided I would just live within the moment.

I jumped up, turned, and leapt into his arms. "You were amazing!"

His chest rumbled with laughter. "It's 'cause you were here."

I kissed him, right there in front of a hundred people gathered in the lobby lounge as they looked on. He smelled clean and his hair was damp as I raked my hands through it. He must have showered in the locker room.

I pulled away just an inch to see his grin. "I'm glad I came," I said.

He hugged me again and kissed my ear. "Me too."

Helen stood casually and said, "Congrats, Seth," before faking an exaggerated yawn. "Gosh, Roddy and I have to get home." Seth and I pulled apart. "Charlotte, you ready or . . . um . . . maybe Seth can give you a ride to our house to get your car? You have plans, Seth?"

He tensed up. "I'll take her . . . if she wants me to."

Helen waved her hand around vaguely. "You two can figure it out."

Roddy came over and smacked Seth on the back. "You killed that ball, man."

"Thanks, bro."

Helen kissed me on the cheek and then kissed Seth on the cheek and whispered something in his ear. We said our good-byes and then they were gone and it was just Seth and me. And I wanted him. I couldn't deny it. He was standing there, humble and unassuming, even though there were at least twenty-five women discreetly moving closer to him in the lounge, hoping he'd shoot them a look or leave my side to seek them out. He acted as though he didn't even notice them. "Thanks again for coming today. You hungry?"

"Yes," I said, my eyes fixed on his mouth.

"Me too," he whispered. "I got a room here tonight."

I nodded. "Before you knew I was coming?"

"No. Just now, when I saw you here. Just after I came in." He pulled a key card from his back pocket.

I laughed. Maybe he was assuming . . . "Getting ahead of yourself, aren't you?"

"Wishful thinking." He moved closer to me and took my hand in his. "I actually don't care anymore how this looks. And yeah, I got the room when I saw you because I want to be alone with you, okay?"

"Okay." I nodded, and then let him pull me toward the elevator bays.

He held my hand all the way up to the twenty-second floor. There was palpable sexual tension in the elevator. When the doors opened, he led me into the hall. "Come on, Charlotte, I want you and I'm tired of waiting."

"We've only been on two dates, technically."

"I don't care," he said with his back to me.

I yanked my hand out of his just before we reached the door to his room. "What if I do?"

He turned to me, squinting, his expression inscrutable. He braced both of my forearms and swung me around so that my back was against the door. Our lips were only inches apart as he held me pinned in place. I felt scared for a second. I looked up and down the hallway but no one was there. He pressed his lips to mine forcefully. We kissed hard, fast, passionately, and I was done for. My body was aching for him. I needed his strong hands on me. I drove my fingers into his hair while he gripped the back of my neck with one hand and my bottom with the other.

He pried his mouth from mine. Breathing hard, he said, "Are you saying you don't want to go in there with me? Because I'll walk you back down and drive you wherever you want or call you a cab."

I stepped aside. All reservations were gone. "Forget what I said. Open the door."

There was a flurry of hands and lips and movement toward the bed. Neither one of us made any motion for a light switch. The Coronado Bridge and San Diego Bay were on display through the large floor-to-ceiling windows, filling the room with a magical glow. He reached behind me and lifted to straddle him as he backed me toward the bed. I pulled my mouth away. "God, it's beautiful out there," I said, panting.

"It's beautiful in here." My shirt went flying across the room as he kicked off his shoes. He set me down on my feet with the backs of my legs against the bed. His deft hands were unbuttoning my jeans with ease, and a moment later I was standing in just my bra and panties. I undid his belt and tugged at his pants and boxers, pulling them down as I dropped to my knees.

When I took ahold of him, he hissed out a breath. "No," he said. He bent, bracing my arms and pulled me up to stand. "What are you doing?" he said.

My face flushed. I was heated but embarrassed. "I thought . . ."

"No, let's kiss." His lips were on mine again, urgent. He somehow managed to undo my bra without me even knowing he was trying. It fell to the floor as he cupped my breast. He bent, kissing it while running his hand up the small of my back. I arched into him. Seth was in charge, smooth, strong, and commanding, the way he played baseball. He laid me on the bed and then stood up straight, drinking me in. When he reached for my panties I covered his hands with mine. "Wait."

"What is it, Charlotte?" His eyes were drowsy with desire.

"Do you really like me?"

"Of course. I wouldn't be here with you right now if I didn't."

He crawled up beside me, propping his head on his hand. I looked down and noticed how painfully turned on he was. "Just give me a second," I said, my chest heaving in and out.

"You were about to go down on me without even hesitating."

"I know."

His fingertips danced across my belly before his hand went sliding down under the waistband of my panties. He dropped his head to my breast, kissing and sucking at my nipple.

After several moments, he whispered, "I'm going to worship you now. Tell me to stop if you want me to stop."

"Ahhh," I breathed out when he touched me down below. I held his hand to me, pressing and guiding.

"Don't," I whispered.

"Don't what, Charlotte?"

"Don't stop."

A second later my panties were gone and then his mouth was on me and my back was arching off the bed. "Jesus. Don't stop. Don't stop!"

When I pressed his head to my body, he hummed in

satisfaction, making my body explode into a million tiny pulses of light. I couldn't make a sound, couldn't breathe; I was falling apart, trying desperately to ride out the waves without screaming. I felt the back of my head digging into the bed while my body quaked and shuddered.

When my brain was able to register my surroundings again, I looked up to see Seth between my legs, sitting back on his heels, looking mesmerized. I was embarrassed, but all I could see on his face was desire. "That was good, right?"

"Yes," I choked out.

"You're stunning," he said. I shook my head. His hand was still on me, moving in slow circles across my sensitive skin. "You are, Charlotte. Why don't you know that?" He blinked. "I want to make love to you."

Warmth spread from my chest to my limbs. My throat tightened. I moved his hand from my body and pulled him up to cover me while I opened my legs wider, inviting him in.

Once we were joined, his mouth was on mine and he was moving gently in and out. He sucked on my bottom lip and then moved to my neck and up to my ear. "God, Charlotte, you feel so good. Too good." He picked up the rhythm.

"Ah" was all I could say. His breath near my ear was making my brain malfunction. I was losing it again, feeling my body tingling around his. He thrust into me once more and then collapsed. I held him to me until our bodies stopped pulsing.

He put his weight on his elbows and leaned back to look at me. There was just enough light in the room to see his serene expression. "That was amazing."

"Yes," I said with conviction between gasps. "Very good."

He pecked me on the lips and then kissed my cheek and lifted himself off me. "Shower?"

"Okay." I followed him into the bathroom, neither one of us self-conscious of our nakedness. I admired how well built he was. How young, virile, and enthusiastic he was once I realized he was turned on again just moments after we were done having sex.

In the shower, he lifted me, pressing me against the cold tile. I wrapped my legs around him and he was inside of me again. "I want to stay here inside of you for a long time."

"I want you to stay there for a long time."

He moved harder, pressing me against the wall. "I really like you, Charlotte. I'm falling for you," he said through ragged breaths. How could he be so open, so honest?

I kissed him, answering his passion without words.

After the shower, we fell asleep naked on top of the covers, tangled up in each other.

16. Good or Bad Timing

Seth was leaving to go on the road in two days. I invited him to come up and stay at my house before he left, and he agreed. I was letting it all happen.

When Seth and I got to my apartment, I was surprised to find Chucky sitting at the bar, eating cereal and reading the newspaper.

"No hot date?" I said, walking through the door.

"Not tonight, Fatbutt." When Chucky spotted Seth behind me, he stood up from the barstool and quickly swallowed a mouthful of cereal.

Seth immediately approached him, hand out for a shake. "Hey, I'm Seth."

Chucky gave him a firm handshake in return. "Nice to meet you. I'm Charles." He pulled Seth toward him and then whispered loud enough for me to hear, "We have mafia ties. Don't forget it, man."

"Oh shut it, Chuck," I snapped.

He shrugged and went back to his cereal. Seth followed me into the kitchen. "You want a beer or something?" I asked.

"Sure," he said. Seth stood awkwardly next to Chucky on the other side of the bar while Chucky flipped through the newspaper. My brother and father read the newspaper every single day. It was like brushing their teeth—and for Chucky and my dad, that's saying a lot. When I handed the beer over the counter to Seth, he smiled his sweet, boyish smile and said, "Thank you." But something caught my eye as I reached across the counter. It was the voicemail notification on my phone.

"Will you excuse me?" I said to Seth.

"Sure." He looked at me peculiarly as I grabbed my phone and headed for the bedroom. I overheard Seth and Chucky making small talk, so it was a relief that Seth at least had that distraction.

I hit the voicemail button and recognized Stacy's voice immediately. "Hi, Charlotte. I talked to Adam. He wasn't sure if it was okay to call you after all this time but he would love to hear from you. I also think you and I need to talk if you do decide to call him or see him. I'd rather not discuss it over voicemail, so if you'd like to call me back, I'll be here for the rest of the night."

I immediately dialed her number. "Hi, it's Charlotte."

"Charlotte, I'm so glad you called. Sorry about all the anticipation. I wanted to go and see Adam myself, and see what state of mind he was in."

State of mind? He is crazy. "Okay . . . and?"

"He was actually in great spirits." She paused for a few beats. "Charlotte, I hate to be the bearer of bad news, but he wanted me to tell you that he's in the hospital. Adam has a stage four glioblastoma."

"Huh?"

"It's a brain tumor. He has cancer, Charlotte."

I dropped the phone. A guttural sound escaped me. I lost my breath, clutched my chest, and felt a sharp pain radiate through my lungs. The wind had been knocked out of me by one sentence.

It all made sense. Quitting his job. The parking tickets. The Post-it notes. His odd behavior, which had seemed like spontaneity in the moment.

When I met Adam, he was already dying. And he knew it.

I finally gathered the strength to pick up the phone and lift it to my ear. "I'm sorry, I dropped the phone."

"I know it's a lot to take in right now. You left quite an impact on Adam. At the time you two met, part of the tumor was pressing on his brain so much that it was affecting his short-term memory. He couldn't remember what day of the week it was, or who he had met five minutes before. He painted a lot of women during that time but remembered none of them but you. He tried to find you. He painted the name Charlotte over and over. He wanted to tell you that, for a little while, he believed the story you two had made up. I don't know what that means, but I guess that will mean something to you."

I was speechless.

Stacy went on. "They removed part of the tumor and now Adam is much sharper, though the cancer is still wreaking havoc on his body."

I couldn't respond. Tears were running down my cheeks.

"Are you there?" she said.

"Yes," I squeaked.

"There's something else, Charlotte. After Adam moved out, he asked me to get rid of his paintings. I didn't have the heart to do it, so I called a gallery owner I know downtown. We went through hundreds of paintings, and she realized they were connected to dozens of murals throughout the city. She alerted some preservationists, who are trying to protect the murals, and now the LA art community is calling him the West Coast Banksy. He wants to keep his identity a secret for as long as possible. If it got out that the artist is dying of cancer, the press would go nuts."

I thought about the wolves. The winged man.

She went on, "But people talk most about the mural of you in the red dress. Adam wouldn't tell me the story behind it, but he remembers why he painted it."

I nearly choked on the emotion rising in my throat. "So where is he? What hospital? Is he dying for sure?"

"It doesn't look good. He gave me a letter to give to you, and I think you should read it before you see him. He's at Cedars."

My brain was so overwhelmed that I had to remind myself to breathe. Seth stood in the doorway. He had only been there for a second, but he was looking at me cautiously.

"I'll come by tomorrow and get the letter and maybe make arrangements to see him. Thank you, Stacy. Thank you so much." I was hesitant to say this last part in front of Seth. "He made a great impact on me as well."

We said good-bye and hung up. Seth was still standing there. He came over and bent his head and kissed me delicately on the shoulder. My throat was tight and I was trying desperately to swallow my emotions. "Tell me what's going on," he urged.

"That painter, the guy I told you about . . . he didn't dog me after all. He was dying; he's still dying. Of cancer. He's been trying to find me but . . . the tumor . . . his memory . . . he couldn't remember . . . oh god."

Seth just stood there quietly.

"His neighbor has a letter for me. I told her I would get it tomorrow and then go see him." I collapsed on the bed.

After a few moments, Seth finally spoke. "Should I go home?"

"No!" The thought of being alone terrified me.

He crossed his arms over his chest. "I don't know what to say besides I'm sorry. I don't want this to affect what we've started."

I didn't want to tell him that it was most definitely going to affect what we had started. Right now, I just wanted him to stay with me.

"I shouldn't be here, Charlotte."

"No. Please. Stay."

He shook his head and turned toward the door.

"You're leaving?" I asked.

"No, I'm going to get you some tissues and water."

I hadn't even realized I'd been crying.

When he came back, I said, "Are you mad?"

"I'm not mad. Of course I'm not mad."

How could I know what Seth was thinking or feeling? Everything that had happened in the last twenty minutes seemed like a dream. I was barely able to get ahold of my own emotions about Adam, the night we spent together, and this new information.

And what was life like for Adam? Was he withering

away, alone and confused in a hospital bed, thinking that we had this amazing connection while I was merrily going on with my shallow life, stalking Match.com and sleeping with baseball players?

"I'll stay if you want me to," Seth said.

"Yes, I want you to stay." *I wish I knew how to be alone.*

"Do you want to get into bed and talk?" he asked.

"Okay."

He turned off the lights and slipped into the bed beside me. We wiggled out of our clothes and lay in our underwear. "I don't know what to do," I said quietly.

"You should get the letter and go see him. He wanted you to have it and he wants to see you. He's a dying man."

"Will you go with me tomorrow to get the letter before you go back to San Diego?"

"Of course."

"Can I tell you something, Seth?"

"Anything."

"I've been all over the place with my life. I've had so many jobs and weird boyfriends. My twenties have been a total joke."

He turned on his side and pulled me into his arms. "So what?"

"Why are you being so good to me?"

"Because I can tell you're a good person. I've had my share of one-night stands and bad decisions. I just try not to dwell on them."

"I've just been lost, you know? Killing time with Helen. I admire her for taking a leap. I could never do that."

Seth tensed. "Did you really fall for that guy, in that way?"

"Does it really matter? He's going to die soon. I usually find a way to sabotage things or seek out the most unavailable people. I did it with Adam without even knowing."

"I can see why he'd be hung up on you, even with a faulty memory. You're kind of impossible to forget. Before I even met you, I couldn't stop thinking about you."

I smiled. There was enough light coming from under the door to see him smile back. Rolling onto my side, I let him spoon me. I wanted to feel like I had done something right, like I deserved Seth spooning me, like I deserved to be Adam's muse.

But I was still conflicted. Would I always be?

THE NEXT DAY, after brunch, Seth and I headed to Stacy's. I knocked on the door. When she opened it, Foxy Cleopatra was at her feet. I bent to pet her. "Hi, Foxy."

When I looked up, I noticed Stacy was staring at Seth—not ogling him, just trying to figure out who the hell he was.

"Stacy, this is my friend Seth." They shook hands.

"Would you like to come in?"

We followed Stacy and sat at a round table. Foxy wouldn't leave me alone. Stacy handed me the letter. Seth stayed quiet.

"I haven't read it," she said. "But if you want to read it here, maybe I can answer some of your questions. I think he wrote it right after that night."

I could feel Seth shift beside me.

"Okay." I opened the letter and read it to myself.

Charlotte. I remembered your name right after you left so I wrote it down. I wanted to tell you but I didn't want to scare you away even more. I have a brain tumor. Like, the really bad kind. That's why I seemed forgetful. My days are numbered, lady. I wasn't joking. I wish I wouldn't have let you go just now. Now I don't know how to find you. Everything before you and I were in that bar is a blur, but everything after is crystal clear. Why is that? Is it because I was so enamored of you that you marked my soul and now I can't get you out of my mind? I hope you come back, but if you don't, I hope this letter finds you. Last night was far and away the best night of my life. I've never felt so connected to anyone before. It was the first time I've ever really been scared to die. I think because it's the first time I've ever really wanted to live. I felt like we had known each other forever. I felt something I didn't think I would feel in this life: love. Like that crazy, passionate shit everyone talks about. You're everything I've ever dreamed of. I know it seems crazy but when you made up that story, at first I believed it and I was confused because it seemed so real, like a memory. And then I realized it wasn't true. I wasn't mad at you for lying, I was sad that I hadn't met you sooner. I was sad that it wasn't real and that I didn't have enough time on this earth to love you well. You lit up my night . . . my fucking life, Charlotte. I don't remember wanting to touch anyone so badly. I would have stayed in this loft with you until the very end, if you would have agreed. I wish I would have asked you.

I'm writing because I wanted you to know that when people talk about "the one," you were my "one." Is that crazy? I know I'm not that for you because you have your whole life ahead of you and we only spent one night together, but I still had to tell you. Please find a nice guy who doesn't give you crap about your toes. They're the most adorable little sausages I've ever seen.

If you're reading this, then I guess I'll see you on the other side. Love, Adam.

He thought he would be dead before I read this.

It's fair to say that by the time I finished reading the letter, I was a blubbering fool. I was hysterical and hyperventilating. It brought Adam back to me, his spontaneity and humor and the way I, too, felt like I had known him my whole life. Seth was rocking me, making soothing sounds and rubbing my arms up and down. Tears were spilling onto the letter, soaking the words.

I crumpled into a ball in Seth's arms, and he held me as I cried myself to exhaustion.

"I need to go home," I said.

"Aren't you going to see him?" Stacy seemed irritated.

"Yes, but I can't today."

"He doesn't—"

"I know, he doesn't have much time left. I will see him tomorrow if it's the last thing I do."

Stacy was still shaking her head when Seth and I left the apartment. He carried me effortlessly up the stairs to my place and laid me down in my bed.

Some time later, I woke up to Seth setting a glass of water on my nightstand. When I opened my eyes and looked up at him, he sat on the edge of my bed and brushed my hair back from my face.

"Hey," he said, his voice low and gentle.

"Hey."

"I gotta get going."

"I know." I glanced behind him to the clock. It was ten p.m. I had slept for three hours after an hour-long sobbing fit. There was a big part of me that wanted to tell Seth that he should move on and forget about us. That he should focus on baseball and his career, instead of sitting here consoling me. But as I looked up into his sincere eyes, his solicitous smile, I saw understanding and a man who cared about me.

"You need to see him, Charlotte."

I nodded.

"If for nothing else, thank him for the mural, but I think there's more to this than that."

"I know." If I went to see Adam, Seth knew there was no way I could just thank him, walk away, and say, *Have a nice death.*

"I'll be on the road for nine days, and when I come back, this will all be a distant memory, right? You'll see him, and then we can move on with our lives?"

I wondered if it would be that easy. I sniffled and wiped my nose with the back of my hand. Seth laughed and then bent and kissed the top of my head.

"Yes, I think so," I said, though I wasn't sure at all.

"I know we haven't known each other that long but I'd like to continue dating you." He lifted my hand and kissed it. "So . . . I need to be sure you know the game plan before I leave."

Of course he does. A flash-forward of Seth coaching our little kid's baseball team flitted through my consciousness. I should have felt good about that, but I was a mess of emotions. I sat up against my pillows. Even though the light from the hallway was illuminating the room enough for Seth and me to see each other's faces, I clicked on the bedside lamp as well, just to make it that much more real.

"Okay," I began, my voice shaking. "Tomorrow you're going to Cleveland and I'm going to see Adam in the hospital."

He nodded once, encouraging me to continue, so I did.

"You'll be gone for nine days, and when you come back, we'll get together and talk about things between us."

"No, that's not what I meant."

"Huh?" *Where is this going?*

"In nine days, I'll come back and we'll pick up where we left off in that hotel room."

I was quiet for way too long. His expression dropped.

"Okay," I said finally.

He leaned in, pecked me on the lips, and then stood up. I watched with no emotion as he walked out of my room. Just before he left the apartment, he called out, "Lock the door, Charlie."

He called me Charlie. Am I going to break his heart?

17. Why We Remember

I walked through the sliding-glass doorway to Adam's hospital room. I couldn't see him right away because the privacy curtain was pulled around his bed, but I could detect movement behind the curtain. And then I heard his voice. He was talking to a female nurse.

"Bald is sexy, right?" he said. I laughed to myself quietly as I waited for the nurse to open the curtain.

"Yes, Adam, bald is sexy," she said, sounding amused.

"I mean, think about it. Bruce Willis, Vin Diesel . . . Natalie Portman . . . Adam Bramwell."

She laughed and then very abruptly pulled the curtain open, the metal hooks screeching along the curtain track, startling me. Suddenly, Adam and I were face-to-face. He was completely bald and had two distinct scars just above his forehead on the left side.

He opened his eyes wide and grinned, but only one side of his mouth went up. I found it completely heartwarming and heartbreaking all at once.

"Hi, Adam," I said just above a whisper.

"Come here, Charlotte." I had been hanging back a few feet, cautious and apprehensive. The nurse, a young, blond woman, appraised me.

"Hello," I said to her as I walked toward Adam.

"Hello," she returned. "I'll leave you two alone. Adam, your lunch will be here in a minute. Do you want me to help you, or . . ." She looked at me. I was looking at Adam.

"I can handle it, Leah, but thank you." He wouldn't take his eyes off me. From what I could tell, he had lost a little use of his left side but he seemed spry and aware.

I stood next to his bed, trying to hold it together until the nurse left the room, and then I started crying.

"Don't cry, please," he said.

"Thank you . . . for painting that mural and . . . for the letter." Tears poured from my eyes.

"Thank you for making my night so starry."

"Why didn't you tell me?"

He shrugged one shoulder. "I don't know. I was scared you'd run."

"It would have been the opposite." I could barely speak.

"I know that, too. I didn't want you to stay just because I had cancer." Adam's eyes were sympathetic. "But here you are." He smiled and then pointed to the scar on his head. "They operated and got some of the tumor out, so my brain works better, but my left side is pretty useless. I was left-handed. I can't paint anymore." He paused. "At least I got to make that one last mural for you before I went into surgery. I'm starting to have seizures more often, so that's a bummer. Oh, and I drool a little now. How's that for progress?"

I laughed because he was smiling the whole time he talked, like nothing could ruin his day.

"So making out is gonna be a little slobbery," he said. "I hope you don't mind."

My lips flattened.

"I'm kidding, Charlotte."

I let out a breath. "Oh. Okay."

"Well, thanks for coming by, and you're welcome for the mural. I figured if I didn't make it through the surgery, you'd have something to remember me by."

"And the letter?"

Adam's warm, chocolatey eyes searched mine. "I meant all of it."

Out of nowhere, I felt the urge to kiss him, so I did. I leaned down, cupped his chin, and kissed him, gently and slowly. The left side of his mouth was a little slack, but it didn't matter; he braced the back of my head and kissed me back.

When I pulled away, he said, "Wow. It was true."

"What?"

"That feeling was real. I didn't make it up."

I closed my eyes. My chest was aching. Right at that moment, a member of the hospital cafeteria walked in with a tray. "It's your favorite, Adam. Chicken fajitas!" the woman said.

"Woohoo!" Adam was genuinely excited. It was charming. "This is the best day ever! Charlotte, sit down, I'll share. It'll be like a date."

This was why I had fallen for him. He was dying in a bed and he was still joyful, buoyant, and charming.

I started laughing and crying at the same time. "Adam, where is your family? How come no one is here with you?"

"My dad can't be pulled away from his job, you know? And all this is too hard on my mom. It's no big deal; I mean, I could live ten more years like this. They don't need to be sitting around waiting for me to die."

He started pulling lids off the containers. I got up, walked over, and began to help him arrange his lunch so he could use his right hand. "Is that true? You could live ten more years?"

He looked up at me, straight-faced. "What, you don't believe in miracles anymore?"

I swallowed hard and noticed that my hands were shaking and my voice wouldn't work.

"I'm kidding. Lighten up, Charlotte." He put his hand over mine and looked right into my eyes. "Relax, okay? I'm probably gonna die soon."

I shook my head. There was a small container of broth. I took the lid off and held a spoonful to Adam's mouth. He opened wide and swallowed the soup.

"I did that for you," he said, smiling. "I don't need you to feed me, but I totally enjoyed it." He held up his right hand. "I can still use this hand, and other body parts, too." He waggled his eyebrows. What was I doing? I was stumbling all over the situation like a fool. I was about to tell him that I had a boyfriend, but I stopped myself. "And, also, the broth is for people who can't have solid food." He lifted the lid off the fajitas. "I got these babies."

I couldn't imagine that Adam was dying of brain cancer. He was chipper and so coherent. "What exactly have they told you about . . ." I tensed up.

"About what?" he said, looking concerned.

"About . . . how long you have?"

Half of Adam's mouth went up.

"Why are you smiling?"

"My beautiful Charlotte. Listen," he implored, "I'm a ticking-fucking-time-bomb, okay? I could be happily enjoying my fajitas and then just"—he shut his eyes and made a croaking sound.

"That's terrible!"

"I'm serious, but it's true for all of us. I'm running out of fucks to give. You could have a stroke or an aneurysm or a freaking heart attack and drop dead right in front of me, lights out."

"And you wouldn't give a fuck?"

"No, I would, but I'm not going to waste one second on the possibility of it happening."

"Adam, please." He was joking but it was hard for me to laugh.

He took a bite of his fajita. I noticed he was trying very hard to keep the food in his mouth. Once he swallowed, he smiled again and said, "It's not pretty but it works. Pull up a chair, Charlotte, you're making me nervous."

"Why would you be nervous?" I reached for a tissue from his bedside table and wiped my nose.

"I don't know. I'm afraid you're going to flee before I have a chance to say good-bye."

If you asked me seven months earlier how I would have described myself, I would have said fickle, indecisive, directionless, shallow, selfish, and utterly, obliviously ignorant of other people's feelings. But all of that was changing, along with the rest of my life. Seven months ago, I might've walked out of that hospital room the moment I laid eyes on Adam. But now I was there with him and I *wanted* to change. To learn from his example.

So I made a decision.

"I'm not going anywhere, Adam. I'm staying with you. I might need to leave to get some of my belongings, but you're coming with me."

"What?" He set down his fajita and reached his left hand across his body, gesturing for me to take it. Squeezing my hand as best he could, he said, "You have a job and a life. You don't need to do this."

"I know I don't need to; I want to. Are you going to tell me I can't?"

"But . . ."

"No, listen. I'm sure you don't need to be in here every second of the day. Am I right?"

"Well . . ."

I took my purse from my shoulder and set it down on the bed so Adam would know I wasn't leaving. "I'm going to talk to your nurse. I'll be right back, okay?"

"Okay."

Adam's nurse was standing right outside his room, talking to a doctor. "Hello." I interrupted them. The doctor was an older woman in her sixties with a kind face.

"Hello," the doctor said.

"Do you need something?" the nurse chimed in.

"I just wanted to know what the deal is with Adam? I mean, can he leave the hospital?"

"Adam's condition is declining," the doctor said. "His parents are paying for him to have full-time care here."

"But he doesn't actually require hospitalization at this point?"

I had never had so much resolve in my life.

The nurse said, "We're keeping him comfortable."

"Okay, I get it. Adam is dying but he's not dead. Can I take him outside? Can I take him for a drive?"

The doctor shook her head. "You absolutely cannot take him off the property. There are all kinds of liability issues. As much as we would all love to give Adam some time away from this place, we just can't do it based on the agreement we've made with his family."

My head dropped to the floor. Just before walking away, the doctor added, "I'm sorry."

When the doctor was gone, the nurse silently followed me into the room. Adam had finished eating and was still wearing a huge grin, which made the nurse smile. "I just realized I haven't introduced you two," Adam said. "Charlotte, this is my favorite nurse, Leah." There was something about Leah that made me instantly trust her. She was older than me, maybe in her midthirties, but there was something in her big bluish-gray eyes that made her seem childlike and honest.

I shook her hand. "Nice to meet you," I said.

"Likewise," she returned. "I saw a picture of the mural. It's beautiful."

"Yes, that was all Adam, though."

"Well, you were quite the inspiration for him."

"Thank you," I said, feeling less than deserving of the compliment.

As she moved around Adam's bed, adjusting his pillows and checking his vitals, she began to ramble. "So, Adam gets intravenous drips every four to six hours. It's pain and antiseizure medication and we keep a line in him for fluids but . . ."

"But otherwise, he's not being monitored?" I said.

"He is. But you know . . ." She hesitated, looking up at me. "I'm monitoring him from the station."

I knew what she was getting at.

She stuck a tongue depressor in Adam's mouth and peered in while she went on. "There's a track out in back that you can take him around in the wheelchair. There's a little garden, too."

"How long can Adam be outside?"

"Well, as long as he's here for his meals and medication. I check in every two hours to take his vitals, but if he skips once, it might be okay."

"Uh-huh."

The whole time the nurse was talking, Adam was just sitting there, happily watching me.

"Charlotte, are you gonna push me around the track?" he said.

"Maybe, if you're lucky."

He winked at me. The nurse was smiling as she left the room.

"What's your plan, small-fry?" he said.

I gripped the handles on the wheelchair and pushed it back and forth a couple of times. "You want to go for a ride, Adam?"

"You're talking dirty now."

I laughed. "Come on, you can stand, right?"

He tore his covers off and swung his legs over the edge of the bed. The nurse returned a second later and, without a word, she unhooked his saline bag, leaving the line in his hand but disconnected. She fiddled with a few other things and then helped me guide Adam into the chair. I put the footrests down and brought his feet up from the floor to rest on the metal flaps. "Your feet are freezing."

"I'll grab him some socks," Leah said. When she returned, she handed them to me and pointed out, in a low voice, "The wheelchair collapses from the lever on the side."

There was no reason for me to know that unless I was taking him in a car off the property. "Thank you. We'll be back in an hour and a half."

"It can get pretty congested on the track. He needs to receive his medication or he'll have a seizure. Just be wary of the traffic. You know, in the hallways and whatnot?"

"Right, hallway traffic."

On the back of the wheelchair there was a little bag with sunglasses, ChapStick, sunblock, and hand sanitizer. "Are these yours?" I said, holding the black Wayfarer shades out to Adam.

"Yep." He put them on and smiled wide at Leah as we passed her on our way into the hallway. "Bye, Leah, see you in a bit," Adam said.

18. Circumstances

I pushed him quickly to the elevator without making it too obvious that we were doing something wrong. The adrenaline rush, on top of my mounting emotions, was overwhelming but gave me a high that felt a lot like love, though I couldn't afford to let my mind go there.

Adam didn't speak. When I reached my Honda in the parking structure, I was thankful that no one was around to see me carting him away in his hospital gown. I pushed him up to the passenger door. In a hushed tone, I said, "You wanna come to my house with me so I can get some things?"

"Yeah, I'd love to," he whispered back. His enthusiasm was sweet. I was worried about taking Adam, but I couldn't leave him. When Leah said they were just trying to make him comfortable, I knew they weren't really preventing anything; they were just managing him toward death. He didn't need to be stuck there. I couldn't believe that he was his mother's only child and she was just going to leave him there to die alone.

As I helped him into the car, I said, "Has anyone come to see you?"

"Oh yeah."

I tried to pull his seat belt across but he gripped my hand. "I can do this myself."

"Okay." I rushed to the back and opened the trunk. The wheelchair collapsed easily, but it weighed forty pounds and was awkward to lift. I hoisted it into the trunk and dropped it in with a thunk before quickly shutting the hatch.

When I got into the driver's seat, I turned the key and was blasted by the stereo. I had forgotten that it was turned all the way up, blaring The Black Keys.

"Agh!" Adam yelled, jumping an inch out of his seat.

I turned down the music. "Oh my god, I'm so sorry, are you okay?"

"I'm already dying of cancer, Charlotte. You trying to give me a heart attack, too?"

"I'm really sorry."

We both laughed. Adam glanced in the back seat and spotted a Padres hat that Seth had given to me. "You a Padres fan?" Adam asked.

"Yeah, you could say that."

"Cool. I like baseball. Maybe we can go to a game, you know, before I . . . before I kick the bucket."

"Adam," I warned, "don't talk like that. And you know I can't take you away from the hospital for that long."

"I know. I just think it would be fun to see a game together."

"It would be." I weaved in and out of traffic as I made my way downtown.

When I pulled into the space in front of my building,

Adam pointed up at the mural of the wolves and smiled. "Hey, I painted that."

"I know. Don't you remember coming here that night when we met?" I turned the car off.

Adam blinked as he stared up at the mural. "No. I remember painting it. When we met, things were getting really foggy for me. I remember being with you at the loft but before that, not much else."

"This is where I live."

"Oh, if I would have known that . . ."

"You would have come looking for me?"

Without looking at me, he reached over and covered my hand with his. "Would you have wanted to be found?"

"I came to the hospital, didn't I?"

"But right after that night?"

"Adam, I thought it was just a one-night stand for you. I had no idea of the circumstances. I was heartbroken."

He looked over at me and took his sunglasses off. "I'm truly sorry. I was heartbroken, too."

"The situation got all messed up," I said.

He put my hand down and looked over. "Yes. It did. We could have had seven extra months together to fall in love. Now, who knows how much time we have."

My stomach dropped, my mouth started watering, and my hands got clammy. "I . . . I . . ."

Adam smiled finally. "I'm kidding. It's sweet that you're taking pity on me now. I'd be bored to death in the hospital. This is like volunteer work for you."

"Stop. I don't pity you. I *like* you," I said, and I meant it.

"Sure you do."

I grabbed my phone from the center console and dialed

Blackbird's. When Jon-Jon answered I said, "Hey, it's Charlotte. I fucking quit." I hung up and looked over at Adam. "See?"

"Wow! I can't believe you just quit like that."

"I learned from the best."

"But how will you pay your rent?"

My expression went blank. *Shit.*

"You know what? Don't worry about it. I have some money I can give you to cover your income for a while. Would a few hundred grand do it?"

I stared at him. He was serious.

"That would cover my income for, like, ten years, Adam. But I'm not taking your money. I want to do this, okay?"

He nodded.

"Now stay here. I'll be right back."

I ran up the stairs to my apartment, where I found Chucky reading on the couch. "Hey, shitbag, can you help me for a sec?"

He didn't look up from his copy of *Dental Practice* magazine. "In that case, Fatbutt, yeah. Anything you need."

"I'm serious." I leaned over the couch and got in his face. "I'm serious. Please. Can you come down to my car and help me?"

He huffed. "With what?"

"Just come with me." I dragged him by the hand. When we reached the bottom of the stairs, Chucky froze. "What is that?" he asked, staring at Adam in the passenger seat.

"It's a human, dumbass. He has brain cancer and he has limited use of his left side. I need you to help me get him upstairs."

Chucky stayed glued to the step he was on. "Are you out

of your fucking mind? Is that a hospital patient? Is he wearing a hospital gown? Charlotte, you've really done it now. What are you doing with him? Please tell me this is for charity or something."

"Listen, it's a long story." I yanked on his arm. "Just come on, help me."

When I opened the passenger door, I said, "Adam, this is my brother, Charles. Charles, this is Adam."

Adam shoved his right hand out for a handshake and Chucky did the same in response. "Nice to meet you," Chucky said hesitantly. He turned and mouthed at me, *Adam?*

"You, too," Adam said.

I helped Adam stand and then slipped one arm around him and anchored his body to mine. Chucky followed suit on the other side as we made our way to the stairwell. Halfway up, Adam laughed.

"What?" I said.

He looked down at the bottom of his hospital gown. "Drafty."

"I bet. Do you want some regular clothes while you're here?"

Adam had gotten thinner since that night we had spent together and he was weaker and far more frail. "I'll be fine," he said.

"Okay."

Chucky was quiet all the way up the stairs. We helped Adam onto the couch, and I handed him the *Dental Practice* magazine. "I'm afraid this is the best literature I can offer you right now. Can I get you some water?"

He looked at the magazine strangely. "Sure."

In the kitchen, Chucky came up behind me. "Tell me

what the fucking deal is. He's looking at you like you're his girlfriend. Aren't you dating Seth?"

"Meet me in my bedroom in a minute."

I handed Adam the water. "I'm going to gather some things I'll need at the hospital for a few days so I can stay there with you."

"Perfect. I'll just read this weird dental magazine. Why do you have this, Charlotte?"

"My brother is finishing dental school. I think I told you that the night we were together?"

"That's right, I remember something," he said, though I wasn't sure if he actually did. He shivered, so I tossed him the skinny blanket I had made during my crochet phase.

He held it out. "This is interesting."

"It's warm. It's a blanket." I could hear Chucky behind me, muffling a laugh. My skinny blanket had become a family inside joke.

I rolled my eyes and scurried off to my room as Chucky trailed me. After closing the door, I pointed at my now derisive brother and ordered him to sit on the bed. I pulled my overnight bag from the closet and began filling it with the things I would need.

"Okay, Charles, listen. That's the guy. The painter. I spent one night with him. He forgot where I lived because he fucking has brain cancer, which I just discovered, like, two days ago. He's the guy that painted the wolves on the outside of this building."

"And he forgot that you lived here?"

"He had a tumor that was making it hard for him to retain short-term memories, but he remembers some of the night we spent together."

"And you like him?"

"Yes."

"What about Seth?"

I stopped packing. "Seth knows. He's the one who told me to go see Adam."

"So you're just gonna leave your boyfriend for a guy you spent one night with? I mean, it's your life, but seriously, you never learn."

"Seth is not my boyfriend. We went on a couple of dates."

"I still think you're crazy."

I went to the bathroom to grab toiletries. As I passed Adam, he shot me a huge grin. When I returned to my bedroom, I sat down next to Chucky.

"Adam is dying, okay? And they don't think he has much longer to live. I'm going to do this. I'm going to take care of him. However long it takes. I'm doing it for me and for him. Do you understand, Charles?"

There was a hint of sympathy on his face. "Dad's gonna freak."

"Why?"

"Because he actually likes Seth."

"He's never even met him. He likes the *idea* of Seth."

"But you said he was a good guy," Chucky argued.

"He is," I shot back. "That's not the point. If Dad understood what I was doing, he'd support me. Now will you go out there with Adam and be nice?"

He shook his head but got up anyway and walked to the door. A moment later I overheard him making small talk with Adam.

When I finished packing, I found Adam and Chucky laughing on the couch. "Can you help us get down to the car, Chuck? I need to get Adam back to the hospital."

"For this guy, no problem."

While Adam stood between us, he leaned over toward me and pecked me on the lips. Chucky caught the moment but didn't say anything.

We helped Adam into the car, then my brother followed me to the driver's side. "I'll talk to Dad. I get it, okay?"

"Thank you for understanding. I have to do this."

"I know. But if you don't really love him, don't—"

"I can't think about that right now, Chucky. It will all make sense someday." I had a moment of déjà vu. Adam had said the exact same thing to me months ago.

"All right, sis." We hugged and it felt awkward but I decided that if I hugged him more often, it wouldn't feel that way. In that moment, I promised myself I would hug Chucky more.

ON THE WAY back to the hospital, Adam was quiet. "Are you okay?" I asked.

"Just feeling a little tired is all."

Thankfully, there was only light traffic. The moment I entered the parking structure, Adam dropped his head and groaned.

"Oh, god, hold on, Adam. We're almost there." I floored it to the second level and zipped into the first open space. I ran to the back of the car and lifted the wheelchair out, then zoomed around to the passenger door. When I opened the door, Adam looked up at me with a pained expression. I bent and reached around his waist. He threw his arms over my shoulders so I could lift him into the chair.

While I was swiveling him over to the chair, his mouth was near my ear. "I didn't picture this part," he whispered. "I don't like it."

I set him down. "You don't like me helping you?"

"It feels shitty. I want to hold *you* up, not the other way around." Until that point, Adam had been all smiles and laughs.

"You're not feeling well. I think you need your medication."

"That's not it," he mumbled as I pushed him toward the elevator.

Back inside his hospital room, Leah, the nurse, came in right away and helped Adam get back into bed. She scurried around, hooking him back up to lines and dialing in his medications. She glanced at my overnight bag and then looked up into my eyes and smiled. "He'll probably nap for a bit from the meds, and then he might need a sponge bath later. Did you want to . . ."

"I don't think Adam wants me to do that."

"What's the difference?" he barked.

"What do you mean, Adam?" I went to the side of the bed.

He scowled. "You or her. It sucks either way. Charlotte, you don't have to do any of this. You should just leave."

"What's come over you? A few hours ago you were so happy to see me."

His eyelids got heavy; he started mumbling.

"Adam?" Leah said. "I'm going to lay your head back

now." She stood on the other side and pressed the button to recline the bed until he was lying flat.

She spoke to me in a hushed tone. "Can I talk to you in the hall?"

I nodded, and then followed her out of Adam's room.

"So," she said, "he has mood swings. I should have mentioned that before. The medication does it to him. You can't take it personally."

"I didn't."

"When he wakes up, he should be in a better mood and then maybe he'll let you clean him up."

"I don't want to do that."

Disappointment crossed her face. "Does that kind of thing bother you? Because . . ."

"Not at all. I just don't want to do it because I want Adam to feel that he has some dignity left, okay? Especially with me. I have a couple of ideas for how to make his last days on earth pleasant." I started getting choked up. "I don't want to be the one who bathes him, or feeds him, or carries him around, okay? I'm just here to be with him."

She was nodding. "I understand. It's my job anyway. I just thought I would ask."

I took a deep breath through my nose and out of my mouth. "I've had a long day. I'm gonna go nap in Adam's room."

I left Leah in the hallway so I could curl up on the horribly uncomfortable mini vinyl couch in Adam's hospital room. Dozing off, I felt a blanket being draped over me. I opened one eye to find Leah standing there. "Thank you," I said.

"No problem."

19. Precisely

It was hard to tell what time it was when I woke up because the room was completely dark and cold. I felt around until my hand hit my purse sitting on a tray. It was five thirty. My stomach was rumbling with hunger and my mouth tasted disgusting. A member of the cafeteria staff knocked lightly on the glass door and then entered with a tray.

"He's still sleeping?" she asked.

"Yes," I said. "I'll wake him in a minute."

"Okay." She left the tray on his table and walked out.

The room was only lit from the stark fluorescent hallway light coming through the sliding doors to Adam's room. I got up off the couch and stretched my aching muscles. When I went to reach for the light, I was startled to find a person standing in the doorway, silhouetted by the light from behind. It was Helen.

I walked toward her. "Hey. Let's go out here; he's sleeping."

In the hallway, I hugged Helen and then pulled away and tried to read her expression. She looked confounded and she still hadn't said anything. "What? Did Chuck tell you?" I asked.

"Yes." She scanned me from head to toe. "You're a mess."

"I don't care."

"So all along he was looking for you?"

"I guess so."

"You kind of were looking for him, too, weren't you?"

"Maybe on the street. I was hoping to run into him."

"I came to see what your plan was," she said. "What are we supposed to tell Seth?"

I crossed my arms over my chest. "You don't have to tell Seth anything. It's between him and me. Anyway, he knows I came here. He told me to come here."

"For what?"

"You seem even less sensitive than Chucky about this. Maybe Seth wanted me to come down here because he's compassionate."

"Well, maybe, but I know for a fact that he didn't expect you to run home and get clothes to move in with Adam in his hospital room."

From the corner of my eye, I noticed Leah walk into Adam's room and turn on the light. He must have been waking up. Helen was still appraising me.

"So how long are you going to stay with him?"

"For the rest of his life." Even as I said it, I knew it was true.

"That could be a long time."

"Not compared to my life," I said.

She shook her head. She was in disbelief. "I just don't want you to mess things up with Seth. It seems like you really like him, and if Adam weren't dying . . ."

"Stop talking about Adam dying. Nothing is certain." I shrugged. "And I'm here because I want to be with him. I'm not here to pity him."

Helen was worried my being with Adam was a result of some fixation I had with getting into relationships that went nowhere. She didn't understand how much I actually liked him.

After she was done thoroughly shaking her head in disapproval, she studied my face. "Should I go say hi? Will he even remember who I am?"

"He might. He might not. It doesn't matter. Come on."

She followed me into the room and stood at the foot of his bed. He was smiling at both of us, waiting patiently for an explanation.

"Hi, I'm Helen," she said.

"Hi, Helen. You can come closer; I don't bite . . . that hard."

She giggled and then moved to his bedside. He could charm even a skeptical Helen. I stood opposite her. He looked up to me as if to say, *Who is this person?*

"She's my best friend. She and I were living together in that apartment. You helped me walk her home the night we met."

He looked over to Helen. Her brownish-blond hair was curled into soft waves on her shoulders. Adam was squinting at her.

"I used to have green hair," Helen offered, trying to help him.

"Really? Green? How could I forget that?"

"It was chartreuse," I said.

"Remember? I was kind of drunk. You gave me a box of Chinese food."

He pointed at her. "Yes, you. I remember you. You were wasted."

I jumped three inches off the floor, "You remember?!"

"Kind of. It's foggy." His brow furrowed and he sucked air through his teeth. "Ouch," he said, holding his hand to his head.

"You okay, Adam?"

I reached over and lifted a cover off a plate. It was beef teriyaki.

"Yuck." His jaw clenched. I set the cover back on the plate and then everything after that happened in slow motion. His arms started jerking, and he slumped down in the bed and his body began convulsing.

"Oh no. Someone help!" I screamed.

Helen ran out into the hallway and started yelling, "We need help in here! Help us!"

I braced the back of his head as he thrashed against the pillow and bars on the side of the bed. Two nurses and a doctor ran in. Leah must have been on a break. One nurse emptied a syringe into his IV line and the other came to my side. "Step away, sweetie, you could get hurt."

"When will it stop?" I didn't recognize my own voice, but I could hear myself. I sounded frantic.

"In a minute. He's slowing down. There you go, Adam," she said to him as she caressed his forehead. His eyes were crossed and he had the scariest, most pained look on his face.

I started crying. "Is he in pain?"

The doctor whom I had talked to earlier answered me without looking up. "He won't remember this. He won't know anything but that he's had a seizure." She turned to the nurse at her side. "Up his dose of valproic acid to sixty milligrams a day. I'll write it up, but let's go ahead and give him twenty right now."

Everyone moved around the room quickly. Adam had stopped convulsing and his eyes were steady and focused on the wall across from him. Helen was standing near the door, stunned. I went to his side and smoothed my hand over his damp brow. His gaze moved to me. He looked like a scared little boy. I bent and kissed his cheek. "You're okay. You had a seizure, but it's over now."

He nodded with wide eyes. I bent again, but this time I placed a kiss on his lips. He was lethargic but he tried to pucker his lips and mimic a kissing sound.

"Charlotte?" he murmured.

"Yes, I'm here."

"I love you," he said. I don't know if what Adam was feeling was love but I knew I felt extremely connected to him, just like the day we first met.

"I love you, too." I kissed his forehead and then glanced to see Helen's shocked face. "I'm going to walk Helen to the elevator. I promise I won't be gone more than a minute."

"Okay." He tried to smile before reaching his hand up and waving sluggishly at Helen. She waved back, still stunned.

"Come on." I pulled her by the arm.

She didn't speak until we got to the elevator bays. "You love him?" she said.

"I have strong feelings for him." I looked at her pointedly.

"Seth will understand. That's all I'm saying about the situation. I don't want to talk anymore about it. I'm going back in there to be by his side. You know where to find me if you need me. Thanks for coming down."

Her mouth was still parted in shock. "Um . . . okay then, I guess I'll tell Roddy to tell Seth . . ."

"Nothing, Helen. You won't tell Roddy to tell Seth anything. I will talk to Seth when he's back from the road."

The elevator doors opened but Helen just stood there. When it started to close, I said, "You better go."

She put her hand out to keep the doors open. "You have your whole life ahead of you."

"Precisely." I gave her a quick hug and walked away.

20. Good and Bad

Adam had good days and bad. There would be times when it seemed like he was a completely normal guy, except smarter and funnier and more genuine than anyone I had ever met. And then he'd have a seizure and get really depressed. They took solid food off the menu for a couple of days after I first arrived. It made him feel like an invalid, even though he wasn't. I snuck In-N-Out Burger into the hospital as often as I could, and on the fourth day, I snuck Adam out to the drive-thru. He promised me he wouldn't touch the food until we were back at the hospital, but he tried to sneak fries anyway. I was worried that he'd have a seizure in the car and choke to death on his food. It made driving in LA all the worse.

He joked, "Mysterious artist dying of brain cancer chokes to death on his double-double with cheese."

"It's not funny."

"It's totally funny. I love this song, can you turn it up?"

I reached and turned the dial up on the Vance Joy song

"Red Eye." Adam bobbed his head to the music. At the stop-light I looked over at him. He was wearing the black beanie my brother had given him, his black Wayfarers, and the hospital gown.

I laughed.

He turned to me and smiled. "What?" he said.

"You're cute."

"Oh yeah? Wanna fool around?" He grinned.

I was glad that Adam couldn't see my eyes welling up behind my sunglasses.

The car behind us honked. I hit the gas and my car lurched forward from the intersection. "How much time do we have?" I asked.

"What? Are you serious?"

"Yes, Adam, I am serious." He was having a good day.

He reached for my phone. "We have like an hour and a half before Leah freaks out."

I knew I was taking a big chance, but how could I say no to him? There was so much joy in him that day just because he got to go to the drive-thru at In-N-Out.

"Okay." I glanced over at him and flattened my lips. "You better not have a seizure on me."

"I can't think of a better place to have a seizure. Although I can see how that wouldn't be much fun for you."

I laughed hysterically. "Oh man, I didn't mean *literally* on me; I meant on my watch."

"Well, Charlotte, I don't have much control over that, but I'll try. You know what helps?"

"What?"

"Alcohol."

"Really?"

As we passed the Four Seasons he said, "Pull in here."

"This is too expensive, Adam."

"What? Are you crazy?" The energy in the car was tangible. "This may be the last time I ever go to a hotel with a girl. I'm paying. I have a ton of money. Come on, Charlotte, please?" His mood was instantly lighter than it had been in several days.

"Okay." I did a U-turn and pulled into the driveway of the hotel.

A valet greeted us right away. "Checking in?" he said, when I rolled down my window.

"Yes," Adam barked over me.

"Last name?" the valet asked.

"Bramwell," Adam said.

The young valet looked at Adam with suspicion but wrote the valet ticket anyway. I got the wheelchair out of the back, then helped Adam into it. He had the In-N-Out takeout bag on his lap. I wheeled him into the fancy lobby and got a lot of strange looks.

At the front desk, the clerk tried to seem normal when she took Adam's credit card.

"The only handicap accessible room I have available is a suite," she said.

"Perfect," Adam returned with his lopsided smile.

The clerk handed over our keys and pointed us to the elevator. As I pushed Adam to the room, he whistled out a song. We entered a lavishly decorated suite with a large living and dining area, a huge fluffy bed, and a giant sunken tub smack in the middle of a bathroom the size of my apartment.

"Find the alcohol, Charlotte!" Adam shouted from the entryway. I found a minibar stocked full.

I grabbed minibottles of tequila and vodka and held them out to Adam. "Are you sure this is okay?"

"Yes," he declared. "Which one do you want?"

"Either one."

I swigged the vodka and he the tequila, and then I wheeled him over to the bar for another round. We ate In-N-Out and laughed and talked and drank a little more. Adam seemed really relaxed.

"Should we take a bath in that awesome tub?" he asked.

"I don't know, Adam. I'd be scared to. What if something happens?"

"Please." His eyes were pleading. "Please. I promise nothing will happen to me."

"Okay," I said but my heart was pounding. I was worried he'd have a seizure and I wouldn't be able to get him out in time.

Inside the bathroom, I filled the tub up with warm water and bubbles. Adam was leaning against the counter as he removed his hospital gown. When he was naked, my mouth fell open in shock. He was much thinner than before. "Big difference, huh?" he said.

I shook my head and tried to will away the tears. I walked toward him, cupped his face, and looked into his eyes. "You're still the most handsome guy I know." It was true. Adam was classically handsome even in his condition. It was undeniable. I kissed him once and then helped him climb into the tub.

Once he was in, he didn't stop smiling. He looked like the Adam I knew from that one night. It seemed like his smile was wider than possible. "Now, are you gonna put on a show for me or what?" he said.

I turned on my heel and glared at him. "Me? No!"

"Well, you have to take your clothes off to get in here. Make it fun."

I huffed. "I'm kind of shy in that way."

"You weren't shy the night we were together."

He was right—I wasn't. I stared at the ceiling, pondering what I should do. I looked down at Adam, who was still wearing a ridiculous grin. *Would Seth understand this part? Was Seth even a factor anymore?*

"Let me find some music." I put The 1975 on the iPod dock in the other room and cranked up the volume. I gathered myself and then went back into the bathroom and tried desperately not to make eye contact with Adam as I began to undress.

"How could you say no to a dying man?"

I pointed at him. "Don't!"

He started laughing.

"You haven't played that card yet so why start now?"

When the music picked up, I peeled off my jeans and watched as Adam arched his barely existent eyebrows and started bobbing his head. He was mesmerized. I lifted my shirt over my head and stood in front of him in my black bra and panties.

"You're beautiful," he whispered.

When I unhooked my bra and tossed it aside, his mouth fell open and his eyes went wide. He was up to his neck in bubbles and it made me laugh. I turned and bent seductively in front of him to peel my panties down.

"Oh my god, Charlotte . . . this is how I want to die . . . with you, standing naked in front of me. Don't forget that part, okay? When it's time for me to go, you have to get naked, just like this, right in front of me."

"That might be a little awkward for the doctors and nurses."

"Come on. Now get in here, I want to touch you."

As I stepped in, he reached both his hands up to guide me. The water sloshed over the sides of the tub, spilling onto the floor.

"Shit," I said.

"It's okay, just come here."

I sat between his legs with my back to his front. He kissed my shoulder and then my neck before slowly moving up to my ear. I shivered when he reached around and cupped my breast. Adam had lost some fine-motor skills in his left hand and he had trouble walking because his left leg wouldn't always cooperate, but in that moment, when we were together and he was kissing me and touching me and our bodies were pressed against each other, there was no cancer, there was no death pending. I could think of nothing else but how right it all felt.

It was impossible not to question myself leading up to that day in the hotel room. I knew Adam and I had something unique, but it was hard for me to describe. If someone asked me why I felt so connected to him, I would say, "I just do, I can't explain it." I knew it had nothing to do with his tumor or the mural. It had to do with that thing, that feeling that allowed me to walk away from my apartment in the middle of the night seven months ago. When I looked into Adam's eyes, I felt like I could see his sincere, genuine soul.

When thoughts of Seth would pop into my mind, I'd be lying if I said I didn't feel a twinge of guilt. I hoped he'd understand, but if he didn't, it still wouldn't change my decision to be with Adam now. It wasn't about Adam's wish, it was about Adam and me and seeing it through. Everyone always said I dated men who were off-limits so that I wouldn't have to get serious about anyone. Adam might have been dying, but he wasn't off-limits. He was baring it all for me and I was going to do the same for him, even though I knew it would break me into a million pieces.

I turned and straddled him in the tub. Our kisses became more demanding. When he touched me down below, I lost all sense of our circumstances. I wanted him and I could tell he wanted me, and nothing else mattered.

"Let's get out of here and go to the bed," he said.

Adam stood and wrapped a towel around his waist. He was strong in that moment. He was driven.

I dried myself off and then met him on the bed. When we ditched the towels, I could see how turned on he was. I climbed on top of him and kissed him hard before sitting up and letting him look at me. My body was totally exposed to him in the well-lit room. He watched with wonder in his eyes. "I'm in heaven, right?" he said. It looked like he believed it.

"Yes, this is heaven, Adam." I bent and clutched his face with both hands and kissed him delicately before moving to his neck and shoulder.

"Mmm, you're an angel for sure," he murmured.

"This is heaven for me, too," I whispered near his ear. A moment later he was inside of me and I was moving on top of him. I was unself-conscious. He gripped my hips and thrust into me, matching my movements. "Adam . . ." I moaned.

I pressed my hands to his chest and moved harder and faster. For just a few minutes the whole world slipped away and it was just the two of us. Adam's body felt warm and strong, for the first time since that night in his loft.

He pulled me to his chest, gripped my bottom with both hands, and thrust harder as I lay on top of him. "Feel me inside of you," he whispered. My mouth was on his neck, kissing and sucking while he continued his steady movements. "Feel me, Charlotte."

All I could do in that moment was feel Adam, everywhere around me and inside of me. I kissed him hard on the mouth. Our tongues twisted as our movements became more urgent. Just when I thought I couldn't take anymore, I felt the tension start to break apart. "Adam . . ." I said with my mouth against his chest. He didn't make a sound, just one last hard thrust and then his hands dropped to his sides. He shut his eyes and turned his head. He was grinning but his arms and legs had gone lax and he wasn't moving or making a sound.

"Adam?" I was smiling at first, but when he seemed unresponsive for a moment I began to panic. "Adam!"

"You killed me," he said softly.

"Open your eyes, you scared the crap out of me."

He looked up and smiled wider. "That was amazing."

"It was perfect."

"I mean, I really thought you killed me, Charlotte. I had already decided it was the best death ever."

I glanced at the clock behind him. "I feel like we should get going," I said.

"Wham, bam, thank you, ma'am. I don't even get a cuddle?"

"We can cuddle at the hospital."

"Come here, calm down. What's going to happen?"

"You'll get in trouble."

"Ha! Are they gonna put me on restriction? I've already been reduced to Jell-O and broth. What will they do next, take away my TV?"

"Maybe they'll tell me I can't stay."

He tilted my chin up so we were eye to eye. "Charlotte, are you worried about that?"

"Of course."

"They wouldn't do that. Plus, my dad is paying for a new cancer wing. They're not going to kick my girlfriend out and jeopardize getting a fancy new Adam Bramwell Memorial Wing, complete with Adam Bramwell paintings."

"Girlfriend?"

He tensed. "I mean . . . friend. Whatever. Hey, you're the one who said you were my girlfriend. Remember that little fib you came up with that night at my loft?"

"I liked that story," I protested.

"Me too." We were silent for several moments before Adam spoke in a strained voice. My face was resting on his chest so I couldn't see his expression, but it sounded like it pained him to speak. "Why does the story have to end?"

"It doesn't," I said immediately.

"Then tell me about our life, Charlotte."

"Really?"

"Yeah."

"Well . . . okay, let me see . . . we moved into your loft together at some point. I loved your loft, by the way."

"Me too."

"So we lived in the loft and then we . . . got married? Yes, we got married. I finally said yes to you."

"Of course. I had to make an honest woman out of you.

But that's not why I married you." The story began to take on a life of its own, with both of us participating. "We got married because we were in love."

"Yes, we were in love."

"Tell me more. Tell me about the wedding and the honeymoon."

"We did our honeymoon first, actually. You surprised me by whisking me off to Paris. We wandered along the Seine and bought trinkets at the bouquinistes. We toured all of the major museums, wandered through Saint-Germain, ate at the brasseries where the American expats used to hang out in the twenties, and spent hours at Shakespeare and Company. Then you took me out on a boat and taught me to sail."

"I did?"

"Yeah, on the French Riviera." I had closed my eyes at that point and was imagining a healthy Adam wrapping a line around a winch as we sailed on the crystal-blue Mediterranean.

"How'd you know I could sail?" he asked. "Did I tell you that?"

"I saw a copy of a sailing magazine in your loft that night."

"So, I taught you how to sail and you were a quick study?"

"Obviously."

"Is that what you want? Is that your dream, Charlotte? To learn how to sail in France?"

Don't ruin this, Adam. I don't like reality very much right now. "I'm just telling you what we did."

"Uh-huh. Okay, go on."

"So you taught me how to sail and then later that day we found a little chapel and we got married."

"That sounds nice," he said, but then he went quiet for several moments.

"It was, Adam. Not just nice—it was perfect."

"Hmm." Several moments passed before he said, "Too bad, isn't it? Too bad it's not true."

I leaned up and kissed him. "We have right now and yesterday and the night we met. That's all real to me, and it's enough."

He smiled piteously. "I know you have someone else waiting for you, Charlotte."

I swallowed. "What do you mean?"

"I mean, you have someone in your life. I overheard you and Helen—"

I put my finger to his mouth. "Shhh. I'm here with you now, Adam. I want to be here with you."

"We should get back to the hospital," he said.

I sat up on the edge of the bed with my back to him. "Please don't do this."

"Do what?"

"Please don't ruin the time we have." I turned to face him. "I love you. That's not a story. That's not a lie."

"You shouldn't. You can't. You barely know me, and I'm dying."

"I know enough . . . and will you please stop saying that?"

"I'm a charity case to you, but I'm not a fool."

"Charity case, Adam? You obviously don't know me. I don't even buy Girl Scout cookies. I fell for you. I haven't stopped thinking about you since the night we met. I just didn't think you were into me. I wished that someone felt like they wanted a future with me and loved hearing my fantasies without getting scared off. No one has given that to me, ever. Not until you. That night was the first time I ever felt worthy. You changed me, Adam, and you're changing me now."

With a furrowed brow, he said, "So you feel like you owe me?"

"We need to get you back for your meds. You're getting grumpy."

I stood and walked to the bathroom to gather our things. Before we left, I took a quick shower and then got Adam into his gown and chair. He sat with me in the bathroom and stared at me in my bra and underwear while I blow-dried my hair near the counter. In the mirror, I saw his face grow penitent as he watched me. Over the sound of the hair dryer, he shouted, "I'm sorry."

"Don't worry about it," I shouted back.

"I ruined it!"

"You ruined nothing!"

"I loved the story, Charlotte! Thank you!"

"I love it, too, and you're welcome!" I still sounded angry, but then in the mirror I could see Adam laughing behind me and it made me laugh.

"You're moody, Adam Bramwell!"

"I know, I'm sorry." He was still laughing.

21. Miracles

It was a miracle, but we made it back to the hospital without anyone knowing we were gone, except for Leah, of course. As we passed her at the nurses' station she rolled her eyes good-naturedly. "You get your hair done out on the wheel-chair track, Charlotte?"

I ignored her and just continued to wheel Adam into his room. "See, no one cares," he said as I helped him into bed. I lay beside him in the crook of his right arm. He held me to his body and for a few minutes it felt like everything was normal, even though we were in a crappy hospital room.

Even with the faint sounds of machines beeping and the medicinal smells wafting through the room, I still felt like Adam was my boyfriend, like we were just two people in love, lying together in the afternoon for a lazy nap. When I felt him doze off, I checked the Padres game on my phone. Seth sat on the bench for the second half of the game due to a wrist injury. I was tempted to text him but I held back.

I would be seeing him in the next couple of days and I was sure I'd have a lot of explaining to do.

Adam had a rough night. I don't know if it was because he had overdone it earlier in the day or if it was because he was getting progressively worse. Probably both. He had three seizures throughout the course of the night. After the third, he cried. I held him and rocked him. He wasn't embarrassed; he was frustrated that he couldn't control his own body. My heart ached for him. I wanted so badly to be strong but when he broke down and sobbed in my arms, I fell apart, too. I felt robbed, victimized because I wouldn't have more time with him.

Both of us were exhausted after that night. We had a couple of mellow days inside the hospital, just watching TV and taking short walks. The day before Seth was scheduled to come back, Adam had the worst seizure yet. He was in his wheelchair when it happened. I couldn't protect him. He fell to the floor and started seizing, his head smacking the tile. I hit the call button before dropping next to him to try and prevent him from injuring himself further. His spasms were so strong that I couldn't do anything besides try to place my hand between the floor and his thrashing head. I ended up with two bleeding fingers and Adam ended up with a gash from his ear to the crown of his head. He felt so guilty about my fingers that he couldn't even look at me for the rest of the night.

The nurses bandaged my fingers and wrapped up Adam's head with white gauze. He was quiet the following day as well, even though I told him over and over not to worry about my hand.

He said sorry at least twelve times an hour until I finally

told him that I would break my other fingers by punching him in the face if he didn't stop apologizing.

Early the following day, he was quiet again and I thought maybe he sensed my anxiety about Seth coming back. I hadn't heard from Seth yet and I was in no place to contact him, so there was nothing to do, really. I selfishly hoped Helen had explained the situation to him so I wouldn't have to do it myself, even though I had asked her not to.

Adam sat in his chair and watched me move around the small hospital room, throwing away trash and straightening up. "What are you cleaning for?" he said.

"Just picking up."

As I walked by him, he grabbed my arm and swung me around to face him. He looked weak. His eyes were hollow and the whites had begun to take on a yellowish tint. I touched my thumb to his bottom lip. "You need ChapStick. Let me get it for you."

"Wait, Charlotte." He reached for my arm and gripped it hard. "Let's get outside. It's a nice day. I want to leave here and put on normal clothes. Please take me away from this place."

"Adam, don't."

"Don't what? This place isn't extending my life in any way."

"You don't know that. I can't take you out of here anymore. I'm scared."

He didn't say anything; he just stared up at me, pleading with his sad eyes.

"Please tell me you understand." I bent down and kissed him. Just a peck on the cheek, but he kept his eyes closed for a long time afterward.

"Will you take me to the bridge? It's sunny out. I need to get out of this room."

He was referring to the long glass-encased footbridge between the north and south towers. Sometimes I would wheel him over there to sit, and he would stare at the cars going by below us. I agreed and took him immediately. When we reached the center of the bridge, I stopped and turned his chair to face the street.

"After we got married . . ." he said, as I stood behind him, gripping the handles of his wheelchair. He was motionless, slumped over and gazing at car after car as they drove by.

"What?" I asked.

"What happened after we got married?"

"Oh, right. We came back and had a bunch of babies."

"How many?"

"Like, five."

"Five? Really? I always thought I would have two."

"We couldn't keep our hands off each other, obviously," I said.

His body jerked with laughter and it was a relief. His spirits had been down since the night after we went to the hotel.

"What are their names?"

"You chose the names, remember?" It was becoming harder and harder for me to talk as I felt a lump growing in my throat.

"Five, hmm. Three boys and two girls."

"Yep, but they're all grown now. They have their own families, their own lives, but we still have each other."

"Life went by fast," Adam said. His voice seemed distant.

I bent and kissed the top of his head. Without looking, he reached back and held my hand on his shoulder. "That's what happens when you live it well, right? When you have someone to love? It goes by fast. You blink and it's over."

"You're making love sound tragic," I said.

"No"—he shook his head—"I wouldn't want it any other way. Tell me about us. What do we like to do?"

"Paint and sail and eat and drink. Just simple things."

"Don't forget about sex," he said.

"Yeah, lots of sex. Before the children were born we were practically naked every second of the day."

"I like that."

"When they got older, we'd sneak away for weekends and leave them at my mom's."

"What are they like? Our children."

"Happy. That's all we wished for. We put our love first and it just spilled over into them and now they're happy."

Tears sprang from my eyes and ran down my cheeks. Isn't that what we all hope for when it comes to our children?

His tone suddenly changed. "That's beautiful, Charlotte." It was like he was waking up from the dream. I didn't want to go back to reality yet, but I knew these fantasies were just to help Adam get his mind off the cancer.

"I can imagine a long life with you," he said. "I can imagine what a great wife you'd be. You're going to make someone a very happy husband."

I pulled my hand out of his. "The story is about you and me." He didn't say anything; he just nodded and then continued to stare out the window. I bent and kissed the top of his head again, and whispered, "It's about us. Don't take that away from me."

From the corner of my eye, I caught a figure walking near the end of the footbridge at the entrance of the south tower where we had come from. I turned and froze when I spotted Seth standing perfectly still, staring at us. He had stopped about twenty feet away.

I straightened my body and turned in his direction like I was going to walk toward him, but I couldn't move. My feet wouldn't work. I mouthed the word *Hi.*

He didn't say anything. He looked upset.

I finally took a step toward him, but he stuck his hand out, stopping me. His lips were turned up very slightly. His gaze moved to Adam, sunken in his chair, and then his eyes were back on mine. Adam wasn't aware of anything going on behind him.

He was still facing out the window, silent. Seth's right wrist was wrapped in a bandage. I wanted to ask him about everything, I wanted to go to him, but before I had the chance, he turned and walked away. He knew.

As I stood there, cemented to the ground, I realized I had thrown it all away with Seth. *Did it matter?*

"Charlotte?" Adam's voice was urgent. My stomach churned with anxiety.

I ran around and bent over near the front of his chair. His eyes were wide. By that point Adam could sense when he was going to have a seizure, so I was certain he was going to warn me that he wasn't feeling well. But, instead, he smiled.

I scowled. "You scared me. Why'd you shout?"

He reached for my hand. "You have to take me somewhere. You have to take me now." He seemed stronger in that moment, more alert.

"Please, Adam, I told you I'm too scared. What's gotten into you?"

When I stood up next to the arm of his chair, he reached for my hand and yanked me onto his lap. "Oh my god, Adam, what are you doing?"

He pressed his hands to my cheeks and kissed me. "Promise me something, Charlotte?"

"What is it?"

His eyes were still wide, searching mine. "Promise me this is the last moment in your life that you will let fear stop you from doing what you want."

"What?"

"Will you do that for me? Stop giving a fuck and take me somewhere right now and promise me you will not be scared of your own shadow anymore. I need a legacy, Charlotte, and I can't make one sitting here in this fucking chair."

"Adam, are you insane?"

"Yes, maybe, who cares? You were all-in that night. Just take me somewhere because I need to do something besides sit here and die, please!"

"If this is about your legacy, you have one. The art world is calling you a genius. When they find out who you are, your paintings will be worth millions."

"I don't care about any of that. Please get me out of here."

I hadn't agreed to anything yet. I wheeled him back to his room, where Leah gave him a dose of medication and his lunch of broth and Jell-O. He slurped it up with a smile and then did a wheelie in his chair and said, "Let's hit it."

"Fine, Adam, but this whole thing freaks me out."

"Just calm down. We don't have much time; we need to go. We need to hit the art supply store first."

"I thought you couldn't paint?"

He smirked, "I'm a genius, remember? I'll figure it out. Let's go."

We hit a Michaels nearby. Adam threw brushes and paints into a basket on his lap as I pushed him through the aisles. Back in the car, he directed me through downtown, until we hit a street near my apartment. "Park here." He pointed.

Directly across from us was the mural of the winged man. "You painted that," I said.

"Oh, I know. That's why we're here. I need to finish it."

I hadn't realized it was incomplete. "But Adam, it's the middle of the day. Someone will see you. If anyone recognizes you, you'll make the news."

"Who cares?"

"At least let me take you to my apartment to get some of Chucky's clothes."

"Fine, but we have to go fast." We went to my empty apartment and grabbed a sweatshirt, jeans, and some slippers from Chucky's closet. Adam was so skinny that his jeans barely stayed up, so I quickly found a belt and then helped him back down the stairs. He was weak but lighter, so I was able to help him easily.

I pushed him over to the mural. In his lap, he carried paints and brushes on a cookie sheet. "I need to sit on the ground. I need to finish the bottom part."

"It's gross on the ground, Adam."

"Jesus, Charlotte, will you just help me?" I helped him to sit on the ground in front of the mural. "You keep watch," he said. I sat in the wheelchair in front of him and tried as best as I could to block his hunched figure, sitting near the wall.

"How's it going?" I asked.

"It's tough," he said. "But it's going to work."

Half an hour went by. I checked my watch. "You okay?"

"I'm done. You can look now."

I stood, turned around, and helped him back into the seat. When my eyes finally registered what I was seeing, I stumbled back and steadied myself against the arm of Adam's chair. He placed his hand over mine. "What do you think?" he asked.

"It's . . . Adam, it's . . ." I couldn't speak.

Before, it seemed like the winged man was looking down at the ground as he levitated from it. Now you could see what he was gazing down at. Adam had painted a little rendering of my apartment building, complete with the frolicking wolves. The winged man was watching over me.

He took my hand in his and said, "No more fear." He kissed my knuckles. "Promise me. Promise me that you'll go on and take everything you want, take what you deserve."

"I promise." My throat tightened and tears fell from my eyes.

I looked down at Adam, who arched his eyebrows and then gestured toward the winged man and said, "I'll have my eye on you."

I sniffled. "Yeah, you gonna keep watch?"

"I'll be very angry with you if you dwell on me, young lady. All the things I said in that letter, I meant. Okay? But I was talking about my life, not yours, and it wasn't some dying man's poetic nonsense. I wanted you to know that I am grateful to you. I'm grateful to you now. I got to experience *it* in this life, and I don't think it's measured with time."

"You don't think what's measured with time, Adam?" My voice was strained.

"Love, Charlotte. Just like we won't be judged by the brevity of our lives, no one will ever be able to take this away from me. Not the cancer, not my death, not your new boyfriend, not your future husband or your future kids . . ."

"Stop, Adam!"

"No, I mean it. I'm not saying it the way you think I am. I'm saying it doesn't matter what happens next. Today everyone is looking for the perfect future and the perfect partner who has it all together so they can feel like the life they dream of is possible, but when you're dying, all you want is a person to love right now. You were my perfect right now that night in the loft, but then I realized something after you left."

By that point I was crying full, quiet sobs. "What did you realize?"

"Come here." He pulled me to sit on his lap. I wrapped my arms around him, curling into a ball. I kissed his neck and then rested my head on his shoulder. "I realized that right now is all that matters for everyone. Even if I had my whole life in front of me the way you do, I wouldn't change a thing." He wheeled us toward the car. "I learned something that night with you. I had spent the years before I got sick trying to build a career that would make me rich because I thought I would find happiness in that. Just like I looked for women I could use as trophies. All of that crap left me feeling empty. I was unfulfilled and I was betraying myself. I only started living once I knew I was dying. That's the reason for all the paintings. The world came to life around me. I could see people for who they were, not what they had. And when I was with you, I felt more alive than ever before." When we reached the car, he wiped tears from my face. "Because you are good, Charlotte. You're a good person and you see the good in other people. You care. You brightened the darkest time of my life."

"No one has ever said anything like that about me. I'm a mess, Adam. I've had five jobs in five years and twice as many boyfriends."

"None of that matters. Why don't you start believing in yourself? I overheard you talking to your mom last night and I knew your boyfriend came to the hospital today. I saw him in the reflection of the window on the footbridge. I saw your reaction and knew it must have been him."

"Oh?" My heart started thumping. "He's not really my boyfri—"

He gestured toward the car. "Let's get going. I need to make some plans." He suddenly seemed more resolute.

I helped him into the passenger seat, put the wheelchair in the trunk, and then slipped into the driver's side. I spent the next few minutes gathering myself. Adam handed me a Kleenex from the glove box. "I better get you back," I said. He reached over and squeezed my hand. I turned to look him in the eye. "What did you overhear?"

"I overheard you telling your mom about Seth and how he probably wouldn't want to have anything to do with you after this was all over. I felt guilty, like it was all my fault. I wanted to call him and tell you to go to him, but at the same time I felt like if he wanted nothing to do with you because of how good and sweet and amazing you are for spending time with me, then he's a damn fool and he doesn't deserve you. Then he came to the hospital and it occurred to me that the doubts had nothing to do with him. It's you. You still don't know what you're worth." He wiped a tear from my cheek and smiled. "So I'm dedicating the rest of my life to proving that to you."

"Adam . . ."

"Don't argue with me. Just drive, lady."

When we got back to the hospital, I pushed Adam past the nurses' station quickly. Leah shook her head and then came into his room a moment later. "You better hurry up and get out of those clothes and back into the gown, Adam."

"Leah," he stated assertively. "I need a pen and some paper as soon as possible." Leah chuckled to herself and then left the room, still shaking her head as Adam stripped away Chucky's clothes.

"But you can't write," I said to him.

"Charlotte, I need you to go home and stay there."

"What?"

Standing near his bed, completely naked, he pointed to the shelf where a gown was folded. "Can you hand me that and then go home and wait until you receive instructions?"

"Receive instructions? Adam," I started to say. I was fully worried now.

"Charlotte, look at me. A human does not get more desperate and vulnerable than this. I'm naked and skinny, my bald head is wrapped in gauze, I can barely stand up, and I'm dying. I'm begging you, please, just do as I say."

"Okay, okay." I handed him the gown and helped him into bed.

"Now go. I have your number. I'll call you. Don't call me."

"This is crazy."

"Just go." He shooed me away, but he was smiling while he did it.

I couldn't laugh even though he was trying to be funny. "What if . . ."

"What if there is a 9.0 earthquake right below us in the next minute? What if the sun explodes tomorrow? What if heaven is real? What if God is a woman? What if the moon landing was a hoax? What if Donald Trump is an alien?"

"No one really questions that last one," I said.

"You promised me there would be no more fear and no more what-ifs. If something happens, then it is exactly what is supposed to happen. Have you learned nothing from me? Now go before grumpy Adam shows up."

I kissed him and left the room without another word. I felt strange walking out to my car alone. It felt even stranger to know that I was leaving Adam in his hospital room alone, and that at any moment he could die and I would never see him again.

22. The Trial

Everyone walks around blabbing about love and life like we all know what it's supposed to mean and how we're supposed to feel. We put these stupid restrictions on our relationships . . . for what? According to whom? God? Society? None of it actually matters because when you have the unfortunate knowledge that you're going to die very soon, none of it applies. Rules are for people with the luxury of time.

Nothing holds you back—certainly not rejection. You've already felt the ultimate rejection. And when you're young, lying in a hospital bed, waiting for the lights to go out because this shitty fucking world has rejected you, there's nothing you can do but try to plant a seed of yourself inside another person so deep that you will undoubtedly live on through them. That's what legacy is. That's what made Adam brave enough to love me.

He may have planted himself inside of every person who viewed his beautiful art and felt moved by it. And in the public sense, that will be his legacy, but for me, his legacy is that he taught me something very important. He taught me that one way to give your life meaning is to teach another person how to look within and love.

I made it back to my apartment and walked listlessly up the stairs, clutching Chucky's clothes Adam had been wearing. When I walked in, Chucky jerked his head toward the door from where he was sitting at the breakfast bar. "Oh man, did he die?" he said with wide, sympathetic eyes.

"No. He kicked me out."

"What? Why?"

"I don't know; he has something up his sleeve." I handed Chucky the clothes.

"Hmm. I was reading a medical journal last night—"

"Shocker."

"Charlotte, listen to me. They're starting a new trial for Adam's exact kind of cancer. I asked him about it when he was here. He didn't want to do it. He's given up."

I shook my head. "He has brain cancer and it's already spread everywhere through his body. He had chemo and radiation and surgery."

"But there's a new trial and he knows about it. He doesn't want to try."

"That is insane. Adam would fight for his life. He's the most vivacious person I know. What's the treatment?"

Chucky walked to the counter and grabbed the medical journal and tossed it to me. "They're doing it at Cedars, on the same floor. He declined to participate. He told me about a study . . . a trial that was coming up, but then he mumbled about the number of fucks he had left to give."

The news devastated me. Would Adam really refuse a possible cure? Or at the very least, an opportunity to prolong his life? He had ordered me to stay away from the hospital until I was told to come back, but I wasn't going to let this go.

I read the study. Some of the cases had yielded very promising outcomes for exactly the kind of tumor Adam had—a glioblastoma. I called the hospital and asked for his room. He refused to take the call, so I told the receptionist it was an emergency.

Finally, he answered. "What's wrong, is everything okay?" he asked, sounding genuinely worried.

"Is there a trial going on there that you refused to participate in? A trial that could possibly prolong your life?"

There was silence on the other end of the line.

"Hello?"

He cleared his throat. "I have some time, I know I do. There's something I really want to do, but I can't do it if I'm being poked and prodded."

I was angry. "So you're not gonna even try?"

He took a deep breath. "If you agree to my plan, I will do the trial, Charlotte. I promise."

It was like the sky opened up. Adam would fight. We could have a future.

"What's your plan?" I asked him.

"I can't tell you yet. Wait for the call."

"Fine." I took a deep breath. I trusted Adam. "I'll wait, but I want to be with you."

He didn't say anything for a long time. "We'll be together."

I couldn't get our moment in the hotel room out of my mind. It was so beautiful, so strikingly different from my time in another hotel room with Seth. Not that it was bad with Seth—far from it; it was exactly what I needed at that moment—but there was more depth of emotion and a stronger bond between Adam and me. I missed him five minutes after I left his side. When I was away from Seth, I didn't yearn for him. I hadn't even chased after him on the footbridge.

I killed time by cleaning up, taking a shower, doing my hair, and going through bills that were piling up on the countertop.

Chucky came out and saw me gawking at the past-due electric bill and the stack of other bills underneath it. "Were you just leaving these here for me to take care of, Chuck?"

"No, I was making a pile for Dad. He's going to float us until September."

"What?" My parents were comfortable, upper-middle-class people with a sufficient retirement. I know paying our bills for a couple of months until Chucky started working wasn't going to break them, but I still wasn't clear as to why they were doing it, except for the fact that they'd do anything for my little brother.

"I told Dad that you quit your job because you decided to play nurse to some artist dude with cancer."

"That's what you said to him, you dick?" I was crushed and my face wasn't telling any lies.

Chucky's expression finally softened when he took note of my anguish. "Not exactly," he said. I noticed Chucky was wearing the tracksuit that matched mine. "I told Dad I thought what you were doing was kind, okay? I said it was big of you." It's hard for brothers, even adult men, to compliment their sisters this way, especially for someone like Chucky who has an extremely large ego and competitive streak.

"Kind?"

"Look, Charlotte, I told Dad the whole fucking story. I said I had met Adam and that I thought what you were doing was really respectable. He agreed and said he'd cover the bills for a while. You should call him and thank him."

I couldn't believe my father would agree with anything I was doing.

"I'll call him. Thanks, Charles."

"I'm sorry." He looked up from the counter. "I'm sorry about Adam and Seth and this whole mess."

"That means a lot to me, but I'll figure it out."

"I know you will."

The best thing a brother can say to you is that he believes in you. It takes more nerve than I'm sorry, or even I love you.

Over the next fifteen minutes, I made three calls. The first was to my dad.

"Hello," he said.

"Thank you so much, Dad, for offering to help me out."

"You're welcome, Charlotte. I'm worried about you, though." His voice dropped.

"This isn't one of my bleeding-heart charity cases, like Curtis."

"I know, which is why I'm worried. I don't want this to tear you apart." My dad didn't ever talk to me about my personal life like this.

I swallowed. "I love him and it has nothing to do with his cancer." The airwaves were plagued with silence. "Did you hear me, Dad?"

"I heard you."

"What? You don't think I'm strong enough?"

"I don't think anyone is strong enough."

"You wouldn't say that if you weren't my dad."

"Daddies want to protect their little girls from having their hearts broken." He had never acted this way toward me.

"It would break my heart more if I couldn't be with him right now. I'm stronger because of him."

"Your mother believes you're doing the right thing."

"But you don't?"

"I just—"

I cut him off. "Please tell Mom thank you for me. I'll come out and see you guys soon."

"Charlotte . . ."

"I have to go, Dad. I love you."

"Love you, too," he said, sounding defeated.

We hung up and a second later I was dialing the hospital. I got Leah on the phone. "How is Adam?"

"He's fine. Hang tight okay? He'll call you in the morning. Get some rest."

"What is going on, Leah?"

"Just trust me. Adam is okay and we have a specialist coming in to do some tests."

"For what?" *He's doing the trial. He has to be. He's setting it up. He promised.*

"It's not what you think. Just hang tight, Charlotte. He'll call you in the morning."

"If anything happens while I'm not there, I'm going to be pissed."

She laughed.

"It's not funny," I said.

"It's only funny because Adam said you would say that. He's okay for now. The tumors aren't growing at the pace we thought."

More hope.

"So are they going to try and remove them?"

"Charlotte, I can't discuss this any further with you over the phone."

"I don't know what he's up to, but I'm not going to be able to sleep at all tonight."

"Try. I'll call you if anything comes up, I promise. And I'll give the night nurse the same instructions."

"Okay fine. Thank you." I hung up.

I went to the kitchen and drank several large swigs of white wine directly from the bottle, then went back to my room and called Seth.

"Hello?" he said.

"Hi. It's Charlotte."

"I know." Awkward silence.

"How is your wrist?"

"It's going to be okay. I sat out two games just to be on the safe side, but I'll be back on the field tomorrow."

"That's good."

"How's Adam?"

"I'm not really sure. He might participate in a trial, a new cutting-edge treatment."

He didn't reply, but I could hear him take a deep, irritated breath. "That's good for him. So that leaves us exactly where I thought. Why are you calling?"

Ouch.

"I guess . . . I'm asking for forgiveness and I'm trying to say . . . I think . . . I guess I'm . . ."

"Just spit it out, Charlotte. What? You realize you weren't really into me?"

"No, that's not it."

"Then what?"

"I just wanted you to know that I'm going to be with Adam. I have . . . *been* with Adam." My mouth filled with saliva like I was going to throw up. I ran to my desk and grabbed the wastebasket, all the while listening to Seth's agitated breaths over the phone. "But Seth, I liked you. I just . . . I can't ask you to wait."

"You have to do it?"

"Yes. But it's more than that. I want to be with him."

Several seconds of silence went by, again making me feel more and more nauseous.

"Okay then . . ." he said. He sounded resigned. "I hope for you and for Adam's sake that he pulls through. I can't imagine your devastation if he doesn't." Before I could respond and convey my utter sadness at leaving things this way, he said, "Listen, Charlotte, I have to go. The team trainer is waiting for me in the locker room."

"Where are we leaving this conversation? I mean, do you forgive me? You don't hate me?"

"This is where we're leaving this conversation. There's nothing to forgive. I don't hate you. You owe me nothing." I detected indifference in his tone.

"You're right, I don't owe you anything. I just thought because we kind of had the beginning of a good thing . . ."

"Yeah, we did. I have to go; the trainer is waiting."

"Okay." I wondered if I was throwing away the one

viable possibility for a real, stable relationship. Seth was the first person I had ever dated who had it all together. It felt like someone had punched me right in the lower part of my stomach.

I got off the phone, feeling even more confused. There wasn't anything either one of us could do. I slept with Adam, I was taking care of Adam, and I was in love with Adam, cancer or not.

That night consisted of me alternating between tossing and turning and crying quietly into my pillow. I slept with my phone right next to my head in case the hospital called.

In the morning, I took a shower and got ready. Exhausted and out of it, I got a text message from Leah, which I thought was strange.

Leah: Hey, it's Leah, Adam's nurse. You can come back now.

Me: I'll be down there soon.

On my way out the door, Chucky stopped me. He didn't say anything; he just grabbed me and hugged me. It was probably the third time in our entire lives that we had hugged.

"What was that all about?" I said.

"Just wanted to hug my sister and say be well."

"You're freaking me out, Chuck."

He squinted. "I just wanted to say I love you."

"I love you, but I'm still totally weirded out."

"You better get going."

"Bye, little brother."

"Bye, sis."

I jogged down the stairs to my car and drove off, wondering what I would be greeted with once I arrived at the hospital.

23. The Plan

When I arrived at the hospital, there was a large crowd gathered outside Adam's room. Some of the women were crying. The world around me started spinning. *Oh no*. My feet felt glued to the floor as I tried to make my way down the hall. I was already crying when Leah met me halfway.

"Who are those people, and what are they doing here?"

She took a step closer to me so that we were inches apart. "That's Adam's mom and dad, and over there is Adam's old boss. The young woman was an ex-girlfriend or something. They're all here to say good-bye."

"Good-bye?" My vision started getting hazy. My head swayed on my neck like it was attached with putty. "Wh-why are you so calm?" As I fell to my knees she struggled to pull me up by the shoulders.

"Charlotte, he's not dead. Stand up, he needs to talk to you." I still didn't understand anything.

Everything was still fuzzy until Leah pulled a smell-ing salt capsule from her pocket, broke it, and waved it in front of my face. My eyes shot open. By that point Adam's mother and father were standing near us in the middle of the hall.

"Is she okay?" his mother said.

"She thought he had gone and you were all here to say good-bye."

His mother had mascara running down her face, but she was smiling. "I'm Deanna. You must be Charlotte?"

I reached my hand up weakly and shook hers. "Yes."

She helped to keep me upright. She seemed conservative, with her natural gray bob, high-necked sweater, and simple makeup.

"Come on," Leah said. "Let's go see our boy." She walked me to Adam's room with her arm around my waist. Inside, I found him standing near the bed wearing a black sweatshirt, jeans, and a baseball cap. Every person gathered around his room seemed somber as I walked by them. They watched me intently. Adam looked better to me, so I wondered why everyone was down.

Adam looked up and smiled. "I'm busting out of here and I want you to come with me. Will you come with me, Charlotte?"

My mouth was open in shock as I tried to find the words to ask all the questions running through my head. "But you—"

"Have cancer, I know. Finally, you're getting it." He jabbed his thumb behind him, pointing to a man hooking his IV line up to a portable device. "Meet Dr. Freedom. We're taking him with us. My dad is letting us use his driver and private jet."

"The jet?"

"I have a plan for us. You said you'd agree to my plan, right?" He sat down on the bed and patted the space next to him. "Come, I'll explain."

"But the trial . . ."

"The trial will still be here."

Everyone but Dr. Freedom had left the room and began congregating in the hall, talking in hushed tones.

"So," Adam said, "I was thinking that I really don't want to stay here any longer. I called my parents and a few other people and—"

"Your ex-girlfriend?"

"Yeah, well, my dad called her." Adam rolled his eyes.

"Is she the runner?"

"Yeah." He looked surprised. "How'd you know that?"

"I have a good memory."

He jabbed my arm with his finger. "Braggart. Anyway, I told them I was leaving, that you and I were going to take a trip, so they came to say good-bye."

"Adam . . ."

Placing a finger over my mouth, he said, "Shh, let's be in the moment now; it's all we have. Will you go with me?" Before I could answer he leaned in and kissed me. What he wasn't saying is that everyone was here to say good-bye in case Adam didn't make it back.

When I pulled away, I said, "But I don't have any of my stuff." I was hoping to change his mind.

"Chucky took care of that. He packed a bag while you were in the shower this morning; he even got your passport for you." I had a passport only because my mom made me get one. I had never used it.

"Chucky went through my drawers?" I imagined him

finding some personal items, taking pictures, and putting it on Instagram.

Adam cocked his head to the side and quirked an eyebrow at me. "He wanted to help. Don't be a brat."

"Fine. So, passport? We're going out of the country?"

"I can't tell you any details. It has to be a surprise."

"We can't be gone long. We have to come back so you can start the trial and get the new treatment. I read all about it. It could save you."

"Don't worry about a thing. We're gonna go have some fun before they inject me with more poison." He smiled wide.

Leaving the hospital was surreal. Each person who was there waiting for Adam to leave knew who I was, hugged me, and thanked me. Most of them were in tears as I pushed Adam in his wheelchair toward the town car waiting at the curb.

We sat next to each other in the back seat and held hands. I put my head on his shoulder and didn't care where we were going anymore.

"Do you believe in God?" I asked.

"Are you worried about my soul, Charlotte?" His chest rumbled with laughter.

I didn't want to ruin the moment, but I needed to talk to him, to see where his head was at. "I guess I'm wondering how you feel emotionally . . . if . . . if you're scared."

"I'm not scared."

My head was still on his shoulder, so I couldn't see his expression, but he lifted my hand to his mouth and kissed my knuckles. "I'll tell you what I think and what I believe as long as you promise that it won't make you sad. We're supposed to be trying to get away from all that sadness. It's the whole point of what I planned."

"I know, I know." I looked up to the driver and Doctor Freedom in the front seat.

Adam lowered his voice to keep the conversation between us. "I believe you have to protect your relationship with God more than any other, Charlotte. Whether you believe in God or not, whether you think God is terrible, truly divine, or absolutely nonexistent, it is the most sacred and intimate relationship we have in our lives."

"What do you mean?"

"I mean the definition of God. It's just something within. That's what I believe."

I pulled away from him to look at his face. He was smiling warmly . . . contently. "So when it's all over . . ."

"Lights out, baby."

I shook my head; my face fell as tears filled my eyes. "No," I said.

"You promised me you wouldn't get sad." He pressed his lips to mine and I felt our tears mixing together on our cheeks as we kissed and kissed.

When we finally pulled apart I said, "Look, now I've made you cry. Don't you want to believe that we'll be together again . . . that we'll see each other again?"

"No, Charlotte." He shook his head and then turned and stared out the window. "I want to believe that you'll go on and live your life. This is mine. This is my right now, and I'm taking it."

Even though I promised him I wouldn't cry anymore, I couldn't help it. I felt Adam was being cheated. It made me angry with God and I wasn't sure how I could repair that relationship, the one I was supposed to protect the most, according to Adam. It was hard for me to understand how he had reconciled that in his own mind.

"You're not bitter?"

"I don't think I have a lot of time to waste being bitter."

He was right. And that was true for all of us.

We ended up at the Getty, standing in front of *Starry Night*—the Munch, not the Van Gogh, of course. Adam insisted on walking instead of using a wheelchair. He stood behind me and said, "I used to think the Van Gogh was starrier, but now that you're standing here, there's no question this one is much brighter." He came up close behind me, moved my hair to one side, and kissed the back of my neck before whispering, "Thank you for that, by the way."

It took everything in me not to start crying again, but I promised myself I would give Adam this last little bit of life to live without constantly reminding him he was sick.

"You're welcome, handsome." I turned around and wrapped my arms around him. We kissed in front of twenty people, and I didn't care.

After the museum, the driver took us to the Observatory at Griffith Park, where Adam got down on one knee in the grass.

"What are you doing?" I gasped.

"Charlotte Anne Martin, there are not enough stars in the sky to match the reasons why I love you. Marry me and make me the happiest man on earth?" He produced a simple gold band from his pocket.

I didn't hesitate. I held my hand out to him. "Yes, I will." It was the easiest decision I had ever made.

He put the ring on my finger. "Good, because they're

getting my father's jet ready for us and we need to be at the Van Nuys Airport as soon as possible." He looked down and laughed at his own helpless state on the ground. "Now, help me up, please."

Doctor Freedom, who I found out was really named Mark, ran over when he saw me reaching down to lift Adam, but Adam held his hand out, waving him off. "Let me kiss my fiancée first!" Mark stood several feet away and tried to act like he was looking at something in the other direction.

I couldn't even guess as to how much they were paying an oncologist to play nursemaid to Adam. Mark was a young, easygoing doctor from Oregon. In the short time that I had known him, I could tell he wanted to be there and that he was fond of Adam. I liked to think he wanted to contribute to the cause. It helped that Adam's dad's pockets were deep; Adam himself had donated a lot of his money before he was even hospitalized.

Everyone coming together for Adam made more sense to me because of Adam's magnetism, his joy, and his courage as he faced what could be the end of his life. It was painfully sad, but also moving and life-affirming for those of us who were lucky enough to know him during that time.

A private Learjet flew us to New York, where we boarded a commercial flight to Paris.

Mark was diligent about administering Adam's drugs while we traveled. Adam and I took up three first-class seats, and if Adam was uncomfortable at all, he said nothing about it. I caught him stealing glances at me every now and then. Out of the corner of my eye, I'd see him smile and I'd smile myself.

When the lights went down in the cabin, Mark took a seat across the aisle from where Adam and I sat. The three of us reclined our chairs and dozed off. Adam's hand clutched mine the whole flight.

Just before we landed in Paris, Adam had a small seizure. Mark calmly intervened, giving another type of drug, which adversely made Adam very groggy. Still, instead of using the narrow wheelchair from the airline to get to the jetway, Adam insisted on walking.

Adam had booked two rooms next to each other in a lavish five-star hotel that overlooked the Eiffel Tower. I didn't think I would see Paris this way, even in my wildest dreams: sitting out on a verandah, staring at the Eiffel Tower's magnificence. Still, a doctor checked the vitals of my suffering fiancé, which wasn't part of the original fantasy. I wish I could say that it was the most romantic time of my life, but it was so equally tragic that it felt surreal and gut-wrenching at times. Yet, there were still moments of magic. I allowed myself to go to that place with Adam. I imagined Dr. Mark wasn't really there, and that Adam and I were experiencing Paris the way I had described it to him.

I had never been out of California before except to visit my aunt in Flagstaff, Arizona, and the three times I had been to Las Vegas. I hadn't even dreamed of going to Europe. I was living in a bubble where I thought everyone exaggerated how amazing the world truly was. You know the people who think seeing it in a picture is like seeing it in real life? Well, it's not. Because when you're there, you're not just seeing it. It's the sounds, the smells of Paris, the way the air feels on your skin, the way the wine tastes different when you drink it from Parisian glasses while sitting in a wicker chair outside a café on a cobblestone street. You can't re-create the hum of a foreign language being spoken over and over itself. It sounds like music. The way the sun rises and sets, the shadows on the buildings, the car horns honking in the distance. It's all different, new, and fascinating to experience when you travel far away from home.

We spent the first few days exploring Paris as much as we could without pushing Adam too hard. On the third day, we got married in a little chapel. He wore a black suit. His hair had started to grow back on his head and face. I wanted to use that fact as some sort of proof that his body was okay. I wore a plain, A-line, tea-length white dress.

Adam and I stood face-to-face while the priest spoke in French to officiate the wedding ceremony . . . *our* wedding ceremony. It didn't matter what language he was speaking; we understood what he was saying. There was a handful of people just sitting in the chapel, and, of course, Dr. Mark looking on as our witness.

In heavily accented English, the priest gestured toward Adam and said, "Your vows now."

While holding my hands and looking into my eyes, Adam smiled and said, "If you told me I could have another life, a longer life, but that I couldn't have you, I'd say no thanks. I'd take you and my short life over and over again."

I started to cry instantly because, even in our vows, there was so much resignation. "But . . ."

He put his fingers to my lips. "Wait, lady, let me say my vows."

I nodded as tears poured from my eyes.

"Every night since that night in my loft, I've fallen asleep thinking about you, standing in front of *Starry Night*—"

I interrupted him by leaning in and kissing him—a full, passionate kiss. I put everything I had into it because the truth was that every night since that night in Adam's loft, I had fallen asleep thinking about being with him, too. Even when I was with Seth, lying in Seth's arms, I would doze off to the image of Adam and me holding hands and kissing the way we were right now.

"No, no," the priest said. "Not time yet."

Adam pulled away and laughed. I was speechless.

"I am totally in love with you, not because you're here right now or because you've taken care of me; it's because when you laugh, it sounds like pure joy. It's because you walk super fast with your head down, and when you stop to look up, you seem surprised every time. Like the world is surprising you with its beauty. I love the way you see the world, Charlotte. That's why I love you. When I thought of you looking at *Starry Night*, it wasn't just that it was brighter to me; it was that I knew it would seem brighter to you. You don't know how beautiful that quality is. You're already so beautiful and kind, but then you have this hope and promise in your eyes, too. And you're also the sexiest woman I have ever known."

"Adam," I chided. The priest shrugged and looked away. At that point I don't think he was too overly concerned about propriety.

"Charlotte, I am so selfish for doing this to you." I shook my head, but Adam continued. "For telling you all of this when I could be leaving you so soon. Until then, I promise to be the best husband I can. Until death do us part," he said with a lopsided grin.

I was not amused. "Don't be a quitter, Bramwell," I said straight-faced. I captured his face in my hands and looked deep into his cozy brown eyes. "Till death do us part is for quitters. I promise to love you forever. As long as there is love in this world, we will be a part of it." I meant it. No matter what happened, I would always love him. I know to others it would seem odd that we fell for each other so easily, even under the worst circumstances, but Adam was exactly the right person for me.

We kissed, and after several seconds, the priest cleared his throat. We let him finish his ceremony. Adam and I walked down the aisle, side by side, holding hands while soft music played overhead.

"Wait," Adam said. He looked up to the dome-shaped ceiling and window blasting light down onto us and just stared for several moments.

"What is it, Adam?" I said.

"Nothing. Let's go."

We headed out to the taxi waiting for us. Dr. Mark let us ride alone but he caught the next one and followed close behind. We held hands the whole way, but we were quiet.

"Adam, I'm afraid you're going to do something really stupid," I said, worried that his silence meant he was making decisions in his mind.

"Like what? I'm not going to kill myself, if that's what you're thinking."

"I know that. I don't want you to give me any of your possessions or try to take care of me after you're gone. I just realized . . ."

"What, that you're my wife now?"

"Yes, exactly."

"I'm not. I'm just going to give you my last million so you can have some fun with it."

"You don't have a million dollars . . . do you?"

"Yeah, probably not. I stopped keeping track of that stuff a long time ago."

"Whatever you have, donate it to cancer research or something. You can't give me your money, Adam."

"Sure I can."

"Adam, I will be so mad at you. Promise me you will not give me a penny."

He laughed. "Okay, I promise you I will not give you a penny."

"I don't want to talk like this anymore. I want to talk about the trial and what we're going to do when we get back and what our plan is."

"I promise we'll talk about that, but not right now."

I shook my head.

"I promise, Charlotte. We'll talk about it."

24. Time to Talk

In our hotel later that night, with Dr. Mark a room away and all of Adam's medications sitting on a bedside table, we made love, slow and sweet. It was sacred. Afterward, Adam was weak but he seemed content. Sometime in the middle of the night, I startled awake, a wave of paranoia racing through my chest. I rolled over and put my hand over Adam's heart to make sure it was beating.

He whispered, "I'm not quite done yet, if you don't mind." He laughed quietly, and I wanted to punch him.

"Not funny. I think we should talk about our plan."

"We have already," he said as his hand moved between my legs.

He was touching me and kissing my collarbone and I was losing all sense. "Don't try to get out of this, Adam."

"This is the best I've felt in a while."

"Ahhh." I couldn't stay quiet. He was moving faster and kissing harder.

It was dark in our room except for the light from the

tower. The window looked like a painting. Everything was still except for us. I could feel myself coming undone. I held his mouth to mine, trying to stifle the moans.

He pulled away and whispered, "I can feel you coming, Charlotte. Let go."

I did, and for several minutes he held me close to his chest. We should have been having the conversation but Adam was doing everything to distract me, even making jokes.

"I can't drive a car, but I can make a woman come in less than five minutes."

I ignored his joke. "When we get back, you'll do the treatment—"

"I think the story goes, we get married, have children, go to concerts together, read in the park, watch our children grow, get old, and sit in rockers on the porch. Sound good?"

"I'm being serious."

"So am I. Worst-case scenario, I die tonight in your arms, which wouldn't be so terrible."

I started crying. "Stop, please. I have a tiny bit of hope to hold on to now."

He pulled me to him and kissed my nose. "You're getting very attached. I can't stand the thought of you being in pain."

I nodded into his chest.

"When you said you'll love me forever—"

"I meant it," I said.

"I want you to say to me that you will be fine and you'll move on and love someone and make a life."

"I've told you that already." My voice broke.

"I need to believe you this time."

It was quiet for several moments.

"I'm afraid if you believe it, then you'll let go."

I know he could feel my tears on his skin.

"I don't think it works that way, doll-face."

"You know what I mean."

"It's for me, Charlotte. It's so I can stop feeling guilty about giving you something and possibly taking it all away. You seemed genuine when you said forever. It scared me a little."

I sat up and straddled his body. "I'm going to kill you myself if you don't stop acting so resigned and feeling guilty. I'm here because I want to be. And I meant it when I said I'll love you forever."

He shook his head.

"Don't shake your head at me."

"Say it," he demanded.

"I'll be fine."

"Say it, Charlotte."

"I will go on."

"That's the only way you can really love me forever; you know that, right?"

"Yes," I whispered, and then cried some more. He pulled me back down to lie on his chest. Moments later he was asleep. I stayed awake thinking about how in the world I would make good on my promise to him if I had to.

I woke to a spear of sunlight shining over my face. Adam was awake already, lying on his side, watching me.

I turned to face him. "How are you feeling?"

His one-sided smirk appeared. "Most commonly asked question of a dying man."

"You're obviously well enough to make jokes, although

your speech is worse this morning than it was yesterday." He was getting harder to understand as he continued to lose feeling on the left side of his face.

"Can you just be my wife today and leave the examinations to Mark?"

I kissed him. "Fine. What should we do with our day, husband?"

He glanced at the clock. "We're traveling. We need to be ready in an hour."

Adam arranged a private plane to fly us an hour and a half away to the Côte d'Azur, aka the French Riviera, where we checked into a room looking right out onto the perfectly blue harbor freckled with sailboats.

I stood on the balcony while Mark examined Adam on the bed behind me.

"What do you see, Charlotte?" Adam said.

"It's mesmerizing . . . captivating. There are buildings of all different colors around us, with tile roofs. The sun is blasting them, making them all look a different shade of yellow, and the water is so clear I can see the reef below the surface. The sailboats look painted, as do the thousands of tiny people on the small stretch of beach below us. It's magical. I've never seen anything like it."

"I wish I could paint you like that," he said.

I turned around to see Adam in his chair, watching me as I stood in a flowing white skirt on the balcony. My hair was dancing on my shoulders in natural, reddish-brown waves. I hadn't worn makeup since we left the States. It just didn't feel necessary anymore. I smiled at him. "You're sweet. You like Charlotte *au naturel*?"

"I like Charlotte any and every way." He wheeled himself

toward me and looked out at the ocean. "You weren't lying, were you?"

I reached for his hand. "It's beautiful, Adam. Thank you for bringing me here."

His hand squeezed mine painfully. I looked down to see the familiar sign of him beginning to have a seizure.

"Mark!" I yelled. He was at my side in a moment, trying to get Adam on the floor.

"Get a pillow!" Mark yelled to me.

Adam was thrashing on the tile floor. The only thing you can do for a person having a seizure like that is to try to prevent them from hurting themselves or you. Mark had no more stops to pull out. He had been giving Adam more medicine than he thought a person could even handle. Still, Adam was holding on. At times, he could barely speak or walk, but whenever I looked at him he still tried to smile. We had to get back; I knew that.

When the seizure was over, while Adam lay in Mark's arms, Mark looked up at me and said, "He's in pain, you know?" Adam didn't say anything. He was still out of it.

I knew he was in pain. I would see Adam wince every now and then, but every time I asked, he would blow it off. He hated the seizures, I knew that. He would be so sore afterward that he would groan in his sleep. He was taking thirty different medications, which all had adverse side effects. I think the only thing truly keeping him alive was maybe the same hope I was holding on to.

"I know he's in pain. What do we do?" I started to cry. "How can we help him? This doesn't feel merciful."

"God is not always merciful."

I thought that to be a strange comment from a doctor.

"I mean, isn't there something we can do?"

Mark shook his head and looked down at Adam. "It's unethical . . ."

"I'm not asking you to do that, Mark! He's going to do that trial at Cedars. There's still a chance for him. I just don't want to see him in pain. We should get back to the States." I was angry, but tears were still pouring from my eyes. It was so painful to watch Adam suffer.

When he started to come out of the seizure fog, Mark looked up at me thoughtfully and said, "What trial were you talking about?"

"He hasn't told you?"

"If you're referring to what I think you're referring to, he applied for it but was rejected."

I started shaking my head.

"Charlotte," Dr. Mark pressed on, "do you know why we're here?"

"No," I squeaked out. I couldn't hear it. I ran into the bathroom where I collapsed against the door and sobbed.

Half an hour later, after trying to collect myself, I came out of the bathroom to find Adam watching me from his chair near the balcony. "You should . . ." He stuttered painfully. It felt like my heart was being ripped out when he struggled to talk.

"Take it slow, Adam." I moved closer to him.

I could see he was trying to find the words. "Ch-change," he said. "Wh-wh-we're going sailing."

I smiled sadly.

"Aren't you hap-happy about that, Ch-Charlotte?"

"Yes, very."

"I–I don't like to see you upset."

"This is hard." The lump was growing in my throat. "It's hard to watch."

"I know, I'm sorry."

"Adam, how can we even go sailing in your condition?"

"I've hired people to-to-to help. Mark knows how to sail, that was one of the pre-pre—"

"Don't, Adam. Just wait until you feel better."

"I'm okay. I was going to say pre-pre-requisites for taking this j-job. Also, he's a genius."

"I wouldn't go that far," Mark said. "But I can teach you how to sail, Charlotte, and for some reason this guy really wants that to happen."

I knew Mark had a wife and small children waiting for him at home; I thought what he was doing was noble. I can't imagine what his interview must have looked like. *Will you take care of this sick man on the French Riviera while teaching his new wife how to sail?* Seemed too bizarre to be real, but I guess every moment with Adam was like that from the time we met.

Adam, Mark, two deckhands, and I went out onto the perfect blue water of the French Riviera and sailed in a beautiful forty-foot yacht for three days. I learned how to raise and lower the sails, change directions, anchor, steer, and all the strange lingo to go with it, while Adam watched in awe from the cockpit. "Charlotte, let's head that way and anchor a bit!" Adam shouted over the wind.

I went to the steering wheel and took over from Mark. "Ready about?" I said. Mark rushed to let the lines out and crank the winch. Adam reached back and helped the best he could from where he was sitting, but he had grown much weaker in those few days. He could hardly do anything anymore. Yet I was still in denial.

We found a calm cove and anchored. Mark jumped in the warm water and swam around before climbing back on board and making lunch for us, all while Adam and I took in the beauty of our surroundings. Later, I sat with Adam on the deck while Mark took a nap down below. Adam was wrapped in a blanket. Even though it was seventy-five degrees, he was getting the chills. I held him.

"You're a regular, pro, Charlotte," he mumbled. "You picked it up really fast. A quick study, just like I predicted."

"It's captain to you, buddy."

"Charlotte?"

"Yes, Adam."

"Mark and my family already know. I want to be cremated."

"Then why are you telling me if they already know?"

"Here, in France."

"No."

"Please, listen to me. I like this spot, for some of my ashes."

"No."

He gripped my face with his trembling hands and said, "And I want to ask you to take the rest to my mother."

"No."

"Then move on, okay? Move on."

"No."

This was the only mercy I could give him, but I was too selfish.

"Charlotte, I'm in a lot of pain."

I began sobbing. "Okay, okay, I'll do whatever you ask." I told him what I knew he needed to hear.

"I love you. You're the love of my life. No one could mean it more." He was struggling so badly to talk.

"Shh. Don't talk."

"I have to tell you that I thought a lot about it and I do think I'll see you again . . . I know I will." I still didn't know if Adam was saying it for me or for him.

"I love you, too, and we will be together."

"We will," he said.

I kissed his face, then pulled him closer to my body and held him to my chest. He closed his eyes finally. I felt him relax.

"Mark," I said in a resigned, beaten-down voice. I had nothing left. Mark came up the ladder from below and saw me holding Adam on the deck.

"I think . . . I think something's wrong," I said.

Mark moved to raise the anchor. I stayed still, holding Adam on the deck as we sailed the calm water back into the harbor. I stroked Adam's face. I could feel that he was still breathing, but it was weak and shallow. When we docked, there was a team waiting to help Adam into an ambulance. He was taken to a hospital nearby.

25. Sapling

Adam Bramwell never woke up again. He died in my arms that night in a hospital bed in France while I cried over him. I stayed with him until they wouldn't let me, and when they pulled me away, I felt like Adam's spirit was inside of me, a part of my soul. I was the last one to touch him alive. He was with me and I was with him. It gave me just a sliver of peace in those moments immediately after he passed.

I had to call his mother. She could notify the rest of the family.

"Deanna. He's gone," I cried.

Adam's mother whimpered and then sobbed before handing the phone to Adam's father. "Charlotte?"

"It's me." I didn't even know his name.

"Was he in pain?"

"No. He died peacefully in his sleep . . . in my arms," I choked out.

He took a deep breath. "Thank you," he said, and then hung up.

Something I would never forget was that Adam smiled more than one would think in his last days on earth. I don't know if he had a glimpse of something none of us get to see, or if he had finally accepted his own fate, or if he was truly happy. All I know is that he taught me about independence and self-worth and about how precious life is.

I cried for days in the hotel room, waiting for Adam's ashes. When you're that low, normal, everyday things we do to stay alive become secondary. I had to remind myself to drink water. It was impossible to eat, but I knew I needed to stay hydrated. I had to remind myself to breathe because sometimes I would find myself holding my breath to avoid crying. The small act of taking a breath would initiate a fit of tears.

Mark traveled back to the States to be with his family while I waited. Alone. It was the hardest thing I've ever done in my life. Everyone I knew called, but words did nothing for me. I lay on the bed, gripping his clothes, smelling them over and over and hoping I wasn't taking his scent out of the material. I couldn't understand how a person could be there one minute and gone the next. I couldn't accept that I would never see him again. I couldn't believe that his body would just dissipate into nothingness. I wanted to hold on so badly, but every time I would get to the point where I didn't think I could handle it anymore, I would hear my promise to Adam. I would hear his voice demand it.

On the fourth day, I gathered myself off the floor and picked up his ashes, chartered a twenty-foot sailboat alone, and sailed into the cove where he and I had last been together. I sprinkled some of the ashes into the water and watched as the light waves carried Adam away. "Good-bye,

Adam Bramwell. I'm not going to cry for you anymore because it's not going to do me any good. I loved you. You're gone." I knew every bit of that was a lie. I still loved him, I would cry more, and he would never truly be gone, but I was trying so desperately to keep my word to him.

I FLEW DIRECTLY back to Northern California, where Adam's parents lived. I rented a car, drove to their house, and walked proudly to the door. I knocked while I held a small gold urn in my other hand. I wasn't shaking. I wasn't scared.

Adam's mother answered the door. "He asked me to bring him home," I said before she could even say hello. I held the urn out to her and she took it. I could tell from the mascara under her eyes that she had been crying.

She reached for the urn. "I don't know how to thank you."

"You don't need to thank me."

"You did something I couldn't do."

"You're right," I said. "But not in the way you think." She was feeling guilty about not being at his bedside.

"Adam and I got married," I rushed to say. "He didn't want anyone watching him die or sitting around waiting for him to die. He knew you were a good mother. He also had a good career and a lot of experiences—more than me, in fact, more than a lot of older people I know. He left a legacy behind in his art, but what I think he really wanted before he died was to be in love. We were in love and it changed me and I'm grateful to him and to you." I didn't cry. I got every word out and I was proud.

Adam's mother nodded, her eyes full of tears. "The doctor left you an envelope. Come in, please."

I followed her past the entryway into the kitchen, where there was an envelope sitting on the counter. "For me? From Dr. Mark?"

"I think it's from Adam," she said with her back to me. "I don't know, I didn't read it." She handed it to me. "Read it in your own time." She walked like a zombie into the living room and placed the urn next to a portrait of a very healthy and handsome Adam graduating from college. She just stood there, facing the mantel, staring at his photo.

"I'm going to let myself out," I said. She didn't respond, but it didn't bother me. I had spent days mourning Adam and carrying around his ashes. I knew there would be more tears over him, maybe at some unexpected time when the image of Adam standing on the corner, lost, holding Chinese food, and smiling from ear to ear popped into my head. Or maybe when I looked at the painting he made of me. I knew it would happen, but for now, I was keeping my promise to him.

When I pulled into the parking space of my apartment building, I jumped out of my car immediately. My jaw hit the ground. Staring up at the wall of my building, I fell to my knees. "No! No!" I sobbed. The wolves had been painted over.

Chucky, who had been standing at the top of the stairwell, rushed toward me. "Charlotte!" he called out. He bent and wrapped his arms around my shoulders. I fell into his chest.

"I tried to stop them. I even called the city, but it's private property and the building owner wanted it gone. I'm sorry, Char."

I stood listlessly. Chucky walked me up to the apartment, his arm hitched around my waist.

I unpacked my bags in a daze, took a shower, sat on my bed, and opened the envelope. Then I began to read the letter:

Charlotte, Thank you for everything. You are now the (I hope proud) owner of a forty-one-foot Alerion sailing vessel, sitting pretty in slip 23 at the Marina Del Rey Harbor. Take good care of her. I know you will. I've also included a check because I lied to you for your own good. Sorry. I want you to spend some of this dumb money. I donated a whole bunch to charity, so please, honor me and use this to get yourself set up in life. Well, I am, in fact, in heaven now. It's amazing. I wish you were here, but don't try skipping any steps, like putting your-self in danger. It doesn't work that way. I'll make you a deal . . . I'll save you a spot on this puffy cloud, for when it's your time, okay? I love you. You were truly my heaven on earth, even if my stint was a bit short. Please keep your promises to me. You know what I'm talking about. Oh, and one last thing, I had the mural changed, the one of the winged man. Honestly, Charlotte, you cannot stay in that godforsaken apartment forever. ;) All my love, Adam.

I was crying and laughing at the same time when I pulled the cashier's check out and saw that it was written for exactly one million dollars. His last million, which I didn't even believe he had. It was signed by Adam Bramwell, and in the comments it said, *It's not a penny.* I held my hand to my heart for several moments until I could catch my breath. When I was calm enough to stand, I stuck the check back into the envelope and threw it on my desk. I walked out of my apartment like a zombie and headed for the winged man. When I got to the corner I saw it. The mural Adam had painted of the winged man was gone, and in its place, just crystal-blue water and the tiny speck of a sailboat. He knew all along.

26. Acceptance

I'm not sure how many hours or days had gone by before I looked up at a crowd of people standing around my bed. There was Helen, Chucky, Mom, Dad, and Jack from the restaurant, which was bizarre.

Helen spoke first. "Hey you." She smiled kindly.

Someone had opened the blinds. I was squinting up at them through the bright light flooding the room.

"Hi."

I noticed they were all wearing the same sympathetic smile. Chucky said, "I got you Cap'n Crunch, if you want a bowl?"

"Why are you all here?"

"You've been asleep for two days, Charlotte. You haven't even peed," Helen said.

I looked at my mom, whose head was cocked to the side.

"I had jet lag," I explained.

My dad leaned over and kissed my cheek. "You need a shower, kid."

Jack smiled wide. "Hi, Charlotte. The restaurant will still have you back if you need to get your mind off things and make some money."

"Thank you, Jack, but I don't need to work and I think I want a dog," I said, rubbing my eyes.

My mother's mouth opened into an O shape.

"A shelter dog. Like a medium-sized dog that likes the water. I have a boat now. I think I'm gonna live on my boat with my dog."

Everyone in the room looked around at each other in a panic.

My mother finally spoke. "Charlotte . . . you've been through a lot . . ."

"You don't like dogs," Chucky said.

"Oh yeah, and I'm a millionaire now." The room went quiet again. "Chucky, I do like dogs. I like dogs and cats, and I want a dog, maybe like a Lab type that would like to go sailing with me."

"You're getting ahead of yourself," my dad said.

I sat up against the headboard. "I'm not. I'm doing what I want. I have money and a boat and I'm going to do what I want." I shrugged.

"It's just not the right time to be making decisions like this, Charlotte," my father said, his eyebrows pinched together in pity and distress.

"You guys," I stressed, "I just spent over a month watching someone who knew he was dying make the most out of the shitty life he was given. I couldn't live alone for one day before this happened. I didn't have an identity. I didn't even know what I liked until I made up a story about it and told Adam, just to make him feel better. I realized I was missing out on all the beauty in this world because I had my head so far up my own ass."

"Charlotte," my father chided.

"You know what he did?" I said. "He made it come true. He made everything I want come true, and if you think I'm going to go back to being the fickle, shallow person I was before, you're wrong. I'm quitting cosmetology school forever. I sucked at doing hair and you know that, Mom." She looked away, a sign of admission. "Just another thing I was preparing myself to fail at because I didn't really want to do it to begin with. Every job and man I've come across I've basically found a way to sabotage. I've made excuses, but I'm done with all that now."

I got up in my sweats and started moving around the room, grabbing things while everyone watched me in shock. In the bathroom, I changed, brushed my hair and teeth, then walked out, past the silent crowd, and reached for a granola bar from the cabinet.

"I'm going down to check on my boat. You're all welcome to join, but you should probably drive separately because I'm gonna take her out for a test run and make sure everything's in working order. Or if you feel like sailing, you can come aboard, but I'm the captain, so keep that in mind. You'll need to refer to me that way and listen to all of my commands. Sailing can be dangerous if you don't know what you're doing."

Whispering too loudly, my mother leaned into my father's ear and asked, "Is she mentally ill?"

My father shook his head. In a normal speaking voice, he said, "Nope."

"Who's coming?"

I think Helen looked the most dumbfounded. My mother

was concerned, but my father looked proud of me for once in his life. Chucky looked good-humored or perplexed—I couldn't quite tell which one.

Jack left and Chucky walked to his bedroom but stopped just before going in. He turned back and said, "So do I need to find a new roommate?"

"I have a million dollars, Chucky," I said, smiling. "I'll pay half the rent until you're a real dentist, okay?"

"Thanks, weirdo," he said, and then shut the door.

It was only Helen and my mom and dad left, staring at me. "You still with Roddy?" I said to Helen.

"Yep." She was looking at me like I was deranged.

"How's Seth?"

"Fine," she said. "Should I call him for you?"

"Nope." I took a bite of my granola bar and spoke with my mouth full. "Your hair looks good, Mom." She had gotten it fixed.

She touched the bouncing curls at her shoulders. "Thanks?"

"Dad, how 'bout those Dodgers? Can you believe it? They're gonna make it all the way."

He nodded continuously for about three seconds.

"Well, it's been real. You're all a joy to be around. I'm heading to the marina. You can follow me if you'd like."

I trotted down the stairs and got into my car. Helen knocked on the passenger window. When I unlocked the door, she opened it and leaned in. "Um, this is weird, but can I ride with you? We're still friends, right?"

"Of course you can, and of course we are. Get in." As she got in, I reached over and caught her and hugged her to my body. "I love you, Helen. You're an awesome person."

"I love you, too," she whispered with emotion.

"Well, the ocean calls. Let's hit it."

On the way to the marina, without shedding a single tear, I told Helen about the last month of Adam's life. I told her about learning to sail and what he had given me. She cried through most of the story.

"You're a widow," she said.

"I am."

"You seem different."

I kept my eyes on the road. "This isn't some existential crisis, Helen. This was just about me not taking responsibility before. Doing things for the wrong reasons, not being able to make decisions. Having no drive to travel, to see the world, to continue learning. Everything I did in the past was safe. The guys I dated were emotionally unavailable to me, and that meant safety."

"Your parents would argue that Adam was the most extreme example of a person who is unavailable."

"I know you think that, too, but you're all wrong. Adam gave everything he had."

"He was dying, Charlotte."

"No, he was living." I glanced at her pointedly and then put my focus back on the road.

It was silent in the car the rest of the way until we pulled into the marina parking lot. "Seth was available but you sabotaged that," Helen added quietly.

I put the car in park and turned my body toward her to look her in the face. "Did I? Did I sabotage a relationship with Seth? Is that what he told you?"

"Not exactly."

"Do you think you're being selfish right now, Helen?

You want me to get with Seth so you, me, Seth, and Roddy can bounce around together?"

"No."

"Good, because I'm not ready to be in a relationship with someone else right now. Is that going to affect the friendship you and I have? Because it shouldn't."

She looked down at her lap to her fidgeting hands.

"What is it, Helen?"

"I don't want to be selfish right now, Charlotte." Her voice cracked.

"Do you want to tell me something about Seth?"

She shook her head. "It's not Seth."

She bent and grabbed her purse from the car floor. She opened a little box, pulled out a ring, and slid it on her ring finger. "He asked me," she said, looking out the window to avoid my gaze. "I didn't want you to see it and get sad."

I took her hand in mine and stared at the modest diamond. "I'm not sad. I'm happy for you. The ring is beautiful and you're going to be a stunning bride, Helen. Congratulations."

When her eyes met mine, I watched tears spill onto her cheeks. "Will you be my maid of honor?"

"Of course. I would love to. I'd be honored." I was holding up strong when my parents pulled into the parking space next to us.

"Have you set a date?" I asked Helen.

"Valentine's Day. We wanted to do it before preseason starts. We're gonna do a destination wedding, somewhere tropical. Maybe Bora-Bora."

"That would be amazing. I can't wait." I truly meant it.

Her smile faded and she shook her head. "Okay, Charlotte.

I'm going to roll with this new version of you, but I don't think your dad is going to be that easy."

My mom was waiting patiently on the sidewalk, but my dad looked irritated. His arms were crossed over his chest and he was scowling.

"I'll have to change his mind," I said.

I found the beautiful sailing vessel, appropriately named *Heaven*, sitting serenely in slip 23. A caretaker nearby spotted me and asked if I was Charlotte. He gave me all the necessary keys and details for my new boat.

"She's a beauty," my mom said as she ran her hand across the bow. It was true. From her smooth lines and deep blue and red lacquer to the hand-polished wood of the cockpit and the gorgeous cabin. The boat was way nicer than my apartment. The boat was nicer than most apartments.

My parents and Helen sat in the cockpit while I familiarized myself with the lines and winches. Everything was electric. Of course Adam had bought me the finest. I motored out of the marina into the harbor, all while my dad watched in awe. That's when it finally clicked for him.

It took a total of three minutes for me to raise the mainsail and headsail. Everything was push-button.

"Char, I can't believe this. You're like a pro. How'd you learn?" my dad asked.

"Adam and Dr. Mark taught me," I said, smiling. "I'll teach you, Dad."

I'd never been close to my dad, but in that moment, I made a deal with myself that I wouldn't put up a wall between us anymore.

When we got out of the marina onto the open water, I set the sails for our tack, cut the engine, and then swoosh . . .

that glorious sound of the wind filling the sails surrounded us in every direction.

"Wow!" my mother shouted, and then the boat heeled dramatically. She gripped the safety lines, looking panicked.

"It's okay, Mom, it's supposed to do that!" As the wind in the sails pushed us forward, we began gracefully skipping across the water. If the ocean were music, sailboats would be the ballerinas. I was never any good at dancing before. Maybe I didn't know how.

"I would love for you to teach me, Char," my dad said, standing near me at the helm.

"I will!" I said, and I meant it.

I sailed them around for an hour or so before tying the boat back up in the slip.

As the four of us stood near my beat-up car in the parking lot, my mom asked, "What's the plan, Charlotte?"

She was concerned. This had all come out of nowhere for her. "I have one, Mom. That's all you need to know."

The three of them left me at the marina. I told Helen to keep in touch and to let me know as soon as she had the wedding location squared away. She told me she didn't want a bachelorette party or a wedding shower; she just wanted me to show up on the wedding day, which was seven months away.

TWO WEEKS LATER, I was standing outside a cage at the Humane Society, staring into the sweet brown eyes of a two-year-old yellow Lab. "Hello, sweet girl."

She wagged her tail.

I said to the young Humane Society employee, "Why doesn't anyone want this dog?"

"I don't know," he said. "There are amazing dogs in here all the time that no one wants."

"I'll take her."

"She has four more days here before we can adopt her out."

Everyday I went back and took her into the play area, threw a ball for her, and brought her treats until I was able to take her home with me. I named her Dora. Yes, after Dora the Explorer. I figured if she was going to be traveling on a boat with me, she should have an appropriate name, besides a chip and all her shots.

Dora loved the water and she was a quick learner on the boat. I had to discourage her from jumping off and going for a swim without my permission, but that was easy because she was smart and followed directions.

I kept to myself over the next several months, living almost a hundred percent of the time on my boat. My father came down on Sundays and I would give him sailing lessons. I practiced on the weekends, going farther and farther on my own until I made my first solo trip to the small island of Catalina. It only took me eight hours, but it was the first time I was far enough out that I couldn't see land for a period of time. I was glad to have Dora. Sailing alone gives you a lot of time to think. My own voice became louder in my head. My own voice should always be the loudest. I stayed that night in Catalina and sailed back without any problem.

My father and Chucky met me on the docks when I returned. As I gently thrust the motor to move the boat into the slip, Chuck ran to one side and my father to the other. I threw out the lines to them so they could tie up each side.

"Proud of you, Charlotte!" my dad yelled to me as he

pulled the line tight. I was beginning to realize that my father was the sixty-year-old version of Chucky, small and fit with a kind-looking face.

I knew they would be there waiting for me but I didn't expect what came next. My brother stood on the dock and saluted me. "Permission to board, Captain."

"Oh shut up, Chuck. Get up here." I motioned for him to come aboard.

"Wow, Fatbutt, I can't believe you did it. Dad tracked you with the GPS."

My dad came onboard next. I knew he was going to track me. There were a lot of safety measures I took before heading to Catalina, but I wanted to see if I could do it on my own.

My father hugged me. "Glad you're back. How was it?"

"As calm as could be. Eerily calm," I said, "and not much of a test."

Chucky and my father sat down opposite each other on the cockpit edges. "Charlotte, we were thinking—"

"That's healthy, Chucky," I returned.

"Dad and I want to sail to Bora-Bora with you for Helen's wedding."

I spun around from my spot on the bow, nearly falling over the safety lines. "Oh, do you? Do you know anything about it? It's not just about putting the sails up. That trip is not leisure sailing. You have to route it based on the wind, time of year, and weather. Everything!"

"Honey," my father said, "I've done the research. I think the three of us can do it. We'll use the Coconut Milk Run. We'll use northeast and southeast trade winds by way of Hawaii. The only thing is . . ."

"What?"

"You'd have to stay in the South Seas for several months before you could bring the boat back up to North America. Or you could leave the boat and fly back to the States with us."

I started laughing because . . . well, the idea was ridiculous, but my father and Chucky sat there looking serious. "You want to drop me off in Bora-Bora for a year with my yacht? Then you two would fly back?" I pointed at them and smiled.

"Well, we were hoping you'd come with us and leave the boat. We'll return when the weather permits and sail her back, if you'd be okay with that. You can't—"

"I'm not leaving the boat in Bora-Bora for a year so you guys can have some great adventure."

"It would be a great adventure for all of us, Char," my brother said. "You can't sail back this way at that time of year. And you can't stay on this boat with your dog for the rest of your life."

The truth was coming out. "Oh, so this is an intervention? A way to get me off the boat? To do what? Normal things single girls do in their late twenties? Go to bars? What? Look for a man?"

"Cut the shit, Charlotte!" my father yelled. "We just thought you'd want to do this. I'm retiring soon and I want to spend some time with my kids. This is the only time Charles will not have a practice to oversee. So you leave the boat? So what. Buy another; you're a millionaire, remember?"

He was losing his patience.

A few moments of silence passed before I walked between them to the steps leading to the cabin below. "I don't think I could handle being on a boat with you two for six weeks, and I don't want to leave this boat anywhere. The answer is probably no, but I'll think about it." At that point I was shouting up at them from the kitchen area.

My father peeked down the steps and smiled at me. "That's all we're asking, for you to think about it. I'd love to spend time with you, kid, both of you . . . before you have families of your own." I turned my head so he wouldn't see the anguish on my face. I had wanted to have a family with Adam.

"What does Mom say about all of this?" I said with my back still turned.

"She thinks we should do it." Of course. My mother condoned everything.

I continued cleaning up. It was hard for me to say no to him, but I thought it unfathomable to stay in Bora-Bora or to leave the boat down there for a year, let alone spend six weeks ordering my dad and Chuck the Fuck around. But I did promise myself that I would at least consider it.

27. Solo

In the mild November chill of Southern California, I sailed solo to San Diego, where I rented a temporary slip near the convention center within walking distance of Helen and Roddy's condo. I was a boat person . . . officially. I started recognizing other boat people. I was part of a community, albeit a very strange community made up of solitary, somewhat introverted people. Something was missing, though, and as much as I didn't want to admit it, I was lonely. I didn't want to believe that it was Adam, because I couldn't bring him back, but at the same time, I knew I wasn't ready to date.

Dora and I met Helen at a small outdoor fish restaurant on Harbor Drive. I was wearing Adidas boat shoes, stretch pants, and a windbreaker pullover. She pointed at me as I walked toward her at the entrance of the restaurant. "Look at you; you're like a salty sea captain, with your dog and shit."

I laughed and then pulled out the tie from my hair,

shaking it in waves onto my shoulders. I missed Helen. I missed her humor and loyalty.

We hugged, both of us vibrating with laughter. "That is true, my friend."

Helen absently petted Dora's head and then said, "Come on in. This is the only place I could find that would allow dogs."

As we talked over lunch, Helen seemed hesitant to chat about wedding details. "Did you find a dress?" I asked her as I popped a French fry into my mouth.

"Yeah, it's simple. Plain. Roddy wanted us to get married in swimsuits."

"I like him!" I said fervently. Helen laughed.

"Well, I'm not having bridesmaids, just you, so you can wear anything you'd like. Seriously, except maybe that wind-breaker." Smiling, Helen looked down at Dora and said, "She's so good, really docile. You want to bring her, too?"

"Maybe. And she *is* a good dog. I can't believe someone gave her up."

"Hey," Helen said, "have you thought about signing her up to be one of those dog therapists?"

"Those what?"

"Yeah, Seth and Roddy do a lot of charity work for Children's Hospital. They volunteer and do events, and since I've been going, I noticed that they have dogs there that are really sweet and loving. They bring them in for the kids who have cancer and are in treatment for a long time."

Helen was talking so fast I could barely understand what she was saying. I was thinking about Adam and cancer wards and sick people and the sadness.

"I don't know, Helen . . ." I let out a long breath and

looked down at Dora's big eyes watching me intently. Her ears perked up like she knew we were talking about her.

"It's called Therapy Dogs International or something. Google it. Just look into it."

"Okay, okay. I'll look into it." I took a sip of water. "So, my dad and Chucky want to sail to your wedding on my boat."

She took a bite of her sandwich and looked away absently. "Yeah, I know."

"Who told you?"

"Your brother called me to get some details about the island we'd be on and where you guys could leave the boat until you're able to sail it back in a year."

"They're crazy, right? Leaving my boat, it's stupid."

She shrugged. "I don't know, I kind of think you should do it. To get all this out of your system." Sometimes Helen didn't realize how obvious she was being.

I laughed. "You guys all think this is some sort of phase?"

She rolled her eyes. "No, not a phase. I know people can change, Charlie; it's just been very drastic. I want my friend back."

"Leaving my boat in Bora-Bora is not going to get you your friend back."

"Then what will?" Her eyes started welling up.

I slumped in my chair. "I'm sorry. I know I've been all over the place. I haven't been a good friend to you. This is supposed to be a happy time for you. Look, I'm going to see if I can rent the slip I'm in down here for a while. We can hang out and I'll check out the dog therapist thing? Okay?"

"Okay." She smiled.

After lunch, I left Helen to go speak to the man who ran the slip rentals and then I texted my brother and dad.

> Me: Fine, I'm in. We sail from
> San Diego on Jan 1.

I knew it would be cutting it close.

> Dad: I'm thrilled. Thank you,
> daughter.

> Chucky: I wanna be 2nd in
> command

> Me: Don't press your luck and
> don't bring any of ur shit
> music either.

> Dad: Language Charlotte!!

> Chucky: What if we encounter
> pirates or mutiny? You'll want
> a 2nd in command.

> Me: Ok Dad is 2nd in command.
> You are a lowly deckhand until
> you can prove your worth.

> Chucky: Aye Aye Captain Fatbutt

Over the next month, I stuck to my plan. I prepared the boat and our meticulous course, tapping every San Diego sailing resource I could find, including anyone and everyone who would be willing to talk to me on the docks. I did several long weekend runs with the boat, some solo, some with Chucky and my dad. I spent more time with Helen, helping her plan the details of her wedding, and I even signed Dora up to be a dog therapist at Children's Hospital.

I avoided Helen when she was with Roddy and I never asked about Seth, and no one offered any bits of information either. I did, however, run into his dog in mid-December. Yes, you heard me right. Obi-Wan is apparently the Jedi Knight of dog therapists.

It was on a Wednesday, two weeks before we were scheduled to leave on the boat and a week before Christmas. Children's Hospital was decked out in holiday décor. I had been visiting the cancer ward with Dora for a month, since she had passed the test to be an official dog therapist. She was a natural, of course. Everyone called her Zen Dora because she was so mellow around the kids. She brought so much peace and joy to the children and, as it turns out, that very thing brought peace to me, a sort of completeness that I couldn't get from being on the ocean or staring at Adam's murals. I was grateful for Helen's suggestion. I wasn't grateful, however, for running into Obi-Wan.

I encountered him in the hospital parking garage where his handler, who was not Seth, was standing with him, next to the elevator bays. There's no way a person can identify a black Labrador mix dog she has never met, unless said person has spent several hours staring at an image of him splayed across the abs of a professional baseball player. Seth's Match.com profile photo displayed all the evidence I would need for dog identification purposes. In this case, because Obi-Wan had a very distinct feature: he had a patch of white fur on his chest in the shape of a light saber. Also, it was slightly phallic in nature, but I would never tell Obi that. It's one of those things I felt kind of gross even thinking about.

His handler, I should mention, because after all, it is the point of this story, was a buxom, blond bombshell.

Fuck you, world.

"Oh, hello," I said to Obi-Wan in my typical high-octave dog-speaking voice. The elevator doors opened and the four of us got in. Dora and Obi-Wan started licking each other's faces and I thought idly that it was like Seth and me licking each other's faces. Then they started sniffing each other's butts. Fantasy breach. I looked up at the handler. "Hi, I'm Charlotte." I stuck my hand out.

She seemed hesitant but reached out anyway, despite her obvious unease. "I'm Sara." She was appraising me; I had no idea why.

"And who is this guy?" I said, even though I was pretty sure I already knew.

"This is Obi-Wan." He looked up at her and wagged his tail. She scratched his ears and said in a baby voice, "Aren't you just the cutest little Jedi?" If the woman wasn't so obviously unaware of her beauty and sort of unabashedly silly, I would have hated her damn guts instantly, but I couldn't hate her for some reason. The dog looked like he was in love with her. Of course he was, who wouldn't be?

As we walked toward the hospital entrance, I looked back at her and smiled. "Have a nice day!"

"You too!" she said as she entered and headed down an opposite hallway.

I stopped and turned to watch her walk away. *Fucking beautiful people. Have a nice life, Sara and Seth . . . and Obi.*

There would be no moping, nor would I make any inquiries. I would continue with the plan.

Christmas came and went. Every single gift exchanged at the Martin household involved our trip to Bora-Bora. I tried to talk my mom into going, but she just kept rambling on about her rotary club responsibilities. Older people take their shit so seriously, though I was actually really proud of my mom for it; we didn't give her the credit she deserved. And if I was like her—slightly directionless—I was proud that at least I knew I had her heart.

We spend so much of our teen years and twenties fundamentally rejecting our parents' philosophies. I'm talking about that period between fifteen and your late twenties when you think your parents are the most fucked-up people because they're slightly flawed. These toxic thoughts create a storm inside of us. We're so terrified that we'll be just like them that we overblow their less-than-perfect characteristics into something worse than they are. But then we hit a certain age and, click, it's as if a light switch flips. Suddenly, our parents don't seem so bad. In my experience, it's called acceptance. We're not born with it, and it takes a while to cultivate.

I think accepting our parents is a way of accepting ourselves. Once we're able to accept them, it's like surrendering or choosing, as Adam would say. That's the moment when we finally say, *This is who I am, this is how I look, this is what I'm good at.* I'm different from my parents, but I'm the same, too. I'm a human, walking around this lonely planet, taking one breath after another, trying to decide what's right and what's wrong. And although they have more life experiences, they don't have the same life experiences.

After Adam, I was closer to my parents. It was undeniable. I was finally appreciating them for who they were.

WALKING TOWARD THE docks on the day of our departure, I could see my father on the bow of my boat, wrapping lines, wearing a satisfied smile. I saw Chucky carrying supplies in front of me, and I watched Dora come out and greet him, then bounce along next to his legs as he continued down the dock. I stopped to take it all in. The sky was clear and crisp. It was a new day. A new year.

A gentle gust of wind caressed my neck, almost willing me forward, but I stayed where I was. "You're here," I said, under my breath. "I can feel you."

Chucky abruptly stopped, turned around, and spotted me standing at the top of the dock, twenty yards away. Carrying a box, he could only motion with his head toward the boat. "Come on," he yelled.

I nodded and closed my eyes. The wind picked up again. "I'm going, I'm going," I said, smiling, thinking about Adam, the smell of the ocean reminding me how connected he and I would always be.

28. Hope

Once we had been on the water for two weeks, Chucky began to think he was Captain Ahab; my dad would just stare out at the ocean, smiling for hours on end. I wondered what he was thinking but never asked. The look of contentment on his face reminded me of Adam. I think when you're done searching for some of the bigger answers, you can experience this sense of awe again, like everything is different, covered in a new coat of paint. I appreciated what this trip was doing for my dad.

For me, I tried to see the beauty in every moment, but it was terrifying when the water was rough, knowing that I was the most experienced person on the boat. But then we'd get through it and I'd feel empowered, so I was getting something out of it, too.

What was even more terrifying was when the water was still at night and there was little wind to carry us. It would be quiet and dark, and we would just float in the middle of the vast sea. Chucky would be reading some dental crap with a flashlight on the deck, my dad would be down below, and I would be at the helm. The moon would glisten on the water and I would squint to make out something in the distance, but there would never be anything. This happened all the time, on almost every calm night. There was no one for miles and miles in front of us or behind us, only the stars above us and a world full of giants and mysteries below us.

It's terrifying what your imagination will make you see.

The weather was fine, although a little chilly. Chucky almost killed my dad one day with the boom while he was tacking. He didn't call out his command, which I had already been on his case for. The boom swung around and my dad turned just in time to duck. Chucky became my kitchen bitch after that. I couldn't trust him with any navigational or operational duties, so he spent his time cooking our meals. It was better this way.

One night while I was lying in the dinette converted into a bed, but which didn't remotely feel like a bed, I thought about my parents and marriage and how I was losing Helen to Roddy and how Adam, my magical dying man, was gone, too. I had Dora curled up by my side, breathing her stinky breath in my face. What was I going to do with my life? I scolded Adam in my head for giving me a million dollars and a boat. It's hard to get motivated when you're a millionaire in your twenties, but I knew the money wouldn't last forever, and really, how could I complain? Poor me: healthy, young, vibrant, and wealthy. I knew I had to invest the money and find something to focus my energy on.

Just as I was dozing off, my dad came halfway down the steps and stopped. The deck lights silhouetted him; I couldn't see his face.

"You up, Charlotte?"

"Everything okay, Dad?"

"Yes."

He came down and sat on the edge of the dinette bed with his back to me. I wished that I could see his face, but I could tell he was struggling to find the right words to say, so I didn't ask him to turn around.

"I just wanted to say thank you, honey." He reached back and put his hand on my head.

"This was your idea," I replied.

"I mean, thank you for teaching me to sail. I love it so much. I didn't know I would."

"Oh." I started to get choked up.

"You're really good at it. I mean, you're a really good teacher, Charlotte. And Dora . . . this dog, man, what a gem." He pet Dora's head. I was officially a dog person and a boat person, and my dad was proud of me. Ask me a year ago if I thought any of this would have been possible.

When I reached my hand out and intertwined my fingers with his, I felt one of his tears drop onto my arm. I didn't know what he was going through, but it was more evidence of just how human he was.

"Is everything okay, Dad?"

His body jerked with silent laughter. "Yes, I'm just really happy and proud of you."

I squeezed his hand. "Thank you."

"I'm going to try and talk your mom into letting me buy a boat, too."

When I sat up and flipped on the light, he turned to me, smiling. I could see moisture still on his face. "You can use my college fund money if she tries to fight you on it," I said.

He laughed even harder. "Oh, darling, that money was gone a long time ago."

I laughed, too, then. "I guess I did the college thing more than most people, but with no real results."

"At least you were willing to explore your options. I have to say, through all of it—nutrition, massage therapy, real estate, cosmetology school—this is the most natural thing I've seen you do, and I just wanted to tell you that."

I nodded as I tucked that one away.

29. Drunk Socrates

Once we docked in Honolulu, in Oahu, and Chucky and I were cleaning up down below, we heard a voice from the dock. "Well, hello there, handsome castaway." It was my mother bantering seductively with my dad. Chucky looked at me and dry-heaved.

"Mom!" I screamed from the bottom of the stairs. Her face lit up.

My dad was already on the dock, hugging her. Chucky and I both jumped off the boat and joined in on a big group hug.

My mom squeaked, "I can't breathe, and the three of you stink."

"What are you doing here?" Chucky asked.

"I missed my family." She looked at my dad. "I missed my buddy." She placed her hands on his bearded face. "I like this . . . rugged look." She winked. I envied my mom and dad in that moment, maybe for the first time ever.

I slapped my brother on the back. "Well, Chucky, I say we get out of here."

We left my parents so they could be alone and Chucky and I caught a taxi to the North Shore, where we proceeded to get drunk on the beach. I kept telling him he could head back to Waikiki, where there was more of a party scene, but he stayed with me.

"I like this version of you, Charlotte. You're fun."

We rode bikes along the road from beach to beach. I sat on the sand at Pipeline in the warm, breezy air, watching the surfers. The water was impossibly blue and the ground was so solid beneath me that it made my own body feel electrified . . . alive.

I bought twelve cheap T-shirts, ate two pieces of haupia pie and a glazed donut from Ted's Bakery, and devoured a basket of shrimp from a food truck in Kahuku before we headed back to our hotel. When Chucky left me in the lobby, he said, "Today was awesome."

"Yeah, I had a great time. Wasn't it kind of cool to see Mom and Dad like that, all in love?"

He squinted. "What do you mean? They've always been like that."

"Well, I guess you lived with them longer so you probably saw it more."

"Maybe." He looked into my eyes for a few seconds—something brothers and sisters don't really do until they're older; when you're young, you're too busy tormenting each other.

"What up, Chuck? Why are you looking at me like that?"

"You're gonna find someone else, Charlotte. It's admirable what you did for Adam, but you still have a lot to offer. Don't give up. And don't settle for some schmuck."

"Adam changed me," I said, looking past Chucky into the distance.

"I think life changed you."

"Okay, drunk Socrates." I smirked.

"It doesn't really matter. Mom and Dad set the bar so high. I think that's why you and I have waited so long to find someone to commit to."

"We're not even thirty yet, Chuck."

"I know, but I'm getting there, you know, to that point of no return where no one will be good enough because I'll be so set in my stubborn ways."

"Well, at least you know it. Still, I wouldn't call your late twenties the point of no return."

"I want to be young with somebody. That's why Mom and Dad work; they have the fantasy of themselves. You need that shit when you get older."

"What does that mean?" I said.

"Ask Mom; she said that to me once. I didn't get it then." He started to walk away. "Wait! Let me get a hug."

He turned and hugged me instantly. It didn't feel weird.

"Get some rest, Fatbutt."

When he kissed my cheek, I giggled. "You too, Shitbag."

THAT NIGHT, IN the privacy of my own hotel room, I had a dream that Adam and I were sailing on the calmest, bluest water. He was lying on the deck with his hands propped behind his head, watching me with a smile on his face. "What are you looking at?" I had said.

"You."

I startled awake at a loud knock on the door. I threw on

a robe and swung it open. It was my mom, wearing a sailor hat and saluting me.

"What are you doing, crazy lady?"

"Captain," she said.

I ushered her in. "What's this all about?"

She came into my hotel room and sat on the bed. "I don't know what you did to Charles, Charlotte, but he got on the first flight out this morning. He said he's going to get Jenn, that girl he sees off and on all the time. He'll meet us in Bora-Bora."

"Really? What a quitter."

"Well, that means you get me, your new deckhand." If I could package the way she looked that day, in that hat, saluting me and wearing the most colossal of cheesy grins, I believe it would do more for depressed people than most pharmaceuticals.

I smiled and said, "I'm happy, Mom. I doubt you could be any worse of a deckhand than Chucky. I didn't do anything to Chucky, by the way. He said he wanted to be with someone while he was young because of something you said to him. That's why he went back, I think."

"Oh." She looked genuinely shocked. "I didn't think he got it. I mean, I didn't really explain it to Chucky in a way that would be clear."

"What do you mean, Mom?"

She looked around my room. "Are you gonna make this bed?"

"The maids do it. Quit trying to change the subject." I sat down in the desk chair across from the bed and swiveled around to face her. "Well?"

"You know my friend Carol?" My mom was talking about

her high school friend who had never gotten married or had kids. She had a few long-term relationships but none that lasted more than a couple of years.

"Yeah, I know Carol."

"Well, she was over at the house one day and had asked me if I regretted getting married so young."

"Okay. I mean, twenty-one wasn't that young back then, was it?"

"No, but I mean twenty-one is young no matter what."

"Cut to the chase, Mom."

"I told her no. I think my exact words were, are you kidding me? Do I regret marrying Jerry when we were in our twenties, lean, beautiful, and dumb? Hell no."

I was shaking my head. "But Chucky—"

"I told Carol I had no desire to have awkward sex with strangers, nor do I reminisce about the awkward sex I did have with strangers before I was married—"

"Mom!" I yelled.

"Just listen. It all goes to shit for everyone anyway. At least I have memories of being young and sexy and doing it all night with your father."

I stuck my hand out. "Stop, Mom, please." It was not what I expected.

"Cut the shit, Charlotte, and listen to me. I tried to explain this to Chucky, in a less graphic way, of course. Apparently, he got the gist of it, although I think it might have taken him a while. I have memories, shared memories with your father." She tapped her index finger on her temple. "I have this up here and that goes a long way when you're trying to ignore your own gray flabbiness. I know how hard this year has been because of . . ."

"You can say his name. Adam."

She chuckled. "I was thinking about the boat, teaching your dad to sail, and Dora, the little canine therapist. I think Adam might have done more for you than—"

"I know," I said instantly. There was no need to talk about it any longer. We understood each other. "I totally get it, Mom. I get what you're saying about Dad and marriage." I might have appreciated the less graphic version more, but oh well.

MY MOM WAS seasick for the first four days on our trek to Bora-Bora. I felt so bad for her, but she made it through, got her sea legs, and eventually became a pretty good deckhand. The trip was smooth. The weather was good for the entire three-week journey from Hawaii.

When we arrived in Bora-Bora, where Helen was to be married in three days, we docked the boat quickly, headed to the overwater bungalows, and checked in. I chose one as far away from my parents as I could—not because I didn't want to be near them, but because I figured they'd want their space after so long at sea.

That night, I met Helen and Roddy in the resort restaurant.

"You look amazing, especially for being on a boat for over a month," Helen said, as we walked to our table. I was wearing a flowing white sundress and sandals. My skin was tanner and my hair, lighter. Helen looked different, too. She was glowing and Roddy was smiling from ear to ear, both of them radiant.

"Well, you guys look pretty darn good yourselves." We all hugged and then sat down.

After we ordered food and drinks, I said, "I got a fuchsia dress to wear for the ceremony, I hope that's okay." I popped a piece of shrimp into my mouth.

Helen looked at Roddy. "That should go fine, right? What is Seth wearing again? Khaki shorts and a black shirt or something?"

I coughed; the shrimp went flying across the room. "Excuse me, what?"

Roddy frowned. "Yeah, khakis and a black shirt. Is that okay?"

"No, it's fine," I said. "I just didn't know he'd be here. I mean, I didn't know he was going to be *in* the wedding."

Helen's eyes were wide, but Roddy looked irritated. "He's my best friend. He's the best man."

"Helen didn't tell me."

"You didn't ask," she countered.

I crossed my arms over my chest. "It's fine. It's your wedding."

"Well, it's not like you two don't get along," she said.

"I just haven't seen him. I haven't said anything to him."

"Well, it's perfect then. You have three days before the wedding to work everything out. He's coming in today," Roddy said.

"Is he bringing his girlfriend, too?" My stomach was doing somersaults. I felt like heaving shrimp all over the table.

Helen looked at Roddy pointedly. "Who's his girlfriend?" she asked.

"He doesn't have a girlfriend, I don't think."

I huffed. "Well, I'm sure he doesn't tell you everything. I met some Sara girl who had his dog at the hospital."

Roddy and Helen looked at each other and smiled. Helen reached out and took my hand in hers. "Charlie, Sara is Seth's sister. Tall, blond, boobs?"

"Yeah."

"Yeah, his sister. See, there's still so much to learn about him."

I will admit now that there was something familiar about her.

"She was taking Obi-Wan to Children's," Roddy added.

"Oh . . . so he doesn't have a girlfriend?"

"Not that I know of," Roddy said.

I wasn't convinced, but at least I could rule out Sara. I was also confused as to why I cared. It wasn't really my business. Seeing Seth no matter what was going to be awkward.

30. New Life

By two in the afternoon, I was thoroughly buzzed on Tahitian rum and tropical fruit. Sitting in my bikini on the deck outside my bungalow, reading an old tattered copy of *The World According to Garp*, I noticed something from the corner of my eye. Across the lagoon sat another set of bungalows, and out on his deck was Seth, waving his arms spastically at me. "Hellooooo, neighbor!" he yelled.

I stood and stared, feeling hesitant to respond. He was wearing only trunks and he was far away, but I knew it was him. I could easily make out the mess of brownish hair on top of his head. Even from a hundred yards away, I could see the ridges in his stomach. I waved, finally. "Hello!"

For me, breaking the glacier I had formed between us was going to take a lot more than a casual wave across a tropical lagoon.

"I'll come to you," he yelled, and dove into the water.

Oh my god, Oh my god! I looked down at myself. I was almost naked. I stood there, slightly trembling, not sure what to do, as I watched his strong body swim quickly through the water in my direction. I walked down to the lower deck right as he grasped the deck railing and hoisted himself up with agile grace onto the wooden platform.

I looked at him towering over me, grinning like a boy who had won first prize. The water was dripping off his perfect body. When he shook his hair out, I flinched. "It feels great. You should try it," he said. He seemed unfazed by what I considered to be a monumentally uncomfortable situation.

"Um, . . . I . . ." The tension, oh god, the confusion. I couldn't tell what I was thinking or how I was feeling. All I could see was his glistening body sparkling in the sun.

"'Hello, Seth, how are you?' would be a good start," he said, smirking.

I blinked, still speechless. *Why is he being so friendly? I broke his damn heart.*

"Charlotte Martin, will you speak? I heard you have a boat and a dog now?"

"Yeah," I said, still stunned at how gorgeous he was. I had conveniently forgotten what it felt like to be in his presence. "Dora is with my parents. How'd you know?"

"Obi told me. He likes her." He wiggled his eyebrows. *Sara must've told him about the run-in at the hospital.*

"Ha!" I said absently, still preoccupied with his stupid muscles.

"Well, I can see this isn't getting anywhere."

He scooped me up like a bag of flour and threw me, not gently, into the air. "Argh!" I screamed as I flew at least ten feet from the deck before hitting the water and sinking straight to the bottom. Seconds later, I heard a crash as the water exploded around me. As the bubbles cleared, I saw Seth swimming toward me with long, expert strokes. The lagoon was perfectly cool and crystal blue. The sun blasted through it, making it possible to see every bit of white sand below us and every tiny tropical fish swimming near us. The word *heaven* popped into my mind as we swam together beneath the surface.

After a few moments, we came up for air.

"You threw me in," I said, breathing heavily.

"Your powers of observation are as sharp as ever, Charlie." He swam toward me and placed his hands on my hips. *Oh god, his hands are on my hips.* He was smiling that boyish, healthy smile, and I couldn't help but smile back, despite my complete shock that he was being so friendly.

I squirmed out of his arms and dove under the water to swim away. He grabbed my foot and pulled me back like I was nothing. I had forgotten how young and virile Seth was. When I surfaced, I was laughing and spitting water everywhere.

He was laughing, too. "Are you gonna keep running away from me? You're easy prey."

"I'm not running, I'm swimming." I broke loose and swam away as quickly as I could back to the bungalow. I could feel him right behind me when I reached the deck rail and lifted myself out of the water.

He shouted up at me, "Okay, now you're running."

I stuck my tongue out at him.

"Where's your boat? Maybe I'll let you take me out on it."

"I haven't even invited you."

"You're feisty today."

"So what." I grabbed a towel and started drying myself off.

"Let's catch up, Charlie. I want to catch up." He sounded more serious now.

I hesitated. Here was this beautiful man, acting as if the last few months hadn't even happened. Was that a good thing? Did I want him to be acting this way? I'd changed so much since the last time I saw him; I wasn't sure if I could go back to the way we were. But Adam's words, and my conversation with Chucky in Oahu, were floating around in the ether of my mind. If Seth wanted to catch up, fine—we could catch up.

"I'll meet you at the bar at five," I said as I climbed the stairs to the top deck. I looked up and saw my parents standing there, staring at us with wide eyes. *Holy shit.*

"Charlotte," my mother said.

"Show's over," I said as I walked past her into my bungalow.

My dad cleared his throat. "I'm gonna head back to our bungalow," he said, and then he skittered away. But my mother stood in my open doorway as I continued to dry myself off.

"That was Seth," I told her.

"I know. Your dad and I watched some of his games."

"We weren't doing anything, Mom."

"I didn't say that you were."

"Even if we were, do I look like I'd care?"

She started laughing. Her laugh grew into hysterics.

"What is wrong with you?" I said.

"Chucky was right." She tried to catch her breath. "You are different." She turned to walk away. "I think I like this new Charlotte," she said as she left the bungalow.

"Then quit picking on me!" I called out as she walked down the wooden deck.

She turned back and made the motion of zipping up her lips and throwing away the key just before blowing me a kiss.

I couldn't help but smile.

FIVE O'CLOCK ROLLED around and I was sitting at the bar in the lobby of the resort in a floral-print maxidress, my hair in loose waves around my shoulders, drinking some concoction with local booze, tropical fruit juice, and a little paper umbrella in it.

"Is this spot taken?" came a voice from behind me.

I didn't look up at him. "Sit. We have much to discuss."

He sat down and called the bartender over. "'Scuse me, can we get a couple of shots?"

"I don't want a shot!" I said.

"You should have a shot, Charlotte."

"I've been drinking since two." I wasn't slurring, but I was squinting hard—my tell. There was no way I was going into this potentially fraught conversation sober.

"Okay, we'll skip the shots. Let's discuss," he said.

We swiveled our stools so that we were now facing each other. His hand was on my bare knee. I glanced at his muscular forearms and felt my jaw go slack.

"You were saying something, Charlotte?"

"If I have that shot, I won't be good at anything . . . including self-control."

"I'm fine with that." He smirked.

"Don't smirk at me. We're supposed to be talking. Quit

trying to distract me with your baseball body and your hand on my knee." I slapped it away.

He laughed. "This is how I see it: I'm just sitting here, waiting for you to talk. You owe me an explanation, not the other way around."

"Actually, I don't owe you, or anyone, anything. I think I made my intentions pretty clear when we last spoke, and I never asked you to wait for me. But fine. I'll tell you what's been going on." I was truly drunk with bravery, in addition to being drunk on tropical cocktails. "I got married to Adam, he died in my arms in the French Riviera, and now I'm a widow."

His expression fell, but he didn't seem shocked; in fact, I saw only compassion in his eyes. "I know. Helen told me, and I'm sorry. And you're right, you don't owe me anything. I just want you to know that I'm here for you."

I waved my hand around in the air. "Maybe you don't understand. I got *married* and all of that," I said, arching my eyebrows. "I. Am. A. Widow."

"I know. Like I said, Helen kept me posted." Just then, the bartender brought us two shots. Seth pushed one shot toward me and held up his own. "Let's toast."

"To what?"

"Widows and bachelors?" He grinned. "I'm sorry. Too soon?"

"No, I'm fine. It's just that . . . why do I feel like everyone around me is going completely insane? Is it this place?"

"You don't want to toast, fine. Let's play a game then." He called the bartender over and asked her to leave the bottle of tequila.

"What's the game, number twelve?"

"You remember my number?"

"Um, yeah? We did date, you jerk." That made him happy. "How was the rest of your season, by the way?"

"I got a contract, actually. I'll be staying in San Diego next season. My average was steady, although now I'm in a bit of a slump."

"But the season is ov—oh, ha ha ha, I get it!"

"We're not really going to have a serious conversation, are we?"

I grinned maniacally.

"Okay, you know what, we're going to play Truth or Dare. If you don't want to do a dare or answer a question, that's fine, but you have to take a shot to make up for it. Got it?"

I was relieved. I couldn't talk about Adam anymore, and I sure as hell didn't want to dwell on the confusing morass of emotions swirling inside of me, further complicated by the fact that Seth would be in Southern California for at least one more year. "Got it," I said.

"I'll go first. I pick dare."

"I dare you to do a striptease on top of this bar," I said, waggling my eyebrows. He reached for the bottle of tequila, poured, and tossed it back.

"Your turn." He smiled, pleased with himself.

"You're no fun. Truth."

"Do you want me to kiss you?" he asked, staring at my lips.

"Yes," I said.

He leaned in and then, suddenly, we were kissing. I pulled away first.

"Okay, now me. Truth. Fire away."

"Why do you still like me?"

"That's an easy one, Char. Because you're compassionate, intelligent, funny; you have insane sex appeal; and you're beautiful. Your turn."

"Truth," I slurred.

"Do you want me to kiss you?"

"Yes," I whispered, growing increasingly bold from the alcohol. And then we were kissing again.

I pulled away and touched my fingers to his lips. "Your turn."

"Dare." He winked.

"I dare you to kiss me," I said.

He took a shot. I gasped. He was such a tease. "Your turn," he said.

"Dare," I said.

"I dare you to take a shot," he said.

I rolled my eyes. "Fine." I took a shot. "You go."

"Truth."

"Did you meet anyone in the months since I last saw you?"

His eyes darkened. "I met a lot of girls. And when I say a lot, I mean *a lot.*" I tried to pull my hand away, but he held on tighter. "But I didn't like any of them, and I started to get it. What you had with Adam."

I looked at him hard. "I fell in love with Adam, Seth. I was in love with him before I even met you. I know that wasn't fair, and I never meant to hurt you, but that's what happened. I fell in love with him and I married him because I wanted to be his wife. And then . . . well . . . he died. And I don't regret a minute of our time together."

He swallowed. "I'm sincerely sorry you had to go through that."

"It was my choice."

"Do you believe in soul mates, Charlotte?"

"I think so," I said.

"Do you want to know what I think?"

"What?"

"I think we have soul mates, but I think we can have more than one, just like we can have more than one career, or more than one hobby, or more than one fucking favorite food. Different people connect to different parts of our souls. I like you, Charlotte. I think you know that. And I want you to have hope that you might fall in love again."

I was speechless, so I did the only thing I knew how to do in that moment: I took another shot. "Your turn."

"Dare," he said.

"I dare you to come back to my bungalow with me." I leaned into him as I said it.

He took a shot and smiled. My eyes opened wider than possible. "You ass! Dare," I said, looking affronted.

"I dare you to go dance by yourself on the dance floor."

"I'm not gonna take another shot." Now I was definitely slurring.

"Then you better get out there and get your tiki on, lady."

I stumbled my way onto the dance floor where they were playing some Polynesian folk music. I tried to remember the dance the sister does in *Dirty Dancing*. I was massacring it while Seth sat smiling at the bar.

"Charlotte?" My mom and dad appeared, seemingly out of nowhere, although I will admit that I was thoroughly sauced by that point. They were sitting at a table near the dance floor. I stopped dancing and noticed that Helen, Roddy, her parents, and more friends were all watching me with amusement.

I threw my arms up. "What? It was a dare!"

Seth was suddenly behind me, propping me up as I swayed. "It's okay everyone. I'll walk her back to her room."

My father strode up and cleared his throat. "Oh, hello, Mr. Martin," Seth said.

"Hello," my father said. They shook hands.

"Charlotte, your mom and I want to discuss something with you, but I don't think it's a good time now. I think you need some rest."

"Oh Jesus, what now?" I said.

"Charlotte!" my mother scolded.

"I'm drunk, you guys. It's not a big deal." Seth anchored me to his side by wrapping an arm around my waist.

My mother stuck her hand out to Seth. "Hello, Seth, I'm Charlotte's mom, Laura." She blushed.

"Oh, Motherrr, are you blushing? He's just a professional baseball plaaayer with twelve-pack abs and perfect hair, get over it!"

"Let's go, drunky." Seth pulled me along.

"Hey, Taylor," my father said, calling Seth by his last name. We turned back to see my dad point to his own eyes and then to Seth's. *I'm watching you*, he mouthed, and then he buckled over and started laughing.

"Your family is totally weird," Seth said into my ear. "I see where you get your sense of humor."

"Yep, they're all right. By the way, it's your fault I'm drunk."

I caught Helen's eye as we left the bar. Seth waved, she smiled, and Roddy laughed.

"I think you had a little too much before I got involved."

"I told you that. Hey, wanna go skinny-dipping?"

"I'm getting you a sandwich and then I'm putting you to bed," he said.

"Killjoy."

31. Adventure

Seth did exactly what he'd said he'd do. He ordered two sandwiches, French fries, and a gallon of water and walked me back to my room, where I began vigorously shoving the food into my mouth.

I held up a French fry. "Do you know how long it's been since I ate anything fried? I don't even wanna eat it because I love it so much."

"Eat!" Seth ordered.

When we finished eating, I brushed my teeth and tore off my dress and threw it in the corner. I stood in front of Seth in nothing but my bra and underwear. He grinned.

"You gonna sleep with me, number twelve?"

"Been there, done that," he said. I socked him in the arm. "Get into bed, lush, I'll tuck you in."

The rest of the night was foggy, but I knew for sure Seth did little more than spoon me. In the morning, he was gone and I was hungover. On my bedside table was a note, a glass of orange juice, and ice water.

You looked so cute drooling all over your pillow. I took a picture of you that I will cherish forever. Roddy wanted me to teach him to surf today, so I had to leave early this morning with him. I am his best man, after all. I think Helen had something planned for you guys anyway. I want to see you later. Don't try to argue or bargain your way out of hanging out with me. I don't negotiate with terrorists. Kisses, Seth.

My head was pounding. I reached for Advil from my purse and swallowed it with a few glugs of orange juice. I could hear voices from outside my bungalow. When I looked out the curtain, I saw my mom and dad sitting in chairs on my deck.

I slid the door open forcefully, still only wearing my underwear and bra. "You guys are seriously everywhere. Have I no privacy? I just spent three weeks on a boat with you two, Jesus!"

"Now you know what it's like to have kids. Put some clothes on, grumpy, and get out here," my mother said.

When I came back out, my father said, "Welcome to the world of the living, Charlotte. It's past noon."

"I had a lot to drink last night."

"We know," they said in unison.

"Seth asked us to check on you. He seemed worried. Should we be worried?" my dad said.

"You guys, I got drunk. It wasn't the first time."

"Well, you sure looked like you were having fun, honey," my mom added with an arched eyebrow.

"Did you guys want to ask me something?" Dora's head

was resting on my mom's knee. "You look comfortable," I said to Dora. Her ears perked up but she didn't move.

My dad began, "I'll just come right out and say it. If you plan on leaving your boat down here, your mom and I will stay and sail her back when the weather permits."

My mouth fell open. Both my mom and dad were staring at me, unblinking. "That will most definitely be months. What about Rotary Club, Mom? And Dad, what about the practice?"

"Fuck Rotary Club, it's boring, and your dad's practice will be fine until Chucky can take it over. It practically runs itself."

"You both are officially never allowed to scold me again for language. I'm a little shocked right now." Just then, I noticed Seth across the way, walking to his bungalow. I was staring at him when I said, "You're not getting Dora, so don't even think about asking."

"We want the adventure, Charlotte," my mother said. She followed my gaze to Seth, who was hanging a towel over his deck rail. He waved and we all waved back, then my mother stood up and came face-to-face with me. She was smiling. "I have a feeling you don't want to hang out down here on a boat for the next five months anyway."

"You're so perceptive, Mother." I kissed her on the cheek. "Fine, you guys can do it. I'll see you at the rehearsal tonight. Come on, Dora," I said before heading inside.

Dora hesitated.

"Come on, Dora!"

She finally followed me inside. When I looked back through the sliding door, my mom and dad were hugging.

I waited for them to go back to their room before I threw on my swimsuit and jumped into the water. Dora and I swam over to Helen's bungalow. No one seemed to be on-site so I started clicking and squeaking like a dolphin. Dora doggie-paddled next to me. When Helen came out, she buckled over laughing. "Oh, Flipper, you're still so good at that."

"Come swimming."

Roddy came out and stood behind her. "Hey, Charlotte."

"Hey, Roddy, how was surfing?"

"I'm terrible at it, but I think Seth had fun. He was beat. You keep him up late last night?"

"Who, me?" I said.

I helped Dora onto the deck and then climbed up myself. Helen said, "I saw Chucky and some girl this morning."

"Did you? I haven't seen them yet. He must have just gotten in," I said.

"They looked super in love," Helen added.

"Really? Good for him. Jesus, Helen, there's love all around, isn't there?" I thought I was making a joke, and then as soon as the words left my mouth, I thought about Adam. And like a giant wave crashing over me, I lost my breath.

"What's wrong, Charlotte?" Helen said, searching my eyes.

"Nothing, I just wish . . . I wish he were here."

Helen's smile was full of compassion. A moment later I felt a hand pressed against my back. "I'm here," Seth's voice came from behind. "Were you looking for me?"

Helen shook her head. "Good timing, Seth."

"Did I miss something?" he asked.

"Nothing," I said, smiling at him gratefully.

"We need to rehearse our nuptials," Roddy added.

"We'll be there in a minute," I told them. Without another word, Helen and Roddy headed down the wooden platform, leaving Seth and me alone.

"This must be Dora?" he said. Her ears perked up. "I can see why Obi's so smitten."

I tried to smile back, but my face wouldn't work. I realized that I was standing in a daze, staring at a shirtless Seth, wearing only his swim trunks and a grin. As quickly as it had entered, Adam's image gently floated away on the waves, and now I was thinking only about Seth and his big, strong body.

"Was I really drooling last night?"

"All over me. It was disgusting."

I felt my face flush. "Stop."

"I'm kidding. Kind of." He took a step forward and pressed his lips to mine, kissed me too quickly, and then pulled away. "You were cute sleeping on me, snoring, drooling. I found it all insanely charming."

I rolled my eyes, and then jumped in the water and swam away. "Come on, Dora! We're outta here." She jumped in too and swam after me as Seth watched from the deck. "I'll see you at the rehearsal."

I didn't look back.

IN TYPICAL HELEN fashion, she and Roddy rapped fake vows in their swimsuits while we all took our places. The rehearsal was just the four of us and the officiant, so there wasn't much to rehearse. I stood across from Seth and could feel his eyes on me the whole time. After the officiant told us what to do, we had dinner in the restaurant, and after that, Helen said, "I'm staying in your room, Charlie. Don't forget."

She kissed Roddy goodnight and then Seth and I were alone . . . again.

"Take a walk with me?" I said.

"I'd love to."

We clasped hands and I led him down a path to the south side of the island where *Heaven* was docked. It was dark, but I knew the boat like I had been born on it. "This is it; follow me."

"Should I call you Captain?" he joked as he stepped aboard behind me.

"Yes," I said seriously. "That's exactly what you should do."

I showed Seth around the boat. He asked a lot of questions about sailing and I told him I would teach him. We ended up on the deck, staring up at the stars, drinking red wine out of paper cups. We were talking, honestly, casually, finally.

"I'm going to fly back to California day after tomorrow," I told him. "My parents are staying with the boat until they can sail it back."

"I fly back the same day."

"Maybe we should try and get on the same flight," I said, "except I'm flying into LA. I need to get things straightened out at my parents' house and then look for an apartment in San Diego."

He reached down and squeezed my hand. "You're moving to San Diego?"

I nodded. "Yeah, I think I am. Too many memories in LA, and I want to be closer to . . . Helen."

"I have three days before I have to go to Arizona for spring training. I can help at your parents' . . . if you want."

"It will only take me a day," I said staring off into the distance. I only had to collect their mail and check up on things.

"And then we can drive down, stop by my parents' house, pick up Obi, and head to my place?" I gave him a side-eye. "Well, I assume you'll need somewhere to stay while you look for an apartment. And I wouldn't recommend staying at Helen and Roddy's honeymoon sex den."

I turned my head to look him right in the eye. "Seth. Are you sure?"

He sat up straight and returned my look. "Never been more sure."

He braced the back of my neck and kissed me, then pulled away gently and whispered, "I have to remind myself to slow down with you." He trailed kisses from my collarbone, up my neck toward my ear. Still whispering, he said, "Will you come and stay in my room tonight?"

"Helen's staying with me tonight. Let me check with her first." He took my hand and led me off the boat.

Back at my bungalow, we found Helen sprawled out on my bed, wearing a cucumber mask, and watching TV. She didn't even need me to ask. "Just go for it, Charlie. I'm dozing off anyway. Need my beauty sleep."

"Don't fall asleep with that thing on your face. You'll prune up by tomorrow."

"It's a hydrating mask."

"Suit yourself," I said before walking out.

Seth was leaning against the rail, squinting at me, looking pensive. "What?" I said to him.

"Nothing, just thinking about my future."

"How's it looking?"

"Brighter."

"Maybe you need some shades."

He smiled. "Can we please go back to my room now?"

Before we could even close the door to his room, our clothes were coming off and we were kissing and laughing. There was an ease with Seth, one that I had yearned for when I first met him.

And as we kissed and kissed, I thought about what had changed. When a person is ready to fall in love, it happens fast. There's no looking back or in between to find empty space where water can put itself to freeze, to crack the two of you apart. There is no void. There's no weighing of options or analysis of pros and cons. Everything is reduced to feelings and emotions and actions that don't need explanation or justification. I felt it with Adam that first night, if only for a second as we stood outside my building. It doesn't always feel like this, it doesn't always feel easy or right, so when it *does* feel this way, you have to seize it. Love is a wordless secret; it's an inside joke. Only the two of you have to understand it.

The door was closed and we were naked. Seth sat on the edge of the bed as I stood between his long, strong legs. He ran a finger down my naked side and kissed my belly. We were limbs and mouths, a tangled, twisted mass on top of sheets. We were promises solidified, named with each kiss, each breath.

WHEN THE SUN came up, a time-lapsed streak over the ocean, we watched the movement of people from bungalow to bungalow like ants from an airplane, so far away from the world that we had created in his room that night. It startled us to think we had to do anything but lie in each other's arms for an eternity. I chose in that moment to be open to all possibilities. To honor Adam and let myself be open to love. To appreciate the fact that Seth was able to accept my love for another man, and to adopt his understanding of life, love, and soul mates. My life wasn't over.

"We *are* the maid of honor and best man," I said.

"I'm not convinced that we have to go," Seth mumbled into my hair as he gripped the back of my knee and pulled my leg over him.

I had my head turned awkwardly to watch the people hurrying past our bungalow.

"It's eleven a.m. We're officially the worst friends ever. Their wedding starts in an hour."

Seth hopped up, smiling. "You're right. I have a feeling I'll be saying that a lot in the years to come."

I smiled back serenely, neither one of us flinching at the breadth of his statement.

Epilogue

Seth

I told her that it was very likely I would never learn to be poetic in our lifetime but that I loved her more than the ocean and Obi and baseball and myself. She responded with, "That, number twelve, is the most poetic thing anyone has ever said to me." She also told me she loved me and that it meant forever.

Charlotte gave me an envelope the day after we got married. She said, "I didn't read this because I promised Adam I wouldn't, and he was my husband and I loved him. I will never break a promise to you, either."

I opened the envelope later that day, read it to myself, and heeded the words I found so beautifully true and full of hope. Then I tucked the letter in a drawer, where I imagine it will stay until I die.

To Charlotte's second husband . . . whoever you are:

Taking care of another person the way Charlotte took care of me doesn't necessarily stoke desire, but we all know that marriage often leads to someone taking care of someone. Hopefully it goes like this: at the end, you're in Boca Raton, in a sun-filled home with slanted ceilings, decorated in pastels and plastic flowers, dusted weekly by a housekeeper. There's bland food but it's plentiful, and there are pink flamingos, lawn jockeys, bingo nights, flu shots, and the occasional evening out, a candlelit dinner where you ask for the low-sodium option. Charlotte gets tipsy on one glass of wine, and after you check your blood sugar, you each have a bite of peanut butter pie and then you hold her hand all the way to the car.

At home you talk about your children, about how they're not all perfect but you love them. You reminisce about your many years of marriage, you imagine yourselves young, and you come together again for the millionth time.

Eventually one of you takes care of the other until the end, but the one who is left will follow soon, and you'll meet up in the same place you've been meeting all these years, which is "somewhere in the middle," with a memory of youth close by.

She gave me this gift before she could have possibly had the wisdom to understand its meaning. I just wanted to say, I hope you know how lucky you are.

—Adam

Acknowledgments

I read the last paragraph of this book again more than a year after I wrote it, and literally minutes before I wrote these acknowledgments. I was trying to remember where I was in my life when I said those words about growing old with another person and wishing for something so simple. And then I remembered that the last piece was about gratitude. Just simply appreciating every breath I take with the people I love by my side.

I am grateful to the readers, bloggers, authors, friends, and family members who have supported me on this journey.

Christina, Jhanteigh, Tori, and Dani, thank you! Jane Rotrosen and Atria, thank you!

To my brother, Rich, this one is for you, maybe long overdue, but I was waiting for the most fitting piece. You're the best brother anyone could ever ask for.

Sam and Tony, world's best teachers and also the joy of my life, thank you.

Anthony, lawn jockeys, bland food, and flu shots sound amazing as long as they're with you.